The Homing
Pigeons...

Praise for the book

"…*The Homing Pigeons* stands out like a stylish bird … A love story that isn't afraid to get its beak wet … A contemporary look at marriage and morality. A tale of two Delhis … high above the crowd of adolescent bestsellers … Bring home these pigeons."
– Ashok Banker, internationally acclaimed, bestselling author

"…the pigeons still pull you in, pained and poignant, with their truth that resembles many our own."
— *HT City*, Delhi NCR

"…an unexpected but stunning story of a love lost and found… The story unravels in the most artistic fashion, surprising you most of the time…delightfully written ending…takes you through the frailties of human behaviour and complicated relationships."
– *Millennium Post*

"…a riveting, easy read… the story will make you turn pages."
– Yatin Gupta, CNN-IBN Live

"This author has the potential to be termed as the Indian Khaled Hosseini."
– Amrit Sinha, Author, *The Last Note*

"To begin with this is one book that has made me miss my metro station twice and the bus stop once."
– Harshita Srivastava, Author, *One in a Million*

The Homing Pigeons...

Not all love stories are perfect, but then, neither are people

Sid Bahri

Srishti
PUBLISHERS & DISTRIBUTORS

Srishti Publishers & Distributors
N-16, C. R. Park
New Delhi 110 019
editorial@srishtipublishers.com

First published by
Srishti Publishers & Distributors in 2013
second impression 2014

All characters in this book are fictitious, and any resemblance to real persons, living or dead, is coincidental. For authenticity and to aid story telling, the author has used places, organizations and institutions that are real, however, there is no intention to imply anything else.

Typeset by EGP at Srishti

To my daughter Aadhira

Acknowledgements

It's probably unfair to say thank you to only a few people but if I were to write everyone's name who has contributed, it would end up larger than the book itself. So, here goes the list.

➢ My wife Puneet, for inspiring me and cajoling me to take this habit of writing beyond a hobby. The countless nights of writing and the move to Ranikhet wouldn't have been possible without your support (even though, you threatened to divorce me a few times).

➢ My sisters Anisha and Sujata, for helping me believe that there is a life beyond the drudgery of a suffocating job.

➢ My mother Varsha, I don't know if I'd have been able to write if you didn't get me into the habit of reading. If you hadn't fought with the librarian at the State Library in Chandigarh to get me an out of turn membership, then who knows…

➢ Shilpa Sharma Sikdar and Shelly Sharma, the two sisters and the two worst beta readers that I have ever known. Yet, you have encouraged me.

➢ Amit Sikdar, my friend, for planting this thought in my mind. I can't forget that evening on your balcony when you said, "Make a living out of doing what you love". You are the next Steve Jobs.

➢ Mr. Vineet Panchhi, my old friend from my BPO days and one of the most versatile people that I have known. When I first spoke about having a book with a soundtrack, people looked at me as if I was crazy. There is only one man who understood. And took it a step further to have an exclusive album created, co branded with the book. I wish to thank you immensely. Vineet is reachable at *vineetpanchhi.com*.

➢ Arup Bose, the editor, and Srishti Publishers for helping me fine-tune this manuscript into what it looks today. Your insights and encouragement have helped me make this piece of writing a novel.

➢ My readers, for being brave enough to pick up a copy from an unknown author. If you like this, I promise to give you better stuff in times to come.

Aditya

This is it. I have been trying to avoid this day for months, but now, it is finally upon me. I call out to the waiter and order my last drink from the last bit of money that I have in my pocket. The void that is created in my pocket is almost as stark as my bank account. I could've chosen to not drink today and lasted another week. The cancer of being broke would've killed me a week later that way.

Just this morning, I withdrew a single one thousand rupee bill from the ATM that now seals my fate. There is a little over thirty-three rupees that I still own but the stingy ATM refuses to part with it.

If my inebriated mind can still calculate, I will have just enough left after this drink to leave the waiter a small, ungracious tip. I can also choose to be ungracious and buy a ride back home. I think that people only need a ride when they are in a hurry or the distance is too great. Neither condition is true for me, so the waiter wins.

I sit alone on an uncomfortable bar stool at Piccadilly Sipper, one of the few up market, standalone bars that exist in Chandigarh. My thoughts wander to this juncture in my life. A little over a year ago, my career had reached its zenith in the fastest-growing sector of the economy – banking. Little did I know that when Lehman Brothers caved in like AIG and Merrill, the tremors would be felt this far out. I was laid off, *restructured* as they had called it, and now my last saved penny is up for grabs.

I always knew this day was going to come, for the signs were always there. First, the credit cards were maxed out, leaving the debt collectors to earn a living out of chasing me. They wanted their money back; I had to sell off my car to stave them off. Despite the momentary respite it brought, the situation didn't improve. In the deep dungeons of a debt-ridden life, there is little respite. The home too was sold; it barely took care of the mortgage. My equity in the home was swallowed by the vicious snake that recession is turning out to be.

When I lost my job, I thought about being an entrepreneur, like my father had once been, but I had no capital and no one wanted to bet on me. It doesn't surprise me. If you present your credentials as someone who has just lost his job, it doesn't inspire an investor's confidence.

I am living off my wife who brings in just enough money from her job to keep our heads above the water. Despite the situation, I am five drinks down, sitting on an uncomfortable bar stool in a seemingly luxurious bar. I shuffle to give my legs some space. The bar is obviously not designed to have customers taller than five feet eight and I struggle to fit in my six foot-one frame.

The bar is located in central Chandigarh which houses the business district. It is ordinary to have the bar full, even on weekdays. But not tonight, for recession hasn't exempted the bar either. The empty tables tell a story of woe and neglect. They aren't used to not being occupied. They aren't used to not being wet. They almost yearn to become a tree again.

When the barman and the half-empty bottles on the shelves stop amusing me, I look around. Of the ten odd people who are here today, two sit at the bar. The lady two stools away from me walks back from the washroom. I can't help but notice that her walk is accentuated. It is seeking attention. She even manages to make a few turbaned heads turn.

She changes her seat, leaving only one stool between the two of us. She looks at me and smiles. I don't, but she still stares at me. It isn't extraordinary for me to invite a stare or two from the opposite sex. A lot of people tell me I am a looker. I am not so sure about today because I haven't shaved in five days and haven't clipped my nails in ten. The maid who comes to clean my wife's home doesn't care. She's the only one who spends time with me these days. I am still wondering if I should've chosen a career in modelling.

An instinct tells me that I am being keenly observed. I don't pay much attention to it for you can never be too sure with alcohol. It can make you hallucinate. I focus on the glass, it's almost halfway down. I don't know why but tears well up in my eyes. I don't know if she sees the tears but she asks me, "Hey, are you fine?"

"Yes, barely," I say.

I bring the old-fashioned glass that holds my drink to my lips. I am happy in my self-pity, wallowing in the mud of my grief, and I don't need a conversation.

"Do you want to talk about it?" she asks.

I didn't say there was anything wrong but she wants me to talk about it. She seems eager to start a conversation. Even if I want to talk, I am not sure that I want to discuss it with a complete stranger. I will have to poke her with the metaphoric pole that will keep her away from me.

"I don't want to sound rude but please leave me alone," I say politely.

"I was only trying to help…," she says. Her words trail off. I don't know if I've offended her.

I could've chosen to be quiet and let the conversation die but I find myself saying, "You can't."

"You never know," she says

Maybe she thinks of herself to be a fairy; one of those who have three wishes to grant.

"Very clichéd, but no, thanks," I say in an even tone. Despite what I am feeling, not a hint of spite betrays my voice. Perhaps it is the humbling brought about by being penniless. I am amazed at my patience. I am still polite, even though the alcohol in my blood stream never lets me be.

"We won't talk about it. But can I buy you a drink?" she asks.

She has her arms up in a defensive gesture, almost as if I have threatened to kill her.

Alcohol is my nemesis. Till about four drinks, I consume it, and then it begins to consume me. I have crossed that mark till which I believe I can think rationally. I am five drinks high. With my last penny gulped down, her offer is tempting. I give in. I have heard of strange things happening. Who knows, she could be a fairy. Maybe this is the first wish she is granting me.

"I'd appreciate that. Thank you," I say.

She beckons the waiter. A thin man with a large moustache, donning a black waistcoat appears by her side. In some way, he reminds me of a shrew. He has trouble understanding what she is saying. In Hindi, I ask him to repeat my drink.

For the first time, I turn around and face her. She isn't good looking in the bookish sense of the word; you know, how the features aren't fit for the face. Yet, there is something attractive about her; it could be the high cheek bones. She is dressed in a charcoal grey business suit with a cream-coloured blouse peeking through her jacket. A pearl necklace adorns her neck. She reminds me of my ex-boss's secretary. I wonder why I always go back to those memories.

I come back to surmising her. The lipstick, now chapped, was a bright shade of red; perfectly manicured hands, burgundy shoulder length hair, conditioned to perfection. Something about her reeks of south Delhi. That place has the highest density per square inch of these stylish women.

I ask her, "Are you from around here?"

"No, travelling," she replies, confirming that my hunch is correct.

"For business or for leisure?" I ask. It isn't important as long as she is here, buying me drinks. I ask her because the least I can do in return for her graciousness is to maintain a conversation.

"A little bit of both," she says. She doesn't find it worthwhile to elaborate

"Where do you work?" I ask

Strangely, our roles have reversed. I am the one asking questions. I was trying to avoid her until five minutes ago. Johnnie Walker can make you do funny things.

"I work with an advertising company in Delhi. I am here for a product launch," she says.

"South Delhi?" I ask her.

She is still nodding when the waiter comes back and places the drink in front of me. I add a little club soda to the drink. While I am happy that I have been able to deduce the mystery of her origin, it leaves me remembering my being laid off from my job in Delhi.

"At least you still have a job," I say dejectedly.

"Why? Did you lose yours?" she asks.

"I did. The bastard fired me about a year ago," I reply.

She has been successful in getting me back to the reality that I have been trying so hard to avoid.

"Jobs come and go. You'll find another one," she says.

"I have lost hope that I will find another one," I say.

I have been trying to get back into a job for about twelve months now. There isn't a contact that I haven't reached out to. There isn't a head hunter who hasn't stopped taking my phone calls. All I have to show for these twelve months of labour are two failed interviews. Both of them rejected me on the grounds that I was 'too desperate'. Hell, I am desperate and can't hide it.

"Don't give up hope," she says. She sounds pompous, like a new priest at his first sermon. It is always difficult for a person with a job to empathize with someone who doesn't.

"Easier said than done," I slur.

I reach out for the Johnnie Walker and gulp the remains of it in one large sip. I am thirsty today. I am the quintessential desert that wants to drown its sorrows in alcohol.

"My name is Adi, anglicized from Aditya," I extend my right hand out to her.

"I am Divya, pleased to meet you," she says and takes my hand.

I can't help but notice the inordinately large rock that adorns her ring finger. Married? Engaged?

"Should I have him repeat your drink?" she asks.

"No, thank you, but I've had my fill. I should get going," I say. I am sober enough to be mindful of not overstaying my welcome.

"Come on, have one. I was just beginning to enjoy your company," she says coquettishly. I think I see her flutter her eyelashes.

I contemplate her offer; what will I do now that I have no money? My future looks a dark shade of black and if the future looks imperfect, then the present must be cherished. I don't take long to give in a second time.

"Just one more, and remind me to drink it slowly," I say.

The effects of the alcohol are apparent in my ever-deteriorating slur.

"We'll have a repeat for both of us. On my tab," she calls out to the barman. He went to a school where they taught him English. He understands.

"I'll be back," I excuse myself

I get up from my stool to find my way to the men's room. I bang into at least three chairs that are not in my way as I make the long serpentine walk to the men's room. I open the fly of my Calvin Klein jeans. It is one of the few prized possessions that recession has been unable to take away. I pee, swaying from side to side. My head is spinning. I look at my reflection in the mirror. My eyes are bloodshot; they could be of a ghost in a horror flick. I know that I should have said no to the last drink.

I wish I had another five hundred rupees that would buy me something to eat. I know that the chef rapes the Chicken Tikkas before he sends them out, even then. Somehow, I make my way back to the bar: a laborious walk, holding on to every piece of furniture that can stop me from falling down. I sit on the stool and continue the conversation with her.

"How'd the product launch go?" I ask.

When it comes out of my mouth, I know it doesn't sound like the question I asked her but I have to talk. She must believe that I am sober.

"Went off pretty well. It's a new brand of lingerie," she says.

The conversation hits a dead end. What can I ask her from here, what's your size?

"Do you have family?" she takes a cue from what I'm thinking.

"I am married; wife works in the media. No kids," I slur.

The barman puts the drinks in front of us. I attempt to put the club soda into my drink. I falter; the club soda spills onto the bar. The barman is trying to clean up when she asks, "Where is she? Why are you alone?"

I want to tell her that we don't get along very well but I think it might be too much tragedy for her to handle.

"She's out covering an event. She's been running the house ever since I lost my job," I say.

"You're drinking?" she asks provocatively.

Even in my intoxicated state, it isn't difficult to figure what she wants to imply. I am living off her money and I am drinking. I am, and worse still, I am not ashamed to accept it anymore.

"Yes. It's not ideal but I'm *dwinking*," I say.

The effects of the alcohol are telling. I am slurring like a man who's just had a stroke. My head spins and I have a sudden urge to spew the contents of my gut onto the bar counter.

I excuse myself and manage to walk like a snake towards the men's room. I vomit at the door. I am relieved, but have some more coming. I gingerly step past the remains of whiskey that lie on the floor, but I have barely walked two steps before I slip and fall on my buttocks. I was a sportsman and I'm used to falling. But yet, it hurts. The Calvin Klein jeans are soaked up in the muck that was once a premium whiskey. Incidentally, this is the last thing I remember.

Radhika

It is freezing out in the open today. The evenings are expected to be chilly in November but this year the cold is bitter. I'm standing alone in a crowd of five people when I see an old man walking towards me. He's wearing a pyjama and has a thick shawl wrapped around him. He's miserably out of place among everyone else sporting their riches. I recognize him as the owner of the farmhouse we're in.

"Who is Radhika Ahuja?" he asks the crowd.

I want to tell him that I am the mother of the woman getting married today. I am the widow of a man who passed away nine months ago. In fact, a very rich widow. My husband died and bequeathed me a house in South Delhi which even in these times of recession is worth a little over ten crores.

I am so bored that I only say, "I am."

"We need an advance," he says

I want to tell him that I don't deal with all this nonsense. I have people who work for me. I only sign cheques because that's what my husband's will wanted me to do. He's left behind a will that leaves me a custodian and the veritable guard dog of his wealth. He's left me in charge until my step-daughter gets married. Incidentally, that day is today.

I am so uninterested that I only direct him to the accountant.
He walks away. He doesn't remember me, but I do.

It was about six years ago when I got married at the very
same place to Vimal Ahuja. He was then, a man in his early
forties, and I was only twenty-five. Back then, the setting had
been similar in this farmhouse on the outskirts of Lucknow.
My parents sat next to me to do the *kanyadaan,* the Hindu ritual
directing the daughter to be donated to the groom. They were
inexperienced; they had two sons before me. They had qualms
that the groom was eighteen years elder than me and had a
daughter, Meera, who was seventeen. They had asked me to
reconsider, but I was sure. After all, he was rich.

The lady in the blue sari asks me, "What's the date today?"

I know it's November, but it leaves me feeling that it's
August. It is almost Independence Day tomorrow. With my
step daughter Meera getting married today, my responsibility
will end. It will leave me with a freedom that I have almost
given up on.

I am logical enough to only say, "It's the eighteenth of
November". I am just about letting out a silent prayer to a God,
who I don't believe in anymore, when a man walks over to
congratulate me. He's the attorney who read out the will after
my husband died. Something about him always leaves me
disappointed. Maybe because he brings out the emotions that
were with me the day he had announced the will. If I say that I
was upset, I'll be lying; I was downright distressed. I could've
gained my freedom a lot earlier if it hadn't been for the will.

I wasn't the only one who was disappointed that day. Meera
was forced to bear with me by virtue of the will. I couldn't
blame her for being dejected. She got the lion's share in the
will. Even then, she felt cheated that I had been bequeathed a
house in South Delhi that could have been hers. She's openly

lamented her father's decision to remarry. It probably hurts her a little more because she knows that I married her father for his money. Meera was even more frustrated when she could neither sue nor show dissent.

It's a little colder now and I wrap the shawl closer around me until it's almost a second skin. I wish I hadn't listened to the fashion designer; the sleeveless blouse is a very bad idea. When I still can't stop shivering, I wonder if it is because of my state of mind.

I walk up to the stage where Meera is sitting. I am only here because of a sense of duty.

Meera and I are like India and Pakistan. We loath each other but are still joined at the hip because of the will. Even in our independence, we are only a day apart. She gets hers today and I get mine tomorrow. I don't know if I believe in hate at first sight, but am sure Meera and I have a relationship like that.

The photographer wants me to pose. I want to tell him that I have been posing for years.

For so long, I have been posing as the trophy wife to a middle-aged man. It could've ended when Vimal passed away in February, ending his long-drawn battle with cancer. But, it didn't. It's left me rich though. Growing up, I had never imagined that I could've afforded all of this and yet, it is mine. Perhaps, it is my destiny to be rich. Maybe, I found the right man. Maybe, this is the reward for leading a loveless life with a repulsive human being.

I look at Vishal, Meera's husband and I can't help feeling for him. The marriage is nothing more than a transaction for Meera to obtain her freedom. Deep inside, I know that the marriage is destined to fail. You never know, Vishal might end up as lucky as I am. He was found within days of the will being announced. It is Meera's desperation to break free of my grasp that has made her find him. Ironically, Vishal thinks that Meera is in love with him. I know Meera too well to be misled.

We are now at the *mandap* and if I put my hand out, I can touch the sacred fire that will solemnize my stepdaughter's wedding. Even then, a shiver runs up my spine. I look around at the crowd that has formed around the *mandap* and find that I am not alone in my misery. The guests are huddled up like sheep around the *angeethis* that are set up. My designer isn't the only one who has underestimated the cold. In sharp contrast, the bride and groom look as if they are under the Hawaii sun. They are absolutely comfortable; not a hint of a shiver, nor a feigned attempt to pull at their clothes.

The priest starts chanting the prayers oblivious to the chattering of the crowd. No one really understands or cares about the *mantras* he is chanting. If he wasn't being paid to do this, he might have refused to perform the wedding. Who doesn't want a little more attention? My mind is elsewhere but I still sit here.

I often wonder why Vimal never saw through me. I am not sure he would have let me control his fortune if he knew. The bride and groom get up from their seats and walk around the fire. They struggle to carry the weight of their heavily-embroidered robes. They sit down momentarily and the priest continues. I wish I had paid him a little extra to wrap up the ceremony faster.

It is unbearably cold now; I wrap the Shahtoosh shawl a little closer to my body to escape the chill and curse the designer again. I detest winters. I wish that I become the bird that flies south for the winters. If I could, I would've changed the seasons so that spring always followed autumn. Despite the cold, I can't stop thinking about Vimal. He had been well-prepared for his death and the division of wealth. Cancer always gives you that opportunity. In giving Meera the lion's share of the wealth, he has left me with an allowance coming out of a trust. The large allowance will leave me with enough money to keep my lifestyle. A lifestyle that allows me to wear a Shahtoosh shawl and maintain most luxuries that money can buy.

The priest concludes the wedding, pronouncing Meera and Vishal man and wife. He puts the *tika* on their foreheads and the crowd showers flowers to signify blessings from the gods. They are naïve. They think that the gods will be able to give Meera a happy married life. I know that it isn't going to be one.

Meera ignores me and goes on to touch the feet of the elders after the wedding. Most brides would be unhappy to leave their father's home, but not Meera. There are no tears that brim in her eyes. No bawling that one expects from a bride as she leaves the familiarity of her father's backyard.

She leaves to consummate her marriage as cheerful as a bird in spring. The half frozen guests wait patiently for them to leave and then almost run to their waiting cars.

It is almost one at night when I stand at the exit and thank everyone for attending the wedding. The last car to enter the driveway is a black, chauffeur driven, 2007 BMW. The car stops besides me and the chauffer opens the door for me. I heave a sigh of relief, now that the marriage is concluded. The conclusion brings with it the end of an era: an era of living sans love, an era of tolerating this woman that I have been forced to call my daughter, and an era of compromise.

Aditya

I can barely open my eyes. Why is it always the same? Why do I always wake up groggy and dehydrated after these drunken nights? From the tiny slits of my eyes, I can see that the setting is unfamiliar. I struggle to get up. It has to be the air-conditioning that always wedges my joints. Clumsily, I sit up in bed, struggling with the sheet that is wrapped awkwardly around me. The synthetic of the sheet causes a rustle against the hair on my legs. Why am I not wearing my pyjamas? I am not even wearing a vest. Hell, not even underwear. It takes me less than five seconds to realize that I am as naked as a jaybird. The pupils are a little larger now, thanks to the shock. I've travelled a lot and I know a hotel room when I see one; that is where I am, the naturally eerie, sleazy hotel room. The radio clock that stands on the mantelpiece says that it is seven in the morning. Then, I see her – the woman that I met at the bar. She is lying right next to me as if she's my wife.

I think back to last night and a familiar feeling grips me. It holds me by the throat and I've never been able to decipher if the feeling is embarrassment, guilt or shame. It is always that same confused feeling on the mornings after these wretched drinking bouts. I vow to myself that I will cut down on my drinking.

The hammer in my head refuses to stop, but I attempt to think about what happened last night. The events play themselves out scene by scene and then there is darkness after I puke. I wish the darkness breaks to explain how I end up in this hotel room, naked, with a complete stranger. I pull the sheet a little further up as if it will undo my crime. It isn't often that I land up like this. I am really not a drunkard.

"Don't bother, there's nothing to hide," *she* calls out from beneath the sheets. I think the person who invented the pronoun must be in my situation. He probably didn't remember her name either.

"What...What happened here? Where are my clothes?" I ask sheepishly.

I need some answers which can confirm that I haven't slept with her. Everything else points in that direction.

"They're at the laundry. You should be thankful that you met me or you'd still be lying in that shit hole where you passed out," she says.

"Thanks. I'm really sorry for what happened last night," I say, even though I don't know what really happened.

She sits up in bed and the sheet that covers her slips down. I can see that she is wearing a black negligee that barely covers her ample bosom. "No wonder they fired you, you dumbass," she says.

I feel slighted by her comment. My natural instinct is to retaliate but the lack of clothes makes me resist. I wrap the sheet around me to search for my clothes even though she's told me that they're at the laundry.

I haven't even stepped out of bed when she says, "Get back into bed, *now.*"

"Lady, I am married," I say.

I'm not sure if married men can't get into bed with strangers but maybe I'm just trying to ignite her morality. By the looks of it, I have been through a typical one-night stand. Even though I don't get along with my wife, I have never been unfaithful. I am a little ashamed.

"You didn't remember that last night?" she asks

"I remember telling you that I am married… The last thing I remember is that I went to the washroom and puked. What happened after that?" I almost cry.

"You passed out and the bar owners were about to throw your sorry ass out on the street. I intervened and brought you to my hotel. I undressed you, sent your clothes to the laundry, cleaned you up and put you to bed."

I am completely horrified. Like I said, this doesn't happen often.

"Since I am neither your wife, nor your mother, nor your lover, I want you to do something for me," she continues

"What?" I ask.

I am a little relieved because I am not sure what a jobless, penniless man can give her.

"Have sex with me," she says without batting an eyelid.

"You can't be serious. I'm really thankful for what you did for me, but this is not right," I say.

It is obvious that even jobless, penniless men can be put to some use.

"Well, that's fine then. You owe me about 500 rupees for the taxi, another 500 for the laundry. I'll give you a discount on my nursing charges. Keep the money on the table and leave. Thank you," she says.

A wave of anxiety hits me when she speaks about the money. I am dead broke; my last penny was spent yesterday and now, I owe her money.

"I don't have the money," I say.

"I know that; I saw your wallet. So take the easy way out," she says.

This is ridiculous, this can't be true. This is too sleazy to be happening in real life. I pinch myself, half hoping that this nightmare will break. I will be awake again, in a real world, where some strange woman isn't making sexual overtures at me.

"I can't do this," I cry like a two-year-old who's been asked to tie his shoelaces.

"Honey, trust me you can, the alcohol has worn off. It's not like last night when you couldn't get an erection," she says.

"Did you try to have sex with me last night?" I shout. Each passing moment is a little more shameful than the last one.

"Of course I did, and you were very willing to do it. The morality of being married wasn't showing under the influence of alcohol. Now, stop being a put on and jump in. The condoms are in my bag," she says.

It is too seedy to be real. I weigh my options; I can borrow the money from my wife but it would mean a lot of explaining. I can bolt out the door, but with no clothes on, I'd be lucky to get past the hotel lobby. Even if I do run with the sheet wrapped around me, the stray dogs that throng the city will rip it before I get past the main door. Really, there are only two options: to talk her out of this, or do it.

"Lady…" I start

"My name is Divya; I think I told you last night," Divya says.

"Sorry, Divya. I can't do it," I reply firmly.

I am standing at an awkward angle, not unlike my situation. I almost feel like a Roman statue – the ones that have a sheet wrapped around them.

"Do you have doubts on your virility? I've got Viagra as well. I wasn't sure how well it would go with the alcohol, so didn't give it to you last night," she says.

Bitch. This woman is a walking sex shop: Condoms, Viagra et al. I am just hoping she doesn't produce a dildo to sodomize me.

"No, it's not that. It's just that this doesn't seem right," I say.

"It's a one night stand; we have sex in the confines of this room. I go back home, you go back home and all's forgotten. That's it!" she says.

Simplistically put, that's it. Most complications in my life occurred when I enhanced my vocabulary to include words like guilt, morals and cheating. Ignorance is definitely more blissful.

"You can make some money too, if you are good. Let's call it the performance incentive," she says, luring me on into immorality.

Money was always a priority in my life but now it is a real need. The last year has been such an eye-opener. When you are living off your wife, you have no rights. I have been living a life of being questioned for every little expense. It has brought me to a point when suicide seems like a viable option. The money can be used.

I look at her. Even without the make-up that she wore last night, she doesn't look repulsive. A thought crosses my mind – what's the harm? We are complete strangers and the moment I walk out of this room, this will be forgotten. Never to be retold. I make my decision.

"Are you coming to bed or leaving? I didn't give standing there and brooding as an option," she says.

Divya is pushy and demanding; I pity her subordinates at the advertising agency. I climb into bed and do what most people count as unethical and immoral. But sometimes, food, water and shelter counts for more than all of these.

Radhika

Iwake up from the deep slumber and my first thoughts are of freedom. In a strange way, I feel like a revolutionary who has fought so long for freedom, that when he obtains it, he doesn't know what to do with it. I have hated this life, of being the trophy wife to a rich, old businessman. And now, that freedom is finally obtained, the elation is so starkly missing.

Even today, I wake up exhausted. The tiredness of the past few weeks refuses to leave me. The planning and execution of the big, fat Indian wedding has left me feeling like a sponge that's been squeezed. I'm happy that the worst is behind me; I only need to send off the relatives.

Out of habit, I pick up the bottle of water that sits on my bedside table and drink until the bottle is empty. At one of those times when I had wanted to become size zero, a dietician had recommended drinking water to speed up my metabolism. Although I still remain a few sizes above zero, the habit clings on. I keep the bottle back, careful to not drop the unused crystal glass.

I get up from bed and stretch to loosen up my taut muscles. The clock on the wall reminds me that it is past nine. I remember my childhood when the school started at seven and I would make it in time. Today, it is unfathomable to even wake up that early. I promise myself that I will wake up early tomorrow and go for a walk. It is my daily ritual to swear that I will wake up in time. Yet, I sleep through the alarm the next morning.

I shower and come out of the bath to face the large dresser. I let the towel drop in the middle of the room. There is a naked, five-foot-six woman in the mirror who refuses to stop staring at me. She looks a few years older than me – maybe she's had a bad marriage. She puts on the foundation to hide the few blemishes on her face – maybe she grew up in the hills where the sun is so harsh. She looks into my eyes – she's got hazel brown eyes. They have a twinkle about them – maybe her bad marriage hasn't left her dead. She brushes down her long, lustrous, brown hair. She can keep them because I am done being a rich socialite. I'm going to get my irritating tresses chopped. She adjusts her sari to hide the few ounces of fat that don't let her look younger. Even then, I think she's beautiful. She sighs, a long wishful sigh. I think she wants to be younger. How do I care? I am still only thirty-one.

I cross four doors on my way to the stairs that lead down to the dining room. Only a few close relatives remain. Vimal's elder brother is sitting at the head of the table. He assumes the role of the head of the household. It's funny how he has suddenly stepped up to that role when I never saw him when Vimal was alive. Breakfast is served – a lavish spread with at least twenty dishes to choose from. A five star hotel would've been proud of this spread. Yet, they find faults – "The *bhaturas* have too much oil", "The *paranthas* don't have enough filling".

Relatives are like that; they can never be happy. One part of me wants to kick them out of the house, but another part of me, the gentler and more patient part calms me down, "They are going to go in any case, and this might be the last time you'll ever see them." Meera and I haven't had the conversation yet, but it is an unsaid understanding that I will need to move out of this house. I suspect that it won't be long before she brings that conversation up.

The waiters bring in a fresh round of *bhaturas* and leave them on the massive dining table. The dining table can seat sixteen, and even then it doesn't fill the room. The room was designed for the Nawabs to hold extravagant feasts and even with the nineteen men and women who sit in the room today, it looks bare. Till about a year ago, there were three people who would sit on this massive table, almost like mice in a grain store. Soon, there will be no one. The house will be locked up unless Meera chooses to rent it out or sell it.

Vimal bought it just after our marriage from a struggling Nawab. The Nawabs are infamous for maintaining a lavish lifestyle. His days of royalty were over when the palatial building had been sold at a pittance. Vimal was stingy but he never lost a bargain. Even after the makeover to remove the signs of decay, there is always a leak somewhere that reminds me of the neglect this mansion has seen.

The relatives make a beeline to their waiting cars. I am not fond of them but out of courtesy, I go down to the porch to see them off. I have to see them leave through the tall gates to believe that they will not come back. They've been around for nearly a week and I am at wit's end in trying to keep them amused. Today, my nightmare will end.

It is bright, sunny and pleasant as the early days of winter are. I call out to Ghanshyam, the servant, who scurries over. He looks hassled and I can empathize with him. He has been as traumatized by the relatives as I have been.

"Ghanshyam *bhaiya, chai*," I say to him.

He nods and rushes back to heed my command. They make me feel like a tyrant who will whiplash them if they don't run away when I ask for something. I sit on the wrought iron chair on the lawns, trying to relax my frayed nerves in the warmth of the sun.

From where I sit, I look at the house that is at least a hundred years old. The architecture is fabulous and looks even more beautiful by night when the light strings that adorn the house are lit. It is quite a sight but it took a fortune to cover the mansion and the lawns with lights. I hate this extravagance for it is so unnecessary. Yes, I can afford it, but somehow my middle class upbringing refuses to understand. At heart, I am still the poor three-year-old girl, who was happy to wear a new dress. I can't forget those days, for they are too severely etched in my memory. It was one of those rare occasions that I had worn new clothes: A soft, pink frock that had small red flowers on it. Even though the heavy sweater was going to cover the flowers, I loved it. My mother had worked by night to have it ready for today. I was turning three and there were preparations for a birthday party. As it turned out, the party was really an overstatement. It was a small event that had four children if you didn't count my brothers, who were five and seven. There were no adults invited, except my uncle and aunt. I wasn't even sure if they had been invited or were in town by accident. They came to Chandigarh pretty often.

"Radhika, don't dirty your clothes. The guests will be coming soon," my mother cried out from the bedroom. She was packing a bag. I was too young to understand if the packing of a bag meant anything but I listened to her. I stepped back from the muddy yard and sat on the small wooden stool in the courtyard of our house, waiting eagerly for the guests to arrive.

I was still sitting on the stool when the children from the neighbourhood came. They were carrying boxes wrapped in brightly-coloured paper, you know, that shiny, cheap thing which shimmers in the light. I remembered when my brother had unwrapped one of those boxes to find a plastic helicopter. I almost wanted to tear the paper apart immediately but when my mother told me not to do it, I didn't. I was still smarting from the spanking yesterday and so, I obeyed.

We went inside to see a cheap cake that had a wafer thin icing. The baker had controlled his costs but created something that hovered between ugly and obnoxious. A plate held *samosas* that slouched, when they really should've been sitting. The crystallized syrup on the *rasgullas* told a nostalgic tale of grubbiness.

It was a shame, but then, what more could you expect from a father who was a cab driver. He'd be up before four and leave for the Chandigarh railway station to pick up passengers arriving on the overnight train. It wasn't short of a miracle that he was being able to provide for a family of five. Within his means, he could only afford a birthday party as extravagant. Even then, I had loved it.

I loved it even more when the guests had left, leaving me alone to open the gifts. My brothers were scavengers, the vultures that hover over the lions to get a morsel of flesh. They waited for something that may not be worth my while, but were disappointed.

In that small one bedroom house in the non-descript by-lanes of Chandigarh, it was nearly impossible to have guests. On the few occasions that we did, we would have to move the furniture to the courtyard. The folding cots were laid out in the drawing room where we would sleep. My uncle and aunt were given the bedroom while we slept on the cots, huddled up together like sardines in a can. It was a difficult fit for two adults and three children to sleep on the two folding cots but we were so used to it.

I woke up to the sounds of my mother weeping. She never really cried. In all that was wrong in our lives, I never heard her cry. I didn't even know why she was crying but I hugged her. She continued to weep while my aunt sat next to her, consoling her. She remained inconsolable.

My father walked into the room. Suddenly and without warning, my mother's bawling died. It was as if my mother had been programmed to stop crying the moment he entered. For a while, there was complete silence until my father broke it.

"Have you spoken to her?" my father asked gruffly

"Not yet," my mother replied, barely able to get the words out of her parched throat.

I thought it was the start of a vacation when my mother said through the tears that had been rolling down her cheeks, "Radhika, you'll have to go with Uncle and Aunt. They will look after you."

It was a December morning when we made the journey in the back of a cranky public transport bus that refused to stop vibrating. Worse still, the windows wouldn't stop the cold mountain air coming in. I was cold and huddled up closer to my aunt. She wasn't doing very well in keeping me warm. The bus reluctantly covered the short distance that existed between my home and my uncle's home. I was blissfully unaware that I would stay here longer than the vacation that I thought it was. Maybe, because of that morning, I have always detested the winters.

Aditya

I wonder if Divya will order a steak for breakfast; she is such a carnivore, a flesh eater. The number of love bites that she has given me leaves me with a risk of being punctured. It is a good thing that my wife Jasleen and I never have sex anymore. Otherwise, my misdemeanour would be very apparent. I am not used to this amount of physical intimacy and even while the pleasures of the flesh are obvious, I feel like a cheap whore for having done the act.

Divya turns over and lies on her stomach. She says, "You're good. Probably one of the better ones that I've had."

This is a shocker. All along, I have been led to believe that the entire episode is an outcome of circumstances. Just how one night stands happen – A lonely guy meets a lonely woman and they end up in bed having uninhibited sex.

"You do this often?" I ask

"About twice a week but lately, work's kept me very busy," she replies nonchalantly.

She speaks so casually that anyone could believe that she is talking about going to the gym. She intrigues me. Even in my wildest dreams, I haven't met a woman like her. I am as curious as a kitten when I ask her, "Do you always pick up guys at bars?"

"No, usually I just pay them in Delhi. I don't know any gigolos in this city. Good thing I found you," she says

I am pretty sure this isn't a good thing, but Jesus, she is interesting. I probe on for the learning. I already know what they call male prostitutes.

"Do you have family?" I ask

"Yes. Parents live in Mangalore. I divorced my husband about four years ago," she replies.

I wonder if she is the stereotype: A single woman whose physical needs compel her to buy satisfaction.

Like a lawyer who has finished examining a witness, I don't have any other questions to ask her. She turns over in her search for the clock, "What's the time?" she asks

I continue to sit in bed, a little dazed and very vulnerable. My hangover refuses to leave me and there's a novice carpenter inside my head. He keeps banging a hammer even though the nail's been driven home. Despite him, I am trying to comprehend what has just occurred.

"It's 8 o'clock," I say. It brings in a realization that I will not be able to run today. I hate it every time I miss my routine. It is an addiction, just as smoking had once been.

"I have a flight to catch; I am going to rush. Just call up housekeeping and ask for your clothes," she says and walks into the bath, naked. I see her jiggling bottom which reminds me of my mother's pineapple jelly. She was such a disaster in the kitchen.

I ask myself – If calling for clothes was this simple, why didn't I just do it before she conned me into sleeping with her?

I am still wrapped in a sheet when the laundry boy knocks on the door. I just open the door an inch to get my clothes back.

I have never liked clothes better than now. I put my clothes on and wait. She is still in the bathroom. One part of me wants to just slip out and melt into the crowd of office goers. Another part remembers that there was some mention of money. I wait.

She comes out dressed in a white bathrobe and looks at me strangely. She probably expected me to have left, but I am still here. I want to know if I have excelled. I want to know if I am eligible for the 'performance incentive'. I almost feel like I'm back at the bank that I got fired from. They would always hang out a carrot and I was always the donkey.

I think it is my imploring eyes that make her walk to the luggage rack. She picks up her purse that is large enough to house a pygmy colony. For an inordinately long time, she fiddles with the bag. I fear that she will con me again by not paying me.

Half her arm is inside the purse and it finally emerges with a fat wad of currency notes. She counts out ten five hundred rupee bills and hands them to me. Despite my atheism, I can't help believing that there is a God. Just last night I was penniless and broke, and now I am earning again, albeit a little dubiously.

"Thank you. It was a pleasure meeting you, and I'm sorry I had to blackmail you into doing this," she says.

It's almost business-like; it's almost like shopping for grocery. I don't know what to say. The events of the last hour have left me speechless. I say to myself that you have to say something. Maybe, a parting speech but the novice in the head won't let me think. Somehow, I say, "Thanks". It's as eloquent as I can be.

I turn around to walk out the door and have almost reached it when she says from behind me,

"Give me your number. Will it be alright if I called you the next time I am visiting?"

I nod my head to jolt the carpenter and we exchange our phone numbers.

"Is it okay if I give your number to some of my friends?" she asks.

I am horrified with myself. I still don't know what I am getting into. I don't quite understand when my morals have faded to this shade of black. Not only have I been unfaithful to my wife, but am consciously degrading myself too. I question myself if it's for the money or is it the sex. I lead a celibate life. Divya thinks I'm good, but I can't have sex with Jasleen. Something inside me stops me from making love to her. In any case, I am sure that I will not have some strange women call me up asking me to have sex with them. I will just have to refuse her.

Instead, I hear myself saying, "Yes".

With that involuntary word, I know that my life will never be the same again.

I exit the hotel and try to find my bearings. I am in Sector 35, where an entire row of hotels stand in line. I wonder why they even have different names when you can't differentiate one from the other. I think about taking a rickshaw, but I prefer to walk. One, it will give me the exercise that I have foregone this morning; and secondly, it will give me a chance to introspect. In the small city of Chandigarh, nothing is too far away. Nor is my wife's home.

I start walking in the general direction of my wife's home, stumbling over the stones that the municipality has so carelessly strewn. My mind fills with questions. I seek answers from myself for what I have just done. My first thoughts are of regret. I know what I have done is incorrect, immoral and maybe even unethical. It isn't right in every way that I look at it. I just know that I've degraded myself. It isn't long before I'm justifying myself. I needed the money and it is definitely better than suicide.

I'm just an average middle class guy. My upbringing doesn't allow me to do what I have done. A thought goes out to my estranged parents. They stay in the same city, less than two kilometres away from my wife's house, but I still don't meet them. I have let them down, I have let my unlovable wife down, and I have let myself down. The cool of the currency notes in my pocket provide a consolation, but even they aren't cold enough to douse the fire that rages inside me. The streets are busy at this hour. Lost in my thoughts, I almost bump into a car as I cross the final street to reach my wife's house.

Radhika

A few years later when the teacher explained the word 'adoption' was I able to appreciate the gravity of what had occurred on the day after my third birthday. I was adopted by my Uncle and Aunt. Even though I was a sapling, I felt uprooted. It was almost a week after our arrival in Solan that I presumed that there was something amiss about this vacation. I wasn't wrong.

My father, or rather my foster father, Rohit Kapila, was the billing clerk in the electricity department. Solan was a small, yet ever-expanding hill station, two hours north of Chandigarh. In those early days, his job didn't pay very well. But somehow, he was able to bring back a gift for me. The gifts weren't extravagant, the poor can't afford to be, but it would be a lollipop one day and candy flosses another. It was a ritual that he refused to forgo.

It wouldn't even be four before I would half hang outside the balcony of the government quarters that were allotted to my father, waiting for his return. The small house on the first floor overlooked the street and the valley below. Even before he had turned the bend, I would run the three hundred metres to be in his arms. I would rummage through the cheap imitation leather bag for my gift. He would carry me home on his shoulders. My biological father wasn't a bad man, but he couldn't be called a good father. For the first time, in my short life, I was experiencing undiluted love. Perhaps it was a good thing that I had been adopted.

My foster mother was quite a novice when it came to raising a child. For one, she didn't know that children need something or the other to keep them occupied. You couldn't really blame her because she didn't have children. She had married my Uncle, now father, over ten years ago and they had been unable to conceive a child. They had waited for her to conceive for over two years, before reaching out to the astrologers. The astrologers had swindled them, taking relatively huge sums of money to perform prayers to appease the Lord and bless them with a child. Only after the Gods had disappointed had they recognized it as a medical problem.

Given her failings as a mother, I didn't have too much to do those days. I would often sit out on the balcony and see the flocks of pigeons that had their nests in the buildings around our house. They were fascinating creatures and I couldn't help admire them. There was something about those birds, maybe their courting, that I could remain on that chair for hours waiting for my father to come home.

My father was an honest, upright man. I don't know why God hadn't given him his own children. I guess God is a little convoluted. He doesn't always favour good people. My father had even been to the PGI at Chandigarh where they diagnosed my mother's problem as an Ovulatory failure. In the early nineteen seventies, the fancier technologies that help infertile couples conceive were yet to be patented. Not that they would have been able to afford it. They had craved for a child, seeing much younger couples bearing fruit, while they continued to be deprived. It was only after I was born that they seriously

considered adoption. I'm not sure my mother was bought into the idea but my father was adamant.

It was only fortunate that I had been born; an unwanted third child to his younger brother. A girl child, to top it, who brought with her the responsibilities of accumulating dowry. They dwelled over the question for over two-and-a-half years before gathering the courage to broach the subject with my biological father. About a month before my third birthday, their desperation reached a peak and during a family wedding, my Papa, as I fondly called my foster father, had taken his brother aside and spoken to him about adopting me.

My day really started when Papa would be back from work. I would usually while away time sitting on the balcony because I didn't have many friends. There were a couple of children in the neighbourhood but they were much older. In the hills, it's difficult to find a playfield. When the boys in the neighbourhood played cricket on the street, I was relegated to field. I didn't know how to and after a few balls were lost in the valley, they refused to let me play with them. With a mother who wasn't the best for company, the pigeons were my only hope.

Most times, I would miss my biological mother. She made a few trips in the first month that I moved to Solan, but those trips had dried up. I was sure that my mother missed me too. I sometimes wish that Papa hadn't spoken to my biological father, Suresh that day. Maybe it was the intoxicant in his blood that had made him agree immediately. He didn't even bother asking my mother. I must have been really unwanted for him to have made a decision that soon. My mother was resistant. I guess, it's the same with the pigeons, for I saw the females fight a cat for their young. Like the chicks fly away, she had let me fly in the interest of the family economics. She had put forward only one request: to keep me for another month, until my birthday.

It wasn't long before I was five and attending school at the Government-run primary school in Solan. Housed in a small dilapidated building with a rustic stone exterior, a small metal board proclaimed its existence. Education at primary school was free – a good thing, because it was the only school that we could afford. My school was a long way away from my home, unless you took the trail through the forest of pine and rhododendron. Every day I would walk back home through those woods, skipping and kicking the rocks that lay on the steep mountain trail, until it emerged out onto the street just below our house. I wasn't afraid at day, but by night I was a disaster.

I don't know why I was such a nervous wreck as a child. I think I feared the ghosts. In the mountains, everyone has a tale to tell. I might have overheard one of those gory stories. The mountains are naturally dark and ominous at nights, and it doesn't take a lot to scare a five-year-old child. I would often wake up in the middle of the night and fiddle with my hair. It was just because my parents slept in the same room that I wouldn't be scared.

It was on one of those nights that I couldn't sleep because my mother was unwell. The next morning, we ferried her to the hospital on the back of a scooter that my father had borrowed from a neighbour. The apathetical nurse kept us waiting for over an hour before the doctor saw my mother. The doctor, who seemed more like a novice intern, checked her and asked a few irrelevant questions before pronouncing his diagnosis – "She is pregnant".

It had to be the way the intern looked that my father was forced to take a second opinion from Dr Mukherjee. It was ridiculously unbelievable that she could be pregnant after all these years.

"I suspect that she's pregnant. The tests will confirm it," he replied.

He obviously did not know what my father would've given him if he had said these words about ten years ago.

"How can that be? She couldn't conceive. We even went to Chandigarh to get her check-up done." I can't forget the look on my father's face at that moment. He was hit by a bolt of lightning.

"You get the tests done, I am reasonably sure that my diagnosis is correct. The tests will confirm it," he reiterated.

The laboratory report came in the next day, confirming Dr Mukherjee's diagnosis. My mother was pregnant. It could almost be a miracle considering that twelve years of a sexually active marriage hadn't led to conception. I was an omen, they said, it was my luck that had rubbed off on them. There was a blissful acknowledgement that there was God.

It was a bright Sunday morning, roughly eight months after my mother's visit to the doctor that the pains started. Mild at first, they gradually intensified until they left her gasping for breath on that dark Sunday evening.

I slept on the chair, to be woken up at dawn by my father. Excited, ecstatic, almost insane, he had transformed from that sombre-looking thirty-eight-year-old into a child who had just experienced his first roller coaster ride.

"You have a sister, Radhika," he said through the tears and the smile that adorned his face.

I rushed into the nursery to see her. She was quite a disappointment. A tiny flailing creature lay in a crib, unconvinced that it had made the journey from her mother's womb into the stark surroundings of the hospital's nursery.

Unsure, if it had gained the right to be called an infant, when it had always been called a foetus. I had expected a larger child, like the ones that they showed in the Johnson and Johnson commercials, but this creature wasn't even close.

I didn't quite like Natasha, my sister, because she took away so much of my father's time. Even before she was born, I didn't quite know what to do once I was back from school. After she was born, I felt neglected. In the little time that my father would have, it left me feeling that I was loved. He would still bring back my gift. He would help me with homework and I wished that he could teach me in school. After all, he was so much better than the teachers at the government school. In school, I made friends but because it got dark so early in the winters, I wouldn't go and meet them after school. If someone asked me who my best friend was, I would say Leechi for I loved the white female pigeon.

Aditya

I enter Jasleen's house. It has ceased to be mine. The day I sold off my house, she signed a lease on this house. Jasleen has no qualms in letting me know, at every instance, that she is running it. I ring the doorbell and she opens it but stands in the doorway refusing to let me enter. I am greeted by a blood curdling glare which demands that I answer her question, "Where have you been all night?"

I want to tell her the truth about the night that has turned me into a gigolo or whatever a male prostitute is called. The truth that she will frown upon and render me a homeless destitute. I choose the comfort of a lie.

"I slept over at a friend's," I say

"Who?" she asks.

She is obviously suspicious. I don't have many friends and the few friends that I do, live in Delhi or abroad. Worse still, I have never slept over at their house. Never.

"Rakesh," I say. I wonder how I come up with such a horribly unimaginative, fabricated name. I am losing my sharpness. The rust of not working my brain is so apparent that it doesn't even allow me to be imaginative in choosing a fictitious name for a fictitious character.

"Who's he?" she asks

"A friend," I say, stating the obvious.

This response is as dumb as Microsoft Office Help; it gives you the most logical answer that doesn't make sense.

I am still standing outside the house while she stands in the doorway blocking my entry. I say to myself that she could be a security guard one day. Outwardly, I am as quiet as a rat. Her build almost scares me – she's five feet nine and almost as broad.

"Never heard of him," she asks. She is still unwilling to accede and grant me entry into the house.

"He's a new friend," I dodge her and enter the house. This move helped me score so many goals on the soccer field and it doesn't let me down today.

She hasn't finished her questioning. She follows me into the kitchen.

"You spent a night at a new friend's place?" she continues the interrogation

The long walk has left me thirsty so I fill a glass of water. I make her wait. She looks unhappy that I am making her wait and a frown appears on her forehead. When she's frowning, she can cause a cardiac arrest. I am immune because I see it every day. I don't want her to be upset lest she turns me out of the house. I keep the glass down even though it's still half full.

"Yes, I attended a party at his place. I had a few too many, so just slept there," I say, straight-faced. I speak with such conviction that a polygraph will fail to catch me lying.

"Ever thought about trying to find work with the same intensity that you drink?" she says

This is so familiar that I am actually beginning to enjoy it. Every conversation over the past year always leads to this point. Every conversation is an opportunity to belittle me.

Every conversation depreciates me. I have reached such a stage of immunity that I can make a self-mutating virus jealous.

"I am trying to network. Rakesh works in a call centre and he will help me find a job," I continue to lie. I finish the glass of water and refill it.

"And what makes you think he'll find a job for a drunken sod like you?" she says.

The male ego doesn't exist anymore. It has been trampled so often that it has preferred to die.

I just nod my head. I want to go some place where she will not follow me; a place that can be locked from inside: the bathroom. Most conversations with her lead me into the bathroom. She thinks I have an irritable bowel syndrome. I know that is the only thing that will distract her from demeaning me.

"I am leaving for work; make sure the maid does the washing and cleaning." She calls out behind me.

"Will do," I say. I am cheerful that I will not have to languish in the bathroom.

She walks out of the door and I lock it. In the confines of the home and with no blaring horns to break my chain of thoughts, I go back to the events of this morning and last night. I feel torn – caught between what my heart thinks is immoral and my brain justifies as essential. I let both of them have a conversation to sort out the mess

"I was wrong in what I did," the heart says.

"In the circumstances, what other options did you have?" the brain asks.

"You could have told Divya to do what she could and walked out the door," the heart says

"Naked?" the brain asks.

The brain has such a bad habit of being logical. The brain hates ambiguity. I think if the brain was a man, he would be an accountant. He'd want the assets and the liabilities to be equal.

"You could have called for the clothes," the heart feebly reasons.

"Who'd have paid for them?" the brain puts it back in its place.

"What you've done is immoral and illegal, its prostitution," the heart says, taking the moral high ground.

"It is a service that you provided her; it's like the bank – they needed you, they kept you. It's just demand and supply. Are we all not whores, in that sense?" the brain is unforgiving.

"Why did you hide it from your wife?" the heart asks.

"Did you tell her why you don't love her or can never love her? There are so many things about you that she doesn't know. Let this be another one," the brain says.

I justify and re-justify my stance on what I had done. Very long ago, someone told me about the Mamma test. If there is something that you are confused about, ask yourself if your Mamma would approve of it. My actions failed the Mamma test. After all, which son can walk up to his mother and say, "Mom, I just had sex for money". It definitely failed the Mamma test.

I wish that it could be a lesser sin, something like lying to my boss, something innocuous that I don't have to hide. I wish I had someone to share it with, maybe even Jasleen. I imagined how the scene would play out when she came back in the evening and I told her, "Jasleen, I was in bed with another woman. But I have the money that you want me to contribute in the house."

I laugh to myself. This will just have to stay inside me.

Radhika

Natasha was over six months old when we made a visit to Chandigarh to meet my biological parents. My biological father Suresh was leaving. Out of sheer luck, he had found a job as a mechanic in the Gulf. His children were growing up and so were their needs. I wondered if he would've left earlier if I had still been a part of his family.

Back in Solan, my father got promoted. They said, it was Natasha's luck that brought them the paltry salary hike. I sometimes wonder if Natasha wasn't born, would his boss have retired. In perfect hindsight, I think I was jealous of her. The undivided love that I was used to had diminished.

I was still in the government school where they refused to teach English. I grew up thinking that it wasn't really a language. My father knew a little bit of it but we wouldn't speak in that language. I was good in mathematics and grasped it well. I could add and subtract even before my teachers at school had a chance to teach it.

Even before I was seven, my mother was pregnant again. She was almost like a dam, holding the eggs behind a concrete wall for all these years, and suddenly, the ovulation had started with a vengeance. While it wasn't abnormal to have three children in those cheap times, there would be a strain on the budget.

We were usually short on money; it always took a lot of thinking to spend. With my mother's frequent pregnancies, a lot of responsibility came my way. I would often go to shop for vegetables at the farmer's market across town. Often, the green grocers would try and steal a bargain from a seven-year-old. I learnt from my father the art of bargaining. I would have a weekly budget. Often, I would save a few rupees from that budget to put into a piggy bank at home.

When my mother's labour started, we were so convinced that it would be a boy that we didn't even think about girl names. We went back to the civil hospital for her delivery and waited while she was in the labour room with my father. After an endless wait, he emerged out of the labour room with mixed emotions; happy, yet a little subdued in expressing it. Elated, because there was another child; disappointed for it wasn't a son.

'You girls have a sister,' he had said, walking away to get himself a cup of tea. The joy that had been him at Natasha's time was missing. He was happy, but he still looked forty. He wasn't that young kid that I had seen him become.

Studying in class 2 of the government school, my routine was still the same, but my father didn't bring the gifts anymore. Maybe for him, it was a struggle to be fair. He would have to buy three gifts for each of his daughters and, therefore, avoidance was best for his budget. Even then, he loved me. It's not always that gifts show how much you love someone. Sadly, I couldn't say the same about my mother.

Often in the evenings, there would be the sound of the two adults at home grumbling. In the two-bedroom government quarter, where the contractors had pocketed the most part of the construction budget, the walls couldn't hold the sounds.

My father would say, "I don't make enough money to raise three children; my salary is quite inadequate."

"I told you not to adopt her," my mother would reply.

I would hear it, but didn't quite understand what they really meant. My father didn't shirk my responsibility that my mother was willing to and would always try and find a solution.

"I think I'll start taking tuitions in the evening to earn some extra money," he replied.

Time passed by and I was fourteen, grown up enough to understand that puberty had arrived. When I think back to myself at that time, I can best describe myself as ugly. I was taller than normal and thin as an eel. Sometimes, I felt like an earthworm.

My hair was the only saving grace on an otherwise unkempt face. It had to be the hormones that covered my otherwise fair face with dark hair. I think it happens to everyone; it's just that some people have a budget to go to the parlour and some don't. I think if I had broken into my piggy bank, I might have had the money to do it. I think mothers teach you this stuff but mine was almost non-existent.

I had been able to break away from the pigeons because my board examinations were scheduled that year and my father would help me at homework after the other students he taught had gone home. I was doing well at school; my grades were amongst the best, except for English. It got introduced when I was eight, maybe nine. I didn't speak it very well, even though I understood it and could write it. In a government school, most teachers can't converse in English and so I had little exposure to the language.

Ashima was now six and Natasha, eight; the bout of fertility that my mother had had was probably seasonal. It was as if the desert had a season of rain and then went back to being a desert. At a time when contraceptives were a rarely-used commodity, my mother had been successful in not being pregnant for over six years - until now.

The frown lines that my father had lost for some time were beginning to show again. The mere thought of providing for another child was giving him sleepless nights. He wasn't getting younger and the small side income that he had coming from the tuitions was already dwindling. The last decade of the century had started and India was increasingly getting obsessed with coaching centres. In these changing times, a part time tutor who specialized in mathematics was having a difficult time making ends meet. Almost forty-eight, and less than ten years away from his retirement, his wife was pregnant. The situation implied that he would have a nine-year-old child and three daughters to marry off after he had retired from his day job. Although there would be a small pension that the government would provide, it would be inadequate. He was ageing faster than his years; the grey tuft of hair were almost white. His financial future was bleak and he still didn't have a plan on how he would be able to manage post-retirement.

The thought of an abortion had crossed his mind, but there was also the matter of progeny, of having a son who could look after him and provide for him when the daughters were married off. It was a gamble –a son would be an insurance policy; but if the child turned out to be a daughter, it would then thrust him into even deeper dungeons of financial instability. Soon, when my board exams would finish, I would study at the Inter College, a higher secondary school that charged fees higher than the school that I was studying in. A fee that he could ill-afford.

In sharp contrast was his brother and my biological father Suresh in Chandigarh. He had gone to the Gulf and worked as a mechanic. He had been able to buy a house in Chandigarh and was on the verge of repatriating to lead a life of retirement. As kids, his brother had been the one who wouldn't study, the one whose only career option had been to be a taxi driver and yet, he had been able to accumulate enough to retire. On the other hand, he, who had been brilliant as a student was still unstable, and unsure of his future.

I wasn't the nervous wreck that I used to be as a child. I overcame my fear of ghosts when I didn't see one for fourteen years. Even then, my habit of fiddling with my hair refused to leave me. I detested exams, not because I didn't study well, but because of the pain of unknotting my tangled hair.

My love affair with the pigeons was dwindling because of my exams. They were loyal, still thronging the building in front of our house. When my father got promoted, he was given a larger flat in the same complex. It only meant that I had to go and sit in the courtyard to see them. Leechi was dead and I had a new favourite – Ehsaan, the grey male.

Aditya

I am accustomed to long walks; I was once a soccer player and that gives me a nervous energy that refuses to let me be home. The walks provide me a release of that energy and are also a refuge from Jasleen. It has been a few days since the events at the Piccadilly Sipper when I take a walk down the cycle track that runs alongside the Rose Garden in Chandigarh. Alone and secluded, the setting is ideal for my thoughts to wander. The ghosts of the events have refused to leave me, although they could've been forgotten. I haven't heard from Divya after that, neither has she given my number to any of her friends. I am almost disappointed in that. I often look down at my phone, expectantly, to see an unfamiliar number flash. I hope that someone, anyone, will call and use my services. The banks don't need me anymore.

In times of adversity, there is a willingness to believe in God. Even an atheist like me wants to believe in a God that I thought had never existed. The time and situation is such that belief is your only saviour. The economic downturn is even worse than was earlier forecast; there isn't a company that is hiring. Most enterprises have lain off people by the thousands. The financial analysts are predicting more doom.

I am more than willing to compromise, in rank and in money, yet that one job is elusive. Anything will do; anything that gives me some money to tide over this period. Like all things that go down and come up, I believe that the economy will be back in shape. I am convinced that I will have a job that will fit my stature, again.

I wonder where I have gone wrong. I have practically tried everything in search for that one job - from the mother-in-law's astrologer to the latest networking website. Nothing is working out.

I quicken my pace; these thoughts always give me an involuntary push. Maybe, it is the frustration of being rejected that's not yielding results. Maybe, it is Karma – a penance of my past sins that is having me endure these times.

Simple luxuries that I had assumed to be needs are luxuries again. I wish I can pull out a cigarette and light it but I don't carry them anymore. I have realized that smoking, apart from what the doctors claim, is an expensive habit for the jobless. I console myself and walk on. I normally turn back from the roundabout that has an ugly igloo sitting on it, but today I cross the main road into Sector 10.

It is past nine, dark and uninviting, yet I walk into the darkness.

I am in an unhappy marriage but can't break away from it. I am dependent on Jasleen even to have a house to stay in. I often wish that I can break away from her as I had done from my parents. I know it will leave me a destitute; one of those homeless beggars who make the subway their home. I shudder at the thought of things being worse than they are today. I am painfully aware that money can buy you happiness or at least enable you to live independently.

I have none and so, this degraded life is now an eternal part of my entity. The five thousand rupees that Divya had given me is all that I have earned in the last one year. Hell, in another world, I used to pay accountants more than that to file my tax returns. I am no accountant. I don't know how to hide incomes and increase expenses. I am a gigolo, a cheap whore that ought to be happy with that sort of money.

I cross the intersection that leads to the Sector 10 market. I am tempted to take the left turn and walk the short distance to the coffee shop at Hotel Mountview. It has been so long that I have had coffee served by a waiter. It has been so long. There had once been a time that I wouldn't have thought twice about doing this. Eating out perhaps is my biggest sacrifice in this ordeal. If I say I love food, it is an understatement. My life revolves around food. I am a voracious, insatiable, experimental devourer of food but that kind must be willing to spend money. And money, I don't have. I am dead broke, living off my wife, without a hope of things being different in times to come.

The five thousand rupees that I had earned are nearly spent. I contemplate making a visit to the bar again. Maybe, I will meet another fairy. Or easier still – I can talk to Divya. It is past nine thirty, a trifle late to be making a call to a relative stranger. Yet, I hit the green button on my cell phone after I bring up her number from the address book. It takes some courage to make a long distance call. I remember the row that had been created when I had spoken to my friend in Delhi. Jasleen hates high mobile bills and I can't afford to upset Madam. To be fair, she has been extremely patient with me but the continued unemployment is stretching her patience. I do not blame her; this is my fate.

Divya answers the phone.

"Hi, this is Adi," I say.

"Adi who?" she says.

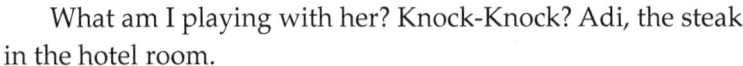

What am I playing with her? Knock-Knock? Adi, the steak in the hotel room.

"Aditya Sharma," I say.

"Do I know you?" her voice betrays no sign of recognition. My hopes are sinking. It must have been a one night stand that I have read too much into. She doesn't even remember me.

"Aditya Sharma from Chandigarh," I say in a desperate attempt to resuscitate her almost dead memory cells.

"Who?" she asks again.

This is futile. I make one last ditch effort.

"You remember that night at the Sipper? When you were here," I say.

"Oh, I'll call you back," she says with a hint of recognition.

I continue to walk down the road that will lead me to Sukhna Lake. I cross another small roundabout. This part of Chandigarh is so unfamiliar. Only bureaucrats and ministers know which sector lies beyond this roundabout. The phone rings breaking the silence of the night.

"Yes, what can I do for you?" she asks.

It is awkward but I try to make it as inoffensive as possible, "I was wondering if you need my services".

"I am not travelling. But, can you come over to Delhi?" she asks me.

"Yes, I'll be there tomorrow," I instinctively say.

How? I do not know. Nevertheless, I jog the four kilometres back home. It is past ten and I stealthily open the door to the house. Jasleen isn't home, so I leave her a note that I have an interview to attend in Delhi and leave the house to take the last train out.

The train rolls into New Delhi station in the wee hours of the morning. It is an unearthly hour to call anyone up, let alone

Divya. I spend two hours waiting for the first rays of the sun on the only available bench, right next to the public lavatory. I try to sleep but the unmistakable stench of urine doesn't let me. I just sit there waiting for the Sun God to arrive.

As dawn breaks out, I make my way to the waiting room. It is grubby, dirty and horrible but even then I shave, shower and change into my business suit. I spray a little bit of the Armani perfume that I have saved for days like today. To a stranger, I will appear as one of those hardworking executives that make their way to their jobs. It is just that my job is not in an office.

Overnight and on the bench, I have reconciled myself that this is the only way forward for me. This is the only way left for me to earn a living. I wait another hour before I think it is prudent to call Divya. She answers the phone in a jiffy, almost as if she is expecting my call. I ask her when it will be convenient for her to meet me. With the timing and venue of our rendezvous decided, I leave the confines of the station on the back of a rickshaw.

I used to live in Delhi. I know this city enough to know my way around. It is best to reach Connaught place on the rickshaw and then take the connecting bus to Greater Kailash.

I look at the piece of paper on which I had hurriedly scribbled down the address. I look up at the board that displays the name of the guest house. The exterior of the guest house looks run down; its walls haven't seen paint in over a decade. I have reached the right place. The guest house, in Greater Kailash, is one of the many nondescript establishments that thrive on lust.

I enter the gate to see Divya waiting for me at the reception. Even before we've had a chance to greet each other, she looks at me from head to toe. "You look very different," she says.

Her revelations don't surprise me. When she last met me, she would've thought twice about picking me up. Today, I am clean-shaven, wearing my best business suit and I also have on a fancy perfume.

To confirm, I ask her, "For better or for worse?"

"Better," she says. When she smiles, she doesn't look so bad. I remember the picture of her when she was luring me into immorality and I only see a monster.

It is apparent that she is a regular at the guest house. The receptionist hands over the keys to a room without bothering to take down her details. I wonder if the fat register that sits on the desk ever gets used at this place.

"My friend owns this place," she says. Does she read minds too?

Contrary to my expectations, the room isn't half as sleazy as I expected it to be. Despite the exterior, the interior seems to be perfect. I look around and see a painting on the wall. It is a print of an M.F. Husain. While I am admiring it, Divya goes into the bathroom.

Is this my cue? Is it time to strip and lay naked on the bed? Is it time to act like a sultry siren? I am not sure what a novice gigolo is supposed to do. I think back to my days in the Philippines. Those go-go girls from the bar – when they came back home with me, did they undress the moment they walked in?

I am still dwelling on Karma and how life has come full circle for me when Divya walks in. I am relieved to see her still wearing clothes. I thank myself for my indecision although it robbed me of her reaction. I would have loved to see her expressions at seeing my entire six foot one frame, naked in the middle of the room.

For the first time, I really look at her objectively. My recollection of that morning is extremely hazy. The hangover and the events of that morning had numbed me. Divya is in her early thirties. Without the heavy makeup, dressed in jeans and a blue polo T, she looks different from what I remember of her. Despite her average looks, she has done well to maintain her body. Even then, I remember the pineapple jelly. The softly accentuated curves of her body give me an unfamiliar feeling of arousal. I don't even remember when I had last heard the call of lust.

"You okay?" she asks. It must be my stare that prompted her question.

"Yes," I make it a point to look away from her breasts when I say that.

"Any luck with the jobs?" she asks.

"No, I don't think I'm going to find one," I reply honestly.

"I know it's difficult. I'm barely hanging on to my own. This recession is such a catastrophe," she says

We sit on the only chairs in the bedroom. She offers me a cup of tea but I decline. We make small talk on the economy and the city. Casually, she reaches out for my tie. She loosens up the knot while continuing to talk. She yanks off my tie and moves to the coat. I am passive. I am not sure what I should be doing. I just stand up from my chair.

She is still sitting and thinks I've stood up because I want my trousers off. She deftly opens my belt and the button of my trousers. She motions me to move towards the bed. I lie on the bed wearing my boxers and a vest that has a fast growing hole. I can't afford to buy a new one. She undresses and joins me.

Not much changes between the last time and this. She is still the same flesh eating animal. The bruises that she had given me last time had taken a week to subside. I wonder what is it about her aggression – why does she have to bite to make her presence felt. Lovemaking can be so much more pleasurable.

She does it again – bites my nipples harder than I had anticipated. Disgusted, I push her to stop my nipples from being severed. She isn't impressed; a resounding slap is her response. A large part of me wants to smack her but an unsaid realization stops me. Knowing that I am the prey and not the predator makes me remain passive.

I am spent, physically and emotionally. I feel humiliated and cheap. She is indifferent when she lights up a cigarette. My last cigarette was over a year ago but I still feel the urge. She offers me one and I can't resist. We continue to lie on the bed, smoking when she says, "I don't know if I told you, but you are really good in bed".

I am not sure if I should be happy about the compliment or be sad about the degradation. I choose graciousness, "Thanks, I am sorry about pushing you off."

"Never do that. Not to me, not to anyone. When you are being paid for it, you do as you are told," Divya says.

This is my first lesson in being a gigolo.

It hasn't been that long but she wants to make love again. She is just insatiable; I find out that day. By the evening, I am limp, dehydrated and hungry.

Just before she is about to leave, she says into my ear, "Have you ever considered doing this in Delhi?"

"Not really. I mean, this is not the ideal career people dream of and plan to execute," I say.

She nods, as if she knows what I am talking about.

"Yeah… but I could get you some clients if you are interested," she says.

Clients, I don't know when that word meant horny women.

"You could be really successful. You have an advantage over the other escorts that women hire. You are good looking, cultured and can keep a conversation. You're not a sex-machine," she says.

I don't know what to say. I keep silent.

"Are you going to be in Delhi for some time?" she asks.

"If you want me to be," I say.

"Stay back. I'll call you," she says.

"I don't have a place to stay," I say.

"That's your problem," she says. She brings out a wad of notes from her pygmy colony purse. I earn another five thousand today, which I think is enough compensation.

Radhika

The board exams weren't the demon that people had told me they were. In fact, they were a breeze and so were the honours when the results came out. I topped the school and was a close second within the district. If my grades in English hadn't pulled down my average, I might even have topped. The school was a little more overjoyed at my showing than I was. To celebrate, they organized a function to felicitate my achievements. The principal of the school was a cautious man when it came to showering compliments but despite his second nature, he was generous in his praises of me.

"She has done our school proud and we wish her success in all her endeavours," he ended the speech, signalling that the few snacks, that a government school on a limited budget could afford, be served to the guests. While people were in conversation with each other, the principal waded through the crowd to find my father and took him aside.

Radhey Shyam Gupta, the principal, was a short, bald and skinny man. A chain smoker who had nicotine-stained teeth, he wasn't setting a great example for the children under his ward.

"I think Radhika is an exceptional student," Mr Gupta

said, pulling out the pack of cigarettes from his trouser pocket.

"I know, her results speak a lot. I am given to believe that she's among the top ten students in the state," my father said.

"I think you should send her to Chandigarh or Delhi to study further, the education here will never do justice to her talent. I can arrange a grant," he said from the corner of his mouth as he lit up a cigarette.

At home, my mother had returned from another one of her now frequent trips to the hospital, this time bearing the fruit of her labour – a son. My father's gamble had paid off and ultimately, he had been blessed with a baby boy. Maybe, it was the coming of the baby that had made my father make the difficult decision or maybe, it was the coming of the grant from the government, but his plans for me were made. I still believe that my mother had something to do with his decision.

He made one trip to Chandigarh to have a conversation with his brother and then, another to meet the principal of a school in Chandigarh. That day, he was only announcing his decision in the presence of his family.

"I have ensured that Radhika gets admission in Chandigarh," he said, "It will be a little expensive but Suresh will keep her."

Chandigarh was a city much larger than Solan could ever dream to be and a place which would hold a fifteen year old girl's fancy. I was excited about moving to Chandigarh, but then there was a hint of sadness to leave everything and everyone that I was familiar with. But then, Chandigarh was only two hours away. I hated to leave Ehsaan and my father. The others weren't really important.

I wasn't a sapling but I again found myself uprooted. It wasn't until the following weekend that we made the trip to Chandigarh, with a bag of clothes that were my only belongings. The welcome that I got from my biological parents was a little subdued. The surroundings were unfamiliar. The small house that I remembered from my childhood had now been replaced by a larger but not so luxurious house. There were three bedrooms in this house, the master bedroom that my parents stayed in and one each belonging to my elder brothers. My arrival had created a feud already. Both of them were asked to share a bedroom so that I could use the third. They looked at me with displeasure – I was unwelcome.

My biological parents Suresh and Sudha displayed mixed emotions. On the one hand, I was their daughter, born of their own flesh and blood and yet, I was a stranger in so many ways. Maybe it was their guilt of having given me away or the cobwebs in their brains, but it prevented them to display their affection, if there was any. The reunion was a little muted than what I had expected it to be.

School started the following day and I was alone in the presence of my biological family. I don't know if it was the unfamiliar bed or the unfamiliar surroundings or just the unfamiliar heat of the plains on that June night, but sleep refused to come. I thought of Ehsaan and how he wouldn't have got his meal today. I was the one feeding the birds in Solan. I sobbed with my head buried deep into the pillow until at some time sleep overtook me.

The first day of school was troublesome, even before I had reached the school. It took a lot to rid my hair of the knots that I had built into them last night. The skirt that the school expected me to wear for uniform was too short for my liking. It was such a stark departure from the salwar kameez that the government school had insisted that I wear. The nakedness of my legs made me uncomfortable and it wasn't until a few hours later at school that I realized that my skirt was the longest, riding two inches below the knees.

Suresh dropped me to Yadavindra Public School where my admission had been secured by my foster father.

I was a new student and as was usual, there was a small induction at the principal's office. The principal introduced me to my class teacher – a Ms Kapoor, a forty something lady, who wore a lovely red Sari and held her hair up in a bun. Sophisticated and suave, she wore rimless glasses that sat on her fair face. I was already impressed because the maid who brought in the tea for the principal was better dressed than most of my teachers in Solan.

"She is your class teacher – Ms Kapoor. She will help you get introduced to the other teachers," the principal said, with a wave of her hand to signify the end of the conversation; a chore had just been finished.

Ms Kapoor escorted me to the classroom filled with over sixty pairs of peering eyes glued on me.

"She is Radhika. She has just moved from Solan and will be studying with you. Try and help her settle in," she said and continued with her lecture. She taught English to the 11th class students that had chosen to take commerce over humanities and the sciences.

There were about twenty-five girls and thirty-five boys in my class. The class' attention was focused on me, despite the fact that Ms Kapoor endeavoured to hold their attention. The English lecture ended about an hour after it had started.

Only in the five minute break before the accounts class started that I made a few introductions; a short girl who sat next to me introduced herself as Shipra and the boy who sat behind me was Aditya. The accounts class started and that was all I could find out until the recess.

The bell rang to signal that it was recess and I opened the tiffin box that my mother had packed for me. Suddenly, the smell of *paranthas* and pickle pervaded the classroom and everyone's attention turned towards me, as if I had committed a cardinal sin. It had been ordinary to do this in my school at Solan and I had expected it to be the same.

"Why don't you go out of the class and eat this stuff?" an anonymous gruff voice from the back of the class shouted out.

"Junglee girl from Solan," said another anonymous girl's voice.

It was obvious why Ms Kapoor had stressed on 'settle in'. Fifty-nine of the sixty students had studied together for the last ten years, they had known each other, they were friends or foes or indifferent to each other, but I was a new entrant and I would need to settle in. I would need to make my place among the other fifty-nine.

"They're crazy; don't let them bother you," Shipra said in a consolatory, sympathetic tone.

"I love *paranthas*. My mother can barely wake up in time to give me this boring butter toast," said Aditya and lunged the three feet from his desk to grab the *paranthas*.

Within the first few weeks of knowing Aditya, I knew he would never become an accountant. Even after studying accountancy for over a year, he wasn't getting any better at ledger entries and would often be confused between debit and credit entries. When you can't master ledger entries, a balance sheet is a distant dream. It wasn't short of a miracle that he had cleared the last exams, barely scraping through with a grace mark from the gracious teacher. And even though his parents had a private tutor coming home to teach him accounts, there was still little hope that he would succeed.

Meanwhile, my grades in English remained poor. How could they be better when all along I had only spoken in Hindi? Ms Kapoor spoke to my parents and offered to coach me. I think people come into your life for a reason. Maybe Ms Kapoor was one of those people who leave an indelible mark on you. Under the pretext of tuitions, she moulded me. Not only did my grades in English improve, but she gave me confidence that I so severely lacked.

It was the early nineteen nineties, a time when India was metamorphosing; when fancy Coca Cola bottles in their bright red crates appeared on the pavements in front of shops. I was going through a transformation too, not unlike the caterpillar, which had never dreamt of becoming a butterfly, yet found itself in the middle of the chrysalis.

Back home, the situation was hardly getting any better. My biological parents were still cold. I wanted to go back to Solan. I wanted to speak to my parents but their visits had stopped and my phone calls went unattended. It was as if I had been estranged; my adopted parents took no interest in my well-being and my biological ones weren't sure of the course they should take.

In the economics lecture about demand and supply, I had learnt that when the demand of a particular commodity drops, the importance or the price of the commodity comes down. In my context, I was the commodity. I had been wanted and cherished until my parents had had their own. And now, as a matter of convenience, when my importance was diminished, I had been sent back to the supplier, my biological parents.

I was still hopeful that it would be temporary but as the days turned to weeks, a fear gnawed me that the laws of economics were true and I was indeed that commodity.

Aditya

I don't have a place to stay, so I check with the clerk at the front desk if I can extend my stay. He confirms in the affirmative. Like a caveman, who has found a cave to spend the night, I venture out for food. The warmth of the currency notes want me to go out and live my life as I once had. I leave the drear of the guest house and walk a couple of miles to go to *Culinaire* in Greater Kailash 2. I love the place, not only for its food but for the memories that I have from that place.

The waiters have changed; they don't recognize me as a regular. I order a raw papaya salad that was my favourite. They refuse to change. They refuse to get an appetizer for thirty minutes. I seize the opportunity and call up Jasleen to tell her that I have cleared the first round of the interview. "I'll just wait here a couple of days for the other rounds to get scheduled," I say.

She doesn't care. I wonder if she thinks of me as furniture. Who really misses a couch being away for a couple of days?

The food is still as good as I remember it to be. The flavourful Thai curry is still as sumptuous as I had known it. After dinner is over, I walk back to the guesthouse.

The clerk wants a deposit and ID. I hadn't bothered to check the rental for the room. At a thousand rupees a night, it could be considered cheap but my circumstances are different. The place is accessible and that I am only going to be around for the next couple of days doesn't make me move out.

I wake up the next morning to Divya's call. "Are you available in the afternoon for a couple of hours?"

I reply in the affirmative.

Divya tells me that she has spoken to a friend about me. "She'll be there this afternoon. Where are you staying?"

I am still lying on the bed and look at the key that lies on the bedside table. It helps me remember the room number.

"The same place. Room 241," I say.

"The going rate is about five thousand an hour but you can easily charge six. However, *we* will wait to hike the rates," she says.

I want to ask her if that is really the rate, why she paid me only five thousand for the entire day yesterday. A commodity, selling by the hour shouldn't ask questions that can harm its chances of selling. I am reminded about a wise saying, 'If you're warm and happy in a pile of shit, keep your mouth shut'. I follow the wisdom.

"And my commission will be ten percent," she continues.

I have found my pimp. I am really and truly on my way. In the thirty hours since I alighted the train, I have a rate, a pimp and a new client. What else can a gigolo ask for?

The dinner yesterday was a little extravagant and I choose to have cheaper *aloo paranthas* at a Dhaba. I know these places. I lived long enough in Delhi during those salad days to know where and how to save money. When my job ended and Jasleen got a transfer to Chandigarh, I was unhappy to leave Delhi. There is so much character that this city possesses.

I am back in the hotel room and flipping through random channels on TV to fill my time. I stop at Bloomberg and find that Citibank has quoted another quarterly loss. Sometimes, I can't stop feeling happy when I hear this about them. It tells me that the Karma theory is true.

I am still burping from the *aloo paranthas* when my cell phone rings. The lady on the line introduces herself as Ratna.

"Just calling to confirm. I'll be there by three," she says.

I think it is wise to brush my teeth before she makes it over. I don't usually brush after every meal but then, it's not often that I have a meeting with a client after lunch.

At the stroke of three, Ratna knocks on the door. It is as if she was waiting outside for it to strike three.

"Hi, you must be Aditya," she says in a funny drawl. Something about her reminds me of a school teacher that I once had.

"Yes ma'am, I am," I say, exactly as I would've addressed the geography teacher.

"Ratna's the name, darling," she says. I am not sure how some people can inspire hate. She is such an impostor. Every word she says is shallow and superficial.

Ratna is in her early forties. She must have been a looker in her heydays. The wrinkles and blemishes that her age has given her, aren't able to take the beauty away. Her body is plump. I am sure that beneath the blue sari, the thighs and calves have cellulite deposits. I am so used to pineapple jelly by now that it doesn't make me cringe. The enormous cleavage that she is using to draw attention to herself, gives away tell-tale stretch marks.

"Divya tells me great things about you," she winks at me as she says that. She is false as hell. I detest her from that moment on. My conscience says something to me about not having to do this. I tell it to shut up.

"Really? And how do you know her?" I ask her. Two can play this game.

"She works in the same office as my husband," she says.

Interesting fact, but how can I make her get rid of this irritating drawl?

In a move that startles her, I pull her towards me and smother her lips with my mouth. It can be construed as a kiss. It is a tool to get rid of this nasal drawl that makes me nauseous. It is like kissing a sponge, so I withdraw. Maybe, the drawl is better.

"And what else did she tell you?" I ask.

"That you are quite charming both in bed and outside," she wants another kiss, so she moves her face at an angle. I ignore her. I am not going to do this again. Even gigolos have preferences.

"And you've come here to verify that she isn't wrong?" I carry on.

"Yes, so should we get started?" she says.

In paying for sex, time is money. She again cocks her face wanting me to kiss her. NO, I am not doing it.

"Sure," I say. I stand here and wait for her to make the next move.

She still has her face at that awkward angle that can give her a crick in the neck. To distract her, I reach out for her sari and let the *pallu* drop to the ground. I am a little more comfortable in being with a strange woman. I'll be honest – there is pleasure in it for me too, but every gyration, every move is meant to give the client more pleasure than it gives me. I finally come and roll over, exhausted.

She looks up at the watch; it is only four. She sits up in bed and asks me, "How long have you been doing this?"

"Just about starting out," I say

"I think you have a bright career ahead of you," she says.

For the first time in the past hour, I don't smell pretence. Even then, the enormity of the situation hits me. This is now my career. I am a professional.

"Thanks," I say with great humility.

"Are you from Delhi?" she asks.

"No, from Chandigarh," I reply.

"Do you have family there?" she probes on.

"Yes."

I reply in monosyllables hoping this conversation ends.

"Your wife?" she asks.

She isn't very bright. She doesn't take the hint

"Yes," I reply.

I feel like I am being interrogated

"Children?" she asks.

"No, don't have any. What about you?" I ask her.

"Yes, they are both studying abroad," she replies.

"Why are you here?" I ask.

"Don't ask personal questions," she says. She is offended.

This is lesson number two in my short career. Do not ask personal questions, just answer them.

Ratna takes great offence to my last question and starts getting dressed. I apologize to her and she softens a little.

"Please walk me down to my car," she says.

Her pretentious nasal drawl is back with a vengeance.

"It was a pleasure having you over," I say in my closing speech

"You are a darling, I'll recommend you," she says.

I am happy to see her drive out in her white Audi. I know the answer to my question: Loads of money, no family and utter boredom. I can't care less if it is any other reason because before she left, she handed me some cash that makes her feel tolerable.

My sojourn in Delhi ends two days later.

I am no accountant but I know that net of expenses and commissions, I have made a good amount of money.

When Divya offers to drop me to the train station, I accept. I still have to pay my broker and pimp her commission. She counts the currency that I give her. She beams and says, "You'll have to move to Delhi, Adi."

Radhika

Shipra and I would take turns trying to make Aditya understand the basic concepts of accounting but he refused to learn. I wondered if he was a little slow or dyslexic when it came to accounts; he had such a huge mental block. He didn't seem dumb when you saw the scores on the other subjects.

"Debit what comes in, credit what goes out," I tried one last time

"Comes in where?" Aditya said

"As an asset," I replied

"Isn't the bank account an asset?" he asked

"Yes, it appears on the asset side of the balance sheet."

"Then don't you credit an account?" he asked.

"Yes, in a non-accounting sense. In accounts, you will debit the bank account."

"This is fuck-all. I don't want to understand this dumb shit," he said faced with his familiar mental block.

"How will you pass?" I asked.

"Fuck knows. I'm going to play soccer. You coming?" he asked unilaterally ending the free class.

Aditya was a great friend, unlike most other boys in the

class. He was loyal and always willing to help. So many times, he would be at fisticuffs with the other boys when they would tease me. I wanted to reciprocate his gesture by helping him in his studies but it seemed like a futile exercise.

We were about three months short of the board exams and he was still struggling with debit and credit entries. The entire class had moved ahead to cash flow statements and analysis of financial statements. I really did want to help him – not only because he was a friend, but because of a certain fondness that I had developed for him. A feeling, that girls my age would best describe as a crush. I wasn't sure if he felt the same and I didn't have the courage to ask lest he take offence. After all, he was precious; the only male amongst the thirty-five who would even speak to me.

On the face of it we were just two very different people – he was hot blooded and aggressive while I was passive and calm; he was indifferent and unattached while I was emotional and grounded; he was strong and athletic and I couldn't run a hundred metres. We were poles apart and yet, opposites attract. It looked like it was always going to be a one-sided affair.

I could be best described as a social misfit in school. I didn't belong amongst the crowd of students who came from rich backgrounds. Maybe, that was that reason why Shipra, Aditya and I made a trio. I still wonder why I never spoke to him about it. It had to be the fear of rejection. I would have, probably, been broken if he had rejected me. Maybe, if my adopted parents hadn't abandoned me, I'd have had the courage to tell him my feelings.

By now, I was convinced that I had been abandoned. I knew that I had been a commodity that was past its shelf life.

It left me shattered and if it hadn't been for Ms Kapoor, I might not have survived. When I had walked into the doors of YPS two years ago, I had been little more than a village girl. She had changed me. I wasn't the same Radhika who wore her oiled hair in braids with red ribbons for company. I wasn't the same Radhika who had worn a skirt two inches below the knees, leaving four inches of unwaxed legs on display. I wasn't the same girl of fifteen who wore a men's vest under her uniform blouse.

I didn't even know when those two years passed. I didn't even know when my friendship with Aditya changed to love. I walked away from school on the day of the farewell – happy for what I had become but sad that I would be separated from Aditya. A little melancholic because I had never been able to tell him what I had felt for him. I think first loves are always like that.

Aditya

On the train back from Delhi, I can't stop thinking about my situation. I question myself to gain a few answers. Yet, I am no closer to an answer. My upbringing doesn't allow me to be what I am. At times, when I'm weak, I remember my grandfather. He had fought the odds and here I am succumbing to them.

My grandfather, Sardar Iqbal Singh, had moved away from a tiny village outside Lahore in Pakistani Punjab. At the time of the Partition, he left behind an ancestral home and large tracts of land. With my father, his only son and his wife in tow, he had braved the refugee camps and the perils until he had reached Delhi. When I was young, he would often sit me on his lap and talk to me of the times that he had seen. The times of distrust, looting and rioting, but the Punjabis are a tough race. They fall down and they rebuild. They lose and they reconstruct. And Sardar Iqbal Singh did too.

He reached Delhi and claimed five acres of land as compensation for all that he had left behind. The land allotted to him was in Uttar Pradesh. A piece that was fertile and well-irrigated. A part of him wanted to remain the farmer that he was, but then sometimes life sends opportunities and one seizes them. He chose to remain in Delhi, sold off the land allotted to him and took a risk by investing every last penny that he owned into a garment-manufacturing business.

The hordes of refugees that had poured into Delhi needed clothes. A small shop in Karol Bagh which housed three tailors and one seamstress was able to fulfil that need. The risk had paid off until he was able to not only provide enough for the family but had enough surpluses to reinvest into the business. It took time, it took long sleepless nights, and it took trips to Surat and Ludhiana. The refugees couldn't afford much and he was forced to procure raw material that was cheap enough to leave him with a margin. He expanded the business to have five shops in the new colonies that were coming up on the outskirts of Delhi and a workshop that could house over twenty tailors. As an outcome, my father, Surjeet Singh was able to receive his education at. Lawrence School in Sanawar and St. Stephens College in Delhi.

His education helped an already flourishing business take bigger shape. His first contribution in expanding the footprint of the business was to procure an export license. Through some of the contacts that he had established at school, the father and son duo were now not only running eight shops in Delhi, but also exporting readymade garments to the United Kingdom and the United States. It was in 1974 that they had consolidated and bought land in Faridabad to set up a factory. A factory, sophisticated enough to house state of the art machinery and large enough to house enough tailors and seamstresses to be able to fulfil the huge bulk orders that were coming in.

My father got married to my mother Gurleen Kaur in 1976.

She was the daughter of an old acquaintance of my grandfather from Lahore. My maternal grandfather had chosen to remain a farmer tilling his fields in Bazpur. It didn't take long for my mother to conceive and before 1977 turned into 1978, I was born and named Gagandeep Singh – an heir to the family business of garment manufacturers and exporters. As a child, I was lanky and thin, which prompted my parents to see the doctor every fortnight. They thought I was suffering from a serious disorder that refused to make me gain weight.

My earliest memories were of my grandfather whom I called Darji. Actually, everyone called him that. We would sit for hours on the jute charpoy as he would recount stories of his ancestral home in Lahore. He would tell me about his fields, the sowing of the land and harvesting of the spoils. He had been successful at business but his heart lay in the joys of agriculture. Darji and I shared a special bond, stronger than I ever did with my mother or father.

My father was a busy man and would seldom be home. His business trips would take him abroad quite often. Like most children, I would look forward to his return when he would bring me back miniature cars, the sorts that were only a dream. We owned a Premier Padmini, a sad excuse for a car but then Maruti hadn't made its foray into the Indian market and the only other option was an Ambassador, a steel behemoth that would need to be warmed up by lighting a fire under the engine. My mother was beginning to take on some of the responsibilities that my grandfather had relinquished at the factory by making short trips out to Faridabad in the Padmini.

I was nearly seven and sported a white handkerchief atop the bun on my head, fastened by many cross running rubber-bands. When I got off the school bus that belonged to the Modern School in Delhi, I was happy. It was the beginning of the Diwali vacation and my mother and I were going to go to Chandigarh to visit my maternal grandmother. My father was in the United States meeting clients. I was a little sad to go away without Darji but my Nani was such a wonderful cook.

The next day was Diwali, the festival of lights. I looked forward to the evening when the entire city would be dressed in lights and the din of the firecrackers would drown all other sounds. My bag of firecrackers was inside Darji's room. It held my fantasy and I would sneak in every so often to check on them. It was finally evening and under the close supervision of my grandfather, I lit a few crackers and then we went inside for the *puja*.

It was sad that Dad had to extend his trip in the States and couldn't be there with us at the time of the *puja*. Although, the festival was Hindu and we were Sikhs, it was still celebrated with the same vigour and intensity as any other Hindu family would.

We were to leave the morning after Diwali and I was made to sleep early that evening. The next morning my grandfather was dressed up even before I woke up; I was dressed in a jiffy and took the front seat in the Padmini before my mother had a chance to object. Darji drove us to the bus terminus, which seemed an awful distance away, even though the traffic was light. My mother touched my grandfather's feet and I hugged him. It was a tough choice between being with him and Nani's *kheer*. He kissed me on the forehead and his parting words were, "Be good, always".

We boarded the bus and were in Chandigarh in about six hours, travelling through a muddy, dusty and narrow highway. Jassi Mamoo, my mother's brother was there to receive us and while he didn't even own a Padmini, he got us home safely on a motor cycle. My maternal grandfather had passed away and his sons had chosen to sell off the lands in Bazpur. They had moved to Chandigarh and ran a grain trade business. The business was struggling and they didn't own a car but they were warm and hospitable people.

There wasn't much to do in Chandigarh, with the exception of food. Jassi Mamoo's son was two years elder than me and he would take me around the colony on his bicycle. He would ride on the seat while I sat on the rod between the handle and the seat. We would return home drenched in sweat and stinking. While our parents would shout at us, Nani would dish out my favourites. The black *dal* with a generous dollop of *ghee* would take away most of the pain of riding the bicycle on the rod.

The vacation was almost over; school would start the following Monday, ending two weeks of a well enjoyed break and Mamma was already busy packing our bags.

It was to be the eleven o'clock train that we were to take back to Delhi. I was awake and ready in time. We were just about to leave for the train station when a phone call changed my life. I didn't understand it then, but our plan was cut short and so were my hair. Indira Gandhi had been assassinated by her bodyguards.

Radhika

"Didi! Meera Didi and Bhaiya are here," Ghanshyam, my late husband's servant brings me back to reality, to the present. I still sit on the wrought iron chair in the lawns in front of the house. I have absolutely no recollection of the time and I look at the pot of tea that has gone cold while I have been reminiscing. I get up and walk in the general direction of the house, still in a trance, remembering what I had once been.

Meera is dressed in a sari, a rich sequined and gaudy piece of cloth that reminds me that money can never buy class. She could almost be one of those cheap, shimmery statues that you get at the Diwali Mela. I may have been one of them if not for my association with Ms Kapoor. Meera's husband tows along, almost lamb-like, behind the proverbial Mary.

I look Meera in the eye; there is a gleam in her eyes today, the twinkle that screams of victory and success. Her eyes say, "I have you out of my life," yet, outwardly she says, "Good function yesterday". I hope she doesn't see the same in my eyes.

I am not sure if she is asking me a question or if it is a statement. I choose to answer it with a simple "Yes" that will fit both bills.

"What's your plan now?" she asks me.

She is obviously not going to beat about the bush. There are no pleasantries or feigned attempts at being polite.

"Well, I still haven't figured it out," I reply truthfully.

While I have known all along that I will have to move away, the details are still hazy.

"Well, I am planning on moving here myself once I'm back from our honeymoon," she says without a trace of emotion.

"I understand," I say, without letting her man feel embarrassed that he will be moving in with his wife, rather than the other way around.

"Well, Vishal wanted me to stay at his house, but it's only got two bedrooms and his parents stay there too. So, it's better that we just move in here," she obviously has no qualms about making her husband feel worthless.

It is a knack that she possesses and loves to display. I have been at the receiving end of this quite often and I know exactly how it feels. I steal a glance in Vishal's direction – he stands there without cringing at the insults that Meera is heaping on him.

"When do you leave for your honeymoon?" I ask.

"Day after tomorrow and we'll be gone for about ten days," she says.

That leaves about twelve days to put down on paper and execute a move of residence. I fiddle with my hair. I always do that when I am unsure or nervous.

Lunch is served – Ghanshyam has put together a vegetarian meal, considering that Vishal is a vegetarian.

"Why've you made vegetarian food?" Meera asks Ghanshyam.

"I thought Bhaiya is vegetarian so…." Ghanshyam begins to explain himself but is cut short when Meera says, "He'll start eating meat".

Vishal doesn't look upset that the woman he has married is going to change so much around him.

They leave shortly after lunch, leaving me a nervous wreck. I am not sure how I will be able to get everything done in such a hurry. I don't even know where to start.

It has been three days since the lunch and I now have a semblance of a to-do list. The list is a mile long and I wonder how I'll be able to complete everything over the next nine days. I delegate more than half of the list to Ghanshyam and the other servants. Gulmohar Park, in south Delhi is going to be my destination.

Secretly, I am happy to break away from Lucknow; the city has never held my fancy. Like Chandigarh, Lucknow is a gossip monger's delight. It is a nightmare to survive the virtual dissection of every move, especially when you are the wife of a leading businessman of the city. The place grants no anonymity and it will be relieving to walk into a store where the store manager doesn't recognize you.

The most important item on my to-do list is something that I will be unable to delegate – a visit to the safety locker of the State Bank of India in Hazratganj. Under the hordes of rich gold and diamond jewellery that are stacked up inside the locker, is a thin silver chain that has tarnished, but still remains more valuable than the millions that the other jewellery is worth.

I leave the house calling the chauffer Ramesh to bring out the shiny BMW onto the porch. It is ironical; my late husband lived the life of a miser for the most part of his life, riding an age old Fiat. It took a lot of coaxing to convince him to upgrade his car, a rare occasion when Meera and I were on the same side of the fence. He had upgraded, going from the Fiat, straight onto a BMW, but died within three months of ordering it. The car pulls over and Ramesh holds the door ajar as I slip into the plush leather upholstery of the back seat.

The locker is only a short distance away from my residence and we cross St. Francis College until I reach the State Bank of India. The manager ushers me in as if I have done him a favour by visiting the branch.

This is another thing that I hate about Lucknow. Everyone is over sweet and unnaturally polite. They almost give me diabetes. I reach into the largest safety locker located within the vault and draw out a small pink coloured box that contains a tarnished silver chain – a gift that Aditya had given me a long time ago. I retrieve the pink box and close the locker. The jewellery is mine to take with me, but it isn't needed. It can stay in the fireproof safe for there are no emotions attached to them. The jewellery is valuable, yet so worthless when compared to a thin, simple, silver chain.

Aditya

Much later in life, I would understand that an ego tussle between a Sikh cleric and the then Prime Minister had changed my life, forever. It started with the Sikh cleric standing for his rights, or that was what he proclaimed, deeming him an anti-national. A holy shrine was desecrated and the Sikhs wanted revenge. The Sikh bodyguards got the community their revenge and then the Hindus wanted their revenge, against my community at large. In the pursuit of revenge, most victims were innocent. They neither believed in the cleric nor in the ability of the Prime Minister, but they were punished. Sometimes, I would wonder if religion was really that important.

The madness manifested itself in the form of riots, arson and focused destruction of property that was even remotely connected with the Sikhs. Our factory in Faridabad and the house were burnt down, with my Darji inside it. It was luck or the lack of it that we weren't in Delhi, where insanity took the most brutal forms.

Our return to Delhi wasn't until two weeks later when some sense of normalcy had been restored. My hair had been cut to a short length and my name changed to Aditya Sharma, through a public notice. It is always difficult to change, especially if it is your identity that changes. Everyone in Chandigarh thought that it was quite unnecessary but my mother was scared. She thought that it was best for me to lose my hair than to lose my life.

Somehow, my mother gathered enough courage to make the return trip to Delhi. We stood in front of the once white coloured house that had been the funeral pyre of my grandfather. Today, it stood charred, black and sooty. My father had received the news too, and had delayed his return from New York. We stood there in silence, grieving for our loss, without a shelter over our heads. A family of garment manufacturers that now only had two suitcases full of clothes.

My father's eyes were cold and expressionless; grieving for a father that he could not give the last rites to. He put some ashes from the charred house into an urn and laid a garland at the entrance of the front door. The next trip was to the factory, an arduous journey on a public bus that would make the Padmini feel like a Lamborghini. The stares on the bus made us more uncomfortable; each stare questioning us how were we still *alive*?

We reached Faridabad and went to the factory on the back of a Rickshaw. We saw more ashes and more charred concrete. We heard more stories of the devastation that had occurred. There were horror stories of how the clothes and the stock of cloth inside had burned incessantly. While I didn't understand much at that age, the impression was grim. Tired of standing, I tugged at my mother's shirt and asked her "What happened to our factory?"

"It was burnt down," she replied.

"Why?" I asked earnestly.

That was a question that most people can still not answer. My mother was no exception. She shrugged her shoulders and turned around, so I couldn't see the tears that were freely flowing down her cheeks.

Ironically, the insurance company that had insured the properties made a killing in the fine print. Of the few exclusions where the insurance policy would not be liable to pay us were the destruction of property arising out of an act of rioting or arson. The loans on the property, the stock of clothes and the advances against expected deliveries, were all the liability of my father. With no assets against them, it took several months to get out of the financial mess that had occurred as a fallout of the arson.

I was admitted to Yadavindra Public School. My mother and I were staying with Jassi Mamoo's family in Chandigarh while my father tried to wrap up his affairs in Delhi. The land took time to sell, and went at huge discounts. The buyers knew my father's situation and the real estate hawks knew that it was a distress sale.

It was only after five months, in the March of nineteen eighty five, that we were together as family. The debts had been paid off, the lands sold and the customers informed. We had no home, no car – not even a Padmini, and only six thousand rupees left to our name.

We rented a house in Chandigarh for two-and-a-half thousand rupees in rent. The landlord asked for a deposit and we paid, not knowing if there would be a way to raise money to pay next month's rent.

Radhika

I wake up tired and wilted even though I have slept for a straight ten hours. The journey from Lucknow was tough – first, the airline cancelled the flight. In these times of recession, business travel has dropped. The airlines aren't getting enough passengers to make the flight from Lucknow to Delhi worthwhile. Very few people from Lucknow are willing to spend money on an airline ticket when a train ticket is about a third of the fare.

Somehow, I got a reservation on the train. I had barely boarded the train when I got the news that there was a minor accident along the route and traffic was delayed. The journey that should've taken no longer than six hours, took ten.

Laxman picked me up from the train station and brought me home. Despite sleeping for ten straight hours, I am still a little weary, probably because of the alien bed. The mattress is sagging and that prompts me to create a new to-do list. Even while some items on the Lucknow list remain pending. I drink the water from the bottle on my bedside and I call out to Laxman to make me a cup of tea.

Laxman knocks on the door and serves me a cup of tea. There is no teapot; just an old bone china cup that is chipped at the edges. I disguise my revulsion and Laxman leaves. I sip on the tea and am tempted to throw it up immediately. It turns out to be tea leaves steeped in milk. The cream in the milk coats my tongue and I leave the cup three quarters full. I am not able to tolerate it anymore.

The weariness refuses to go without a cup of tea and I go down the wide staircase to the hall. I vaguely remember the kitchen being beyond the hall. I walk into the kitchen and I feel like an alien. I don't even remember when I last saw the insides of a kitchen. Cooking was never my forte or passion. I open the cabinet and the door almost disintegrates in my hand. I peer into the dingy cabinet but I can't find a kettle or a sauce pan. The cabinets are decaying. I wonder how many termites share this home with me. I call out to Laxman who is outside tending to the kitchen garden. He runs the few steps to come back into the kitchen, panting. The *beedis* that he reeks of aren't helping his stamina.

"Where's the kettle?" I ask.

"We don't have a kettle," he replies.

"A saucepan? How did you boil the milk? Sorry, the tea?" I ask.

He opens another cabinet. The handle on the cabinet comes off when he yanks it too hard. He brings out a freshly washed, almost wet, yet dirty saucepan with a broken melamine handle. He holds it out for me without an iota of disgust.

"Is this the best that we have?" I ask. Even before he answers, I reach my hand out for the shabby container that faintly resembles a saucepan.

"Yes. Otherwise there is the *patila*," he reaches into the cabinet again, his head completely inside the hollow, before he emerges with a huge brass pot. The brass pot is tarnished. It hasn't been used in ages. I am not surprised because it's big enough to serve an army.

"No, this will do. Where are the tea leaves and milk?" I ask. I move towards the sink to scrub the saucepan that I have in hand. It will have to be changed but till then a scrub will do.

I turn around to see Laxman pulling at the door of the refrigerator. The door almost drops off the hinge. I can't control myself any longer. I almost shout when I say, "Why is everything in shambles? Why don't you get this repaired?"

"Madam, it only came off last week. I'll get it repaired," he says. His voice is a whisper. I don't want him to run away. I don't want him to become a Ghanshyam who saw me as a tyrant. I control my anger. Laxman isn't to blame because when my husband had been alive, he would come to Delhi alone. Once or twice a year, I would accompany him, but I had never bothered to venture anywhere near the kitchen. If Laxman knew any better, why would he be working as a help?

I make the tea, putting in just a dash of milk. I carry the cup back to my room and sit on the bed. I can't help praising myself for the tea. It's been a while since I entered the kitchen but the tea is perfect.

The house is an independent house built on a plot of three hundred and sixty square yards. The architect has done well. He's built a duplex structure to leave enough room for a kitchen garden and a front lawn. I love the porch that overlooks the front lawn. Even on my trips with Vimal here, I would often sit on the rocking chair while he was gone. When his will was announced, I was happy that I didn't get the mansion in Lucknow. This house is better. It's smaller and easier to manage. It has three bedrooms which is also a luxury. I don't think I will ever have as many guests.

I step out to the balcony that opens out from the master bedroom. From where I stand, I can barely make out the street in front of the house. The high boundary wall almost blocks out the view. I look at the lawn. It's been neglected for so long that weeds overshadow the little grass. I know that there's a lot of work to be done. If the kitchen cabinets are anything to go by, the termites would have done more damage than the cabinetry in the kitchen. I make a mental note to try and arrange a contractor who can help me make the changes.

I shower and dress and sit alone in the den. If the handle on the shower hadn't come off while I was bathing, I may not have made this a priority. I ponder over a to-do list.

I write 'renovating the house' at top of the list. There's also the matter of buying a new car. I scribble on a yellow legal pad that I found in one of the drawers. I look up from the pad, trying to get my thoughts together. A question arises: what will I do now that I am away from everything familiar? I choose not to answer the question because it can be procrastinated. I owe myself better living quarters first.

Aditya

I am not sure if Punjabis are enterprising or merely resilient but it wasn't long before my father was creating a business out of nothing at all. He could have chosen to work a job; it would have given him the security of a salary. Instead, he employed a tailor, took cloth on credit and converted the unused servant quarter on the terrace into a tailoring shop. He arranged a buyer for the finished product and had Jassi Mama become a guarantor. All this, when he didn't know how he was going to pay next month's rent.

I continued to school at the Yadavindra Public School, in short, YPS. The tuition was steep, given our circumstances. My father refused to compromise on education. The school was an educationist's dream that had gradually taken on commercial overtones. They ceased to exist as just another school being run out of residential premises. Even when they had bought the land they still didn't have enough to construct a building. The school sent a notice to all the students' parents to voluntarily contribute to the cause. There was hardly anything voluntary about the demand and my father was willing to sell my mother's jewellery for the deposit. He always said, "We can eat less but not compromise on education".

My grades were among the best until the tenth standard and I was a sportsman, leading the school team in soccer. For my sins, I chose to study accountancy.

I never could fathom why I needed to study those damned debit and credit entries. I revelled in hating the subject, knowing that my future depended on it.

Between my hate for the subject and the pleasures of soccer, I met Radhika – a new joiner in class eleven, who was as misfit in the class of sixty as a penguin in the Sahara. At best, she was a village belle who was rudely thrust into the urban landscape, with snobbish, noveau rich, spoilt brats for company. I had half a mind to ignore her or taunt her like the others but the smell of *paranthas* enticed me. I didn't know if it was her mother or someone else who cooked them but they were heavenly. The stuffing of potatoes was admirably spiced up to leave a lasting sensation on the tongue. I was evil; I knew that the *paranthas* would be in constant supply over the next two years. So, it was best to befriend her.

My mother, despite her best qualities, had failed to inherit her mother's culinary genius. Unfortunately for her, my taste buds were oversensitive. She would *attempt* to make good food. Her attempts would be shot down by my criticism until her demotivation had led her to delegate the duties of the kitchen to the maid.

Radhika was a welcome change from the maid's cooking. It was much later that I began to notice the face and the person behind the tiffin box. The face was beautiful, although it did need a little brushing up – the eyebrows had never seen a beautician's thread and the facial hair had never been bleached. As the two years progressed, she changed in her appearance. It was as if she were the statue that the sculptor creator was polishing, to smoothen out the edges. The changes weren't sudden; they weren't apparent, but subtle. One day it would be her hairstyle and then the facial hair would blend in with the skin.

She helped me with my nemesis, accountancy and I would feed on her tiffin. I didn't even know when we became friends or when I got attracted towards her. I didn't know when I developed a fondness of her. On more occasion than one, I thought about telling her what I felt, but then I was a little afraid. At heart she was still rural; I wasn't sure how she would react to any of my overtures. I still remember the last few days of school after which I hadn't seen her for a very long time.

"Will you participate in the fashion show?" I asked Radhika.

"Yes, and you?" she asked me in return.

It was the school farewell set in the mid-nineties; the most fashionable event on the agenda was a fashion show. It was a display of the finest suits and saris that our parents could wrap us in. I had chosen to wear a charcoal black suit over a pin-tucked white shirt and matched it with a red bow-tie that had once belonged to my father. Already, the tailors at dad's shop were stitching it.

"I will," I replied, sounding more carefree than confident.

The practice for the fashion show started the next day, the outcome was the crowning of a Mr and Ms YPS. The fashion show would bring an end to years of studying at YPS. The last two years would also mean an end. It would mean an end to an unfulfilled desire of loving a woman – Radhika. It would all end with a fancy cat-walk routine on the make shift stage at the lawns of Yadavindra Public School. Only memories would remain.

The farewell party, a weak replica of a prom, began in the mild sun of that February afternoon – a time when one isn't sure if it's cold enough to keep your sweater on or warm enough to wear a t-shirt. My father dropped me to the school on his faithful scooter, the machine that had been running for over twelve years and despite its coughing, so reminiscent of old age, refused to die on him.

I saw her; she was almost like Madhuri Dixit in the movies. You know, how the long hairs fly in the wind when the actress makes her first appearance. Her peach chiffon sari ballooned up as it caught the wind.

She reached the parking lot of the school where a few classmates stood, accompanied by very caring mothers who were adjusting safety pins on the saris of their little girls.

She towered over the crowd, a shade over five and a half feet but still tall enough to dwarf the crowd. I felt a familiar longing of reaching out to touch her; of kissing her until one of us collapsed on the ground, breathless. Every eye that existed in the parking lot turned towards her, some stopping momentarily and some continuing to admire the beauty of this young woman.

She walked in my direction and I felt myself burn with desire. I looked into the side view mirror of the nearest car in the parking lot – to get a sense of reassurance that the blushing of my skin didn't give away what I was feeling inside. I was still a light shade of pink, but my heart was the deep red of burning embers. "All set?" she asked me in the same nonchalant way that she would always address me.

"Yes, sort of," I replied.

"You're becoming Mr YPS today," she stated, knowing that I probably stood no chance.

"If I get past the first round, I'd call it an achievement," I replied.

"You'll make it; you're the best," she said.

"Let's go," I said, and we walked the fair distance across the lawns to where the event was being staged, leaving behind a large gathering of girls, women and safety pins.

The music started – the cacophony of Roxette singing "It must have been love…," a bitter reminder that the end was near of a love that had never seen a beginning. I was painfully aware that I might hardly see Radhika again, except for the few times that we would meet at the examination hall.

One part of me wanted to express myself – to tell her that I wanted to be with her and to date her. I sometimes even imagined myself being married to her. I guess that's how first love is. Yet, the other, saner part of me said that this was the last day of school. We would go our different ways after the exams were over, in search of our education and a means to a livelihood. In the process, we'd meet people who possibly, would be more interesting. Maybe, they would be interesting enough to fall in love with. The pain lingered on, of not being able to garner the courage to express what I felt for her. I felt the agony of never being able to dance with her to the tunes of old English songs. I felt anguished that even if I met her later in life, I wouldn't be seventeen.

The evening ended when Radhika was crowned Ms YPS. She walked away in the glory of being crowned, far away from my life. I wipe the one tear that has broken my command and made it to the corner of my eye, mourning the loss of my first love. The love that had never been expressed.

Through the tears, I look out of the window to see that the train has stopped at Chandigarh. I have returned to the city where my first love had happened. So much has changed during this time. Today, I am not the young Sikh boy who had come here on vacation with his mother. Today, I am a gigolo.

Radhika

My social life after my marriage with Vimal was non-existent. He wasn't the sorts who would go out and meet a lot of people. When you don't meet a lot of people, there is a very likely situation that friends are hard to come by.

The very few friends that I have are either out of touch or very far away. Despite the fact that Lucknow was a nightmare that I wish would end, Delhi is beginning to become a horror, sans company. It isn't by accident that I find Shipra. It is the result of a careful search on Facebook that lasts many hours as I navigate through profiles of many similar named people until I find her profile. She now calls herself Shipra Ramachandran Sidhu. I think it's funny that she has married a meat-eating Jat Sikh. She was a Tamil Brahmin who would frown on us meat eaters. Shipra looks ravishing in her profile picture.

She is wearing a kanjivaram sari that suits her wheatish complexion. I send her a friend request and wait for many days before she replies. I read the message that gives me her phone number and I feel like calling immediately but I hesitate. I can't really say why I feel that hesitation. It takes me a week to get over my reluctance to call her. I had sent her my number too but she hasn't called. Maybe, she's as hesitant. My loneliness gives me the courage to call her.

There was so much in common between us in school, yet, we are now so far away, so distant. The void of the years leaves us as strangers. The conversation helps us bridge the divide of the years. I invite her over and she agrees to make a trip the following weekend.

As I learn, Shipra now lives in Delhi for about two years. She is married to a Colonel in the Indian Army – Karambir Singh Sidhu. The phone conversation ends with only an introduction to him and I wait eagerly to host someone at my dingy home. I haven't yet been able to find a contractor who is willing to help me renovate.

The days pass by in preparing for company. I don't sit on the porch so often. I have been shopping for cups and plates and saucers. I want to impress them because they are my only hope of finding company. It was my birthday two weeks ago and I was alone. There was no birthday party. Not even one that had four children come with plastic helicopters. There were no phone calls to wish me and that's when I knew that it's time to change. I am thirty-two now and maybe, a little wiser. I want people around me and Shipra and her husband are the only ones who can keep me away from the porch. Laxman shares my eagerness; he is as perplexed at seeing my forlorn face on the porch, as I am making it.

The weekend arrives and the couple does too; Colonel Singh is dressed in a tweed coat that is so becoming of an Army officer. Around his neck, he wears a silk scarf that has stripes running across it. He's almost as tall as Aditya. It makes him look handsome and I'm happy that Shipra found him.

Shipra is dressed in another one of her south silk saris. It's a red and black silk sari which has a golden border running the length of her *pallu*. I don't know why I didn't ask her and she never told me on the phone but she has kids. In fact, she has two of them – twins, a boy and a girl. They are so alike that it's difficult to make out if they actually have a different gender. I wasn't expecting the kids, so I panic a little. I am not sure how I can entertain them. Laxman is a saviour; he takes charge of the kids immediately. He's converted a wooden plank into a bat and borrows a ball from the neighbours. He and the kids play cricket on the front lawn which leaves us alone to have a conversation.

Shipra is still the same. Her hair is still as short as she used to wear them in school. She's matured like a good wine. The *kajal* that she wears in her eyes makes her look beautiful. I don't know what it is about South Indians that they have the most beautiful eyes. I turn on the heater. As November's turned to December, it's become wretchedly cold. I can't help feeling jealous that Shipra doesn't feel cold in her sari while I sit huddled in layers of cloth. I can't help feeling fifty years old in the company of these young people. The last few days have made me age.

She introduces me to the Colonel and tells me how they met in college. Her father was posted in Chennai as was his. They fell in love and the affair lasted many years before they were married. They both came from an Army background and had travelled India, as most Army children do and that is where the similarities ended. They were from different religions, regions, cultures and traditions. Somehow, their magnetism and love kept them together. As they recounted, they had had a difficult time convincing each other's parents until they had eloped. It was ten years ago that they married. I can't help thinking that some people are so lucky that they can marry the people they love.

Laxman hit the ball too hard and it's lost in the bushes somewhere. They search for it but can't find it and so, have to give up their game. It's probably best because it is past one and I am hungry. He goes into the kitchen and serves us lunch. The conversation continues on the dining table. It isn't until dessert is served that the conversation veers towards Aditya. It has to – he was such an important part of our trio in school.

"Are you in touch with him? I haven't met him since school," Shipra asks.

It was such a long time ago. I think the year would've been 1999. Almost five years after my last meeting with him at the notice board of the school when the board results were announced. I had topped the school and he, thanks to accountancy, had barely scraped through. I wasn't sure if I ought to be happy to see my result or grieve with him for his result. He seemed happy; he had run the risk of failing altogether and took consolation from the fact that he would see the face of a college, as against repeating the class. We went home, and lost touch, not seeing each other until then.

I didn't know if it was an optical illusion or if it was really him. It could've been someone else with an uncanny resemblance to Aditya. It was his walk that gave him away; that same lazy, relaxed gait of a sportsman. We were at the Radisson in Delhi, attending the induction training organized by Citibank. Citibank, at the beginning of every year, would aggressively raid almost every business school worth its salt and recruit some of the best students available. I had been hired from the Punjab University Business School and given a posting at the Chandigarh Branch of the bank.

It was normal to have a week of orientation for fresh recruits at their place of posting before the rigorous, induction program would start. By design, it was a five week long program that would introduce the recruits to the policies of the bank and the conduct that was expected of them. Gradually, it would move to the technical know-how of the designated area of operations.

I had reached Delhi a night before the training on the Shatabdi Express. I was met by a waiting car at the train station that took me to the Citibank guest house in Vasant Vihar. I had never been to Delhi before. Most of my childhood had been spent in Solan and then, Chandigarh. I was accustomed to seeing ghost towns at nine but Delhi was bustling.

I couldn't stop staring out of the window at the bright lights and the fast cars. The car hurtled through the wide roads of Lutyens' Delhi and I couldn't help admiring the wide roads. Awestruck, I took in the sights and sounds, paying scant attention to the girl besides me. Roshni was another recruit who had made the journey with me. We checked in at the guest house and had barely caught some sleep before hustling to the training program that morning.

Aditya made his entry, amongst the last people to enter the hall. He made a cursory glance at the five tables and the five people at each table. His eyes met mine for a split second but didn't show a hint of recognition or familiarity. Maybe, I was mistaken. Maybe, it wasn't him. The morning session started with a round of introductions and he stood up boldly. In a loud booming voice he announced himself as Aditya Sharma, putting to rest any doubt that it was him.

The morning session was a disaster – The tiredness of the night before, the more than uncomfortable chair and the ranting of the head of Human Resources had my body craving for coffee. I wasn't the only one in that situation; most people in the room looked tired and bored. If the HR head was anything to go by, the trainees weren't sure if they had made the right career decision in joining the bank.

Twenty-five pairs of droopy eyes can have a profound effect on the speaker. Mr Kumar looked at the steward for help who nodded that the coffee was ready. We filed out of the hall into the lobby, longing for caffeine to add some colour to the drab start. It was in the coffee break that we met. It was a little awkward in meeting each other after so long.

"Hi," I said, extending my hand out to him. I could've been warmer but in that formal setting, I wasn't. I think it was the unfamiliarity that existed between us that stopped me. It had been five years and I wasn't sure if we had changed.

"Hi, what a pleasant surprise," he said, holding on to my hand.

"I know. It's a small world," I said.

"So, where…" we both started, and stopped simultaneously. He smiled sheepishly.

"Where are you staying?" he asked me.

"At the Citi guest house in Vasant…." I said.

I couldn't remember what the place was called.

"Vihar?" he asked me.

"Yes," I replied.

"It's a short break; let's meet for coffee after the training and we can catch up. I'm stepping out for a smoke. See ya," he said and stepped away.

"You smoke?" I wish I could've seen my expression then. No one in my family smoked and it was just strange for me.

"Yes, bye," he said, unperturbed with that expression. It must be the same whenever he told a woman he smoked.

The day stretched on – the HR head was unforgiving. Most policies and benefits that he outlined that day would come into force after ten years of continued service: the sabbatical and the superannuation. It was ironical that he would speak of the separation policy at the induction, but he did it with disdain. The day wore on until it was nearly six – a day completely wasted by Mr Kumar. The truth was that if it had taken a test of the entire group, most people would have failed miserably.

We stepped out of the Radisson to see that the rush hour traffic was jamming up the highway in front of the Radisson. Aditya went past the many rows of parked cars until he reached the inconspicuous parking lot for two-wheelers. The architect who had designed the building was wily – the parked motorcycles and scooters could hardly be seen, leaving the majesty of the five-star hotel intact.

He kick started the bike into action and drove to the main porch where I stood with a couple of our colleagues. We bid our goodbyes and I sat on the back seat of his bike. Weaving dangerously through the rush hour traffic, we reached Basant Lok: A shopping complex in Vasant Vihar, where the newest store of Barista had just opened. We parked and strolled through the crowd of movie goers until we reached Barista.

He ordered a café latte for himself and I was content to sip on an iced tea. We recounted from the time when we had last seen each other at the notice board. He told me that it had taken a lot out of him to go back home and announce the results to his parents. He was afraid of their wrath. It was only when he got admission to St. Stephens in Delhi that they were a little happy. The soccer that had so contributed to his poor result had been his eventual saviour. He got through a reserved seat on the basis of his sporting abilities.

He moved to Delhi in '94, living in a hostel that provided food, water and shelter and hardly anything besides that.

"Life was tough then. I used to work weekends as a waiter for the embassies," he said.

"Why?" I asked.

"My father wouldn't pay my alcohol bill," he replied straight faced. He was funny.

It wasn't a difficult choice for him to abandon accountancy. He had majored in Psychology.

He said, "The good part about the subject was that you can get away with a little ambiguity. It's not like a balance sheet where the Assets and the Liabilities have to work in tandem."

I laughed remembering the disaster that he was when he would try and make sense of journal entries.

I always knew that he would do well. He was too smart to be bogged down by accountancy. He had excelled and had gone onto to do an MBA. In the final year, he had been selected off the campus by Citibank and offered a Management Trainee position out of the New Delhi branch. He had joined a week before me and had been thrust into the induction program that we were attending together.

We ordered another round of coffee and I told him my story of the hiatus. He dropped me back to the Citi guest house and rode back home. I was still standing at the gate when he left making me wonder if my meeting with Aditya could be called a date.

Aditya

Back in Chandigarh, I dwell on the possibilities in front of me. I can either move to Delhi and work as a gigolo or continue to be in Chandigarh. I can continue to live the low life which I have been used to living. The lure of money is stirring, especially coming off a lean period. I know that the more practical option is to move to Delhi but how can I ever explain this to my wife.

Despite my hardest tries, my conscience refuses to die. Often, it throws up strange words that I don't want to listen. Guilty, cheat, immoral and illegal it says. Whenever these words sound in my ears, I turn on the music a little louder. It drowns out the sounds of the soul.

I came back from Delhi yesterday but haven't had a chance to talk to Jasleen. I decide to approach her while she sits in the lobby, sipping on a huge mug of tea. I pull up a chair and try my best to appear confident.

"I got the job," I lie.

"That's great news, when do you start?" she asks me. Her words and her expression don't match. She doesn't seem excited about my employment. I guess she's not used to seeing me as an equal. I will be an equal if I start earning again.

"In a week's time, I'll have to move to Delhi," I say.

"I won't be able to come; it's not a great time to ask. My employers are letting people go," she says. I haven't asked her to move but she's telling me that she won't.

I think I know this already. I am happy that it will mean a break away from her. It will mean that I have the freedom of prolonging my *career*.

It takes me two days to pack everything that I will need for a bachelor's abode – a thin cotton mattress and a blanket that will help me fight the November chill. I put in more than a few clothes. I don't know when I will next be in Chandigarh. I book my tickets on the train to Delhi. I have a little more money on me this time and I choose to travel by the Shatabadi express. I have things planned; I will initially go and stay with an old friend until I can find a place for myself.

Out of duty, I kiss Jasleen in a passionless way. She is equally cold in her response. I say my goodbyes and walk to the waiting auto rickshaw. She doesn't bother walking out and quickly shuts the door on my back. I am not sure who amongst us is happier.

The auto rickshaw drops me at the train station. I enter the station and look up the leader board. The train is late by about half an hour which isn't abnormal. I sit at the Chandigarh railway station thinking about what lies ahead of me. Not in my wildest dreams have I ever seen myself as a gigolo and even then it is my truth. It must have been destined that I be at the bar when Divya was there. It had to be fate that I am looking forward to moving back to Delhi.

The train arrives and despite the short stop and the swarming crowd that wants to enter simultaneously, I am able to enter. I arrange the luggage on the overhead racks. Before I sit, I take another look at the train ticket to reconfirm that I am on the right seat. I take off the blazer that I have on and prepare for a nap on the way to Delhi. I sit down and recline my seat. The seat next to me is empty until a middle aged lady comes and sits on it. She is one of those eager souls who look for company on train journeys. The sorts, who see this as a chance to befriend their co-passengers.

She has no respect for my plans of sleeping and chatters away to glory. In the first five minutes of meeting her, I know that her husband is in Chandigarh. She is going to visit her son in Delhi who works as a software engineer in a multi-national company.

She asks me, "Where do you work, *beta*?"

My mother is estranged and I am not used to be called *beta*. Her question makes it apparent that I will have to lie again. It will be too scandalous to stay with the truth. On the other hand, the truth will also stop her from elongating the conversation. It will help me get a nap that I want. I choose to be truthful.

"I work as a freelance gigolo," I say with a straight face. I almost make it sound like I am a copywriter.

"What is that?" she obviously hasn't heard the word before.

"A male prostitute," I tell her in earnest.

"You mail prostitutes? How?" she looks bewildered.

"Just like you have female prostitutes, I am a male prostitute," I reply, still looking her in the eyes.

This time she understands. I see her expressions change – shock, that turns to bewilderment and then to disgust.

The train has started moving and there are still a few empty seats in the compartment. She makes a beeline for the one seat farthest from where I am sitting. Often, she turns back to see me, as if I am a Martian that has attacked Earth.

Notwithstanding her stares, I now have more space to stretch my long legs and sleep on the way to New Delhi.

I reach New Delhi station and promptly make my way to the address that my friend Birendra Singh Bhatoliya had given me. The address in West Delhi is a small apartment on the second floor of an independent house. The way to the apartment is almost like an obstacles race. First, the gates – there is a small gate nestled within a locked ugly iron gate. It is about four feet high and I have to double over to get my six feet something frame through it. With the luggage in hand, it is an even more arduous task. Then, the stairs – a steep flight of stairs stand ahead of me. I can either take my luggage or myself upstairs. I almost feel like my father's old scooter. A few years after the farewell in school, it would stop running if anyone sat on it.

I make two trips upstairs, taking a bag each time I go up the stairs. I ring the bell. A man in boxer shorts and a vest, quite underdressed for this November morning, stands in front of me. He opens the door and hugs me. I am a little taken aback by his sudden show of emotion. Yes, we were close in college and a few years after, but that was a while ago. I was very hesitant in asking him for a favour. Given my circumstances, I had unashamedly asked him if I could stay with him.

Birendra Singh Bhatoliya was a subject of ridicule from the moment he had stated his name on the campus. In a college filled with urban, common names, Bhatoliya was unique because the weighty, royal name belonged to a meek, thin and tall human being. His parents were thinking wishfully when they had given him the name. In the twelve years that had passed by since college, the name still tickles my funny bone. Especially, when I associate the name with the man standing in front of me, clad in boxer shorts and a thin, worn-out vest.

"How've you been?" he asks me.

"Very well. You?" I ask in return.

"Hanging in there buddy. Each day I walk out of this house and make my way to the office. I know that it could be the last day I'm going there," he says.

His story is the same as mine; just that what had happened to me isn't somebody's reality yet.

"I know what you're saying, it's a tough economic situation we're in," I make a feeble attempt at consolation.

"Where is this company that you've found a job? I am really interested in knowing which company is still hiring," he asks me.

I want to tell him the truth that there isn't such a company. There isn't a whiff of a chance that any offer letters are being printed. There isn't a tree being felled to make the paper that the potential offer letter will get printed on. I don't.

"It's a company in Gurgaon, Aztec software. They are just venturing out into the BPO space and think that the recession will be over by the time that they have the project off the ground. I sure hope that they are right." I have prepared this part well. Over the past couple of days, I have practiced it to make it sound more authentic than it actually is.

"Yes, I hope so too. My job is at risk; maybe you can send them my resume," he says.

This is unexpected, so, I just nod. He shows me around the house, not that there is too much to show around. It is a small one bedroom apartment. It has a single couch in the drawing room and a rickety bed in the bedroom; there is hardly any other furniture except the two plastic chairs and a table that rocks.

Birendra has wisely, never married. While most friends have put it down to his inability to woo a girl, the truth is that he is still independent. He can still make his own decisions and he can still, at a moment's notice, move a city or a job. Unlike the rest of us, who are weighed down by our marriages and the baggage that comes with it, he is a free man.

"What'll you have for lunch?" he asks me as if he is a culinary genius

"Beef Stroganoff," I reply.

He doesn't know how to make it and we settle for yellow *dal* and rice. I cut a raw onion into pieces and serve it with green chillies to mask the ostensibly bad taste.

Radhika

After he had dropped me at the gate of the guest house, I went past the landlord's fierce Alsatian tied to the trunk of a large palm tree. I went upstairs to the first floor of the large bungalow that had been leased by Citibank to cater to the many visitors that would throng the headquarters of the bank. I changed and came out to find Roshni, the girl from Chandigarh, sitting on the dining table

"Good date?" she asked.

"Date?" I questioned her and myself.

"Ya, that's what we thought," she said. The length of the *'ya'* was directly proportional to her eagerness to pry into my personal life

"He's just an old friend from school," I clarified. I didn't sound very convincing when I said it.

She looked at me, a little disappointed and deeply saddened. She had lost out on a bedtime story and promptly went into the other room leaving me alone in the drawing room.

I sat on the couch, surfing through some of the most ridiculous television programs ever created. There was nothing that held my attention and I called out to the caretaker to make me a cup of tea. It was a habit that I followed from the nights when I would study.

I bolted the bedroom door and turned off the lights. At the train station, I had picked up a novel by Sidney Sheldon. I snuggled under the covers and started reading in the light of the table lamp that rested on the bedside table. Like most characters in his novels, the ones that I was reading about were in bed, making wild, passionate love. I loved reading Sheldon, even though he would always turn his characters into bunnies that were ready to reproduce. It wasn't long before I closed the book; I was too distracted. I turned off the table lamp and attempted to sleep.

My thoughts went back to Aditya – he was even more handsome than what I remembered of him. He was tall, lean, and athletic. His skin had a richer tan than what he had in school. It was almost the colour of that rich caramel sauce that I had had with ice cream. He wore his jet black hair differently now. They were longer than the mushroom cut that he would sport in school. The new hairstyle matured him. The baby face had matured too, making him a man worth dying for. I wasn't sure if he knew that he could arouse a woman's sexuality. I think he did, for why else would he have that air of arrogance. Alone on the bed, I thought of him walking into the training room. He had worn a light tan trouser and a spotless white shirt. Unconsciously, I fantasized about his body under the white shirt until we were the characters of the Sidney Sheldon novel, making uninhibited, unbridled love.

The crush that I thought had passed when we passed out of school was still alive and I was feeling it. Despite the tiredness and lack of sleep the night before, sleep refused to come. Maybe, this was what love did to you. I didn't know the feeling; I had never experienced it but it must be this. I had a sudden longing to call him. I looked at the watch; it was a little after midnight, a trifle too late to listen to the heart's whims. I tossed and turned some more, looking at the watch intermittently, calculating the time that I would have to sleep, if sleep did come.

It wasn't unnatural to wake up tired and lifeless. I'd had less than four hours of sleep. Already late, I rushed into the bathroom and got dressed. Roshni sat at the breakfast table and eyed my swollen eyes suspiciously.

"Didn't get too much sleep, did you?" she smirked. It was the smirk of someone who understood what had kept me awake all night.

"No, it's the new bed. Always have trouble adjusting on the first couple of nights," I lied.

"He's quite a looker, your friend," she said laying special impetus on *friend*. Either she was a psychic or could see right through me. She reached the darkest corners of my soul where I hid my little secret.

I ignored her comment, not knowing if that would fuel her anxiety or kill it. We made our way to the waiting car and were at least fifteen minutes late for the training. Today's training was being conducted by the head of branch banking. He was a surly man with thin, vicious-looking lips. He was to give us a brief overview of the products and services that the branch offered to its customers. He looked at us from above the rimless glasses that he wore on the edge of his nose. It was a discerning look to signal that he did not appreciate our unpunctuality. I apologized, and found my way to the empty chair at the back of the room on the table where Aditya sat.

He looked at me, feigning that he was still interested in the lecture. A small smile appeared on his face, a genuine smile to indicate that he was happy to have me for company on his table.

He scribbled on the thin notepad that hotels provide and turned it towards me. It read "What happened?"

I pulled the notebook in my direction and scribbled on it, "Didn't sleep very well. Woke up late."

"You look tired," he scribbled back on the sheet.

"I am. Tough night," I wrote back.

"If the two of you have stopped exchanging notes, I'd like you to give me the names of three liability products that Citibank offers," Mr. Garg, the head of branch banking hollered.

Fortunately, I remembered, but the virtual rap on the knuckles succeeded in keeping me away from the notepad. At least for the rest of the morning session, we stayed away.

It was in the afternoon tea break that he asked me. "What's the plan for the evening?"

"No plans. I don't know anyone here. I guess I'll go back to the guest house, read and sleep," I replied.

"Have you been to Delhi before?" he asked.

"No, this is my first time," I replied, hesitatingly, as if it were a crime to not have visited the city.

"I could show you around, if you're interested," he said.

I wasn't sure why I accepted immediately. Maybe, it was his company that I had enjoyed last evening or maybe, there was something deeper that I could not understand yet.

"We could go out, but want to catch up on my sleep," I said, trying to be a little more reserved. Even when I said it, my eyes were sparkling, excited by the mere thought of seeing the city.

After the day was over, he pulled the motorcycle out of the parking lot and we went to Dilli Haat – a street food plaza and a craft bazaar from each state of India. Each stall held my attention – be it the Rajasthani stall that sold the camel leather *juttis* or the Kashmiri stall that sold the pashmina shawls. I was like a small child whose attention span would last a few seconds, before moving onto another wonder.

We had dinner of *Rista* and *Gustaba* – fragrant Kashmiri meat balls in gravy. We made our way back to Vasant Vihar, where he dropped me and made his way back home. I was still wondering if this meeting could be referred to as a date. It was apparent that we both enjoyed each other's company, but wasn't a 'date' meant to be a form of courtship? And were we really courting each other?

Aditya

The morning after my arrival, I wake up to the sounds of a thin man scampering in the drawing room to be dressed in time to go to work. I look at the watch besides the couch that I have slept on; it reads eight twenty five. It is a Monday and although it has been a long time that Mondays have ceased to make a difference in my life, I still hate them. If inexplicably, Mondays were people and had a face, I would gladly punch them.

"I am already late. Just fix up something for breakfast. What time do you need to go to work?" Bhatoliya cries out while combing his hair.

"Four o'clock," I reply. Assuming that I do have a job offer at Aztec Software, four in the afternoon is probably the best time to go.

"Leave the keys under the brick," he says and runs out of the front door. It leaves me wondering which brick he is referring to. The truth is that even if I leave the door completely ajar, burglars will probably leave without taking anything. There is hardly anything to take away from the apartment.

I switch on the radio, an old transistor from the middle ages which stalls and has to be beaten up to life. It refuses to take a

FM frequency and the only option is to listen to a presenter on All India Radio. The faceless voice is giving out information on which seeds to sow in this season. Bhatoliya doesn't even possess a TV; I wonder what he does for entertainment. I reckon that he must be earning a decent salary and could afford it. Where is the money going?

I make a phone call to Jasleen, my first since leaving Chandigarh on Sunday morning. I think that the only reason that I want to call her is that it will give her one less reason to crib.

"Hello," I say into the mobile phone. In the many ways in which telephony has evolved, a solution to the crackling is yet to be found.

"Aha, look who is calling! So, you finally found the time?" she replies back sarcastically.

"Sorry, I got busy. How are you?" I ask.

"Settled in?" It is that awkward moment when a question is answered with another.

"Yes," I reply.

"I'll talk to you later. Driving. Bye," and she hangs up the phone. The conversation that has shown so much promise of being converted into a row fizzles out.

I pick up the phone again and call Divya.

"Hi," I say. I assume my deepest, huskiest, sultriest voice when I say it.

"Hi! Are you in Delhi?" she asks me. She is probably in a meeting, the voices in the background certainly sound like she is.

"Yes, came yesterday," I say.

"I'll arrange something; wait for me to call," she says and hangs up. I am getting accustomed to women hanging up on me.

I unpack my bag and bring out a black t-shirt and a pair of jeans. It is still warm during the daytime and a t-shirt will do. In case my escapade does extend into the evening, a wind cheater will suffice. Delhi is always warmer than Chandigarh.

I shower and dress and wait for Divya to call back. It is painful to be in a house bereft of any form of entertainment, especially when you are expectantly waiting for a call that has no timeline to it. I thank God for the man who invented cell phones and lock up the house. With the key in hand, I search for the elusive brick to hide the keys under.

I find the brick – a half broken piece that rests obtrusively on the niche below the electricity meter. The brick is so apparent, that it is the first place a stranger's eyes will rest on. Hiding a key with a key chain under the brick isn't the smartest idea but Birendra's instructions were explicit. I do as I was told and leave the house, uncertainly. I am not sure where I am going but am desperate enough to leave the desolate apartment.

I have just reached the corner of the street when a familiar number flashes on my mobile phone screen. The name "Divya" confirms it.

She speaks in a hushed whisper. It is obvious that she has excused herself from the meeting to arrange a side income for herself.

"I'm sending you an address, reach there," she says. "The rate today is seven thousand; I take fifteen percent," and she hangs up without giving me a chance to negotiate terms.

I get the message and make my way to the rendezvous. It is an address in Aurangzeb Road, one of Delhi's posh colonies. It is a residential address and probably my first house call.

*

The last few weeks since I have moved to Delhi have been exhausting. Unexpectedly, my schedule is keeping me very busy. Divya has lived up to her promise in providing me an endless supply of women. Frankly, I had never thought that there were as many desperate women who would pay to have sex. I was ignorant until now.

It is one of those rare evenings in the last three weeks that I have no appointments. I choose to laze all day in bed with only a book for company. It is in the evening that I finally push myself into the shower. I come out of the bathroom with only a towel wrapped around my waist when I see a forlorn, brooding character sitting on the bed.

"What's wrong?" I ask.

"It has finally happened. My company gave me the pink slip," Birendra says.

"Why? I thought your industry was unaffected by the recession," I ask.

Birendra worked for a fast moving consumer goods company. The likelihood of people not brushing their teeth or not having a bath due to the recession was remote. His job was insulated, unlike bankers like me, who lived off the interest of subprime credit.

"I don't know, I thought so too, until the son of a bitch called me into the office and told me that I needn't come from tomorrow," he says.

"Did they give you a reason?" I ask.

"Yes, the recession; it's the most convenient excuse everyone has these days," he replies. He is holding his head between his hands. Despite the sombreness, he reminds me of an actor from the mid-fifties who specializes in tragedy.

"Cheer up, it's all going to work out," I say. I try to sound optimistic but I know it is in vain. I know the feeling and it is terrible. I was close to tears when I had been asked to leave.

"How come you didn't go to work today?" he asks.

"There's some work over the weekend, so my boss thought it would be best for me to take a day off during the week," I lie. I am lying with so much confidence these days that I can become a specimen for a multiple personality disorder.

We step out for dinner to the nearby *dhaba* to enjoy a sumptuous meal of mutton curry and *rotis* – they are the only highlights of an otherwise melancholic day. The food that I had so missed when I was jobless is returning to my life. The mutton is a little overcooked and spicy but even then, it almost gives me an orgasm. My mouth is burning long after the meal and we make the short walk back from the *dhaba*. We stop to a get a sweet *paan* at the cigarette shop. I need something to help me douse out the fire of the green chillies. While the *paanwaala* puts in the right amounts of *kattha* and *choona,* I light a cigarette and inhale. I am back to smoking regularly. Everything that I had forgone to save money is re-entering my life.

"Can you refer me for a job at your company?" Birendra asks.

I want to tell him that there is no such company but I say, "They are just a start up; they don't have any revenues coming in. I'll try."

"If they can hire you, they obviously think that there is potential. Please try and push it."

"I will," I say half-heartedly.

I hate to lie, especially to a friend. But such is my destiny that I cannot confide in anybody.

Radhika

Yes, I was in love with him. It was love the first time that I had let him walk away in school. It was love now that I was going to leave behind when I would make my way back to Chandigarh. I had struggled to decode the gene that dealt with emotions. Initially, I thought that this strange feeling could be called a crush. I rationalized and waited a few weeks until it didn't feel like an infatuation. I thought it was a strong liking, a kind of adoration of meeting someone who is familiar. Now, when I looked back at the events of the last five weeks of the training, I knew that I was in love.

If I hadn't looked at the watch, every day, five times between five and six, in anticipation of the day to end, I might have thought otherwise. Every day, I would eagerly wait for the training to end so that I could spend the evening with him. When places like Dilli Haat started to prove very expensive we found the Indian Coffee House in Connaught Place. The place we were at, ceased to make a difference. I realized that it was his company that made the evenings so likeable.

It was my conversations with him that made me realize why I loved him. He had the gift of the gab. His humour was dark and wicked and it would make me laugh. He could make me laugh until I cried. Sometimes, even when he wasn't funny, I would laugh. He could even make the most mundane things sound funny – the gatekeeper at the Radisson was a walrus because of his indomitable moustache; the waiter was a catfish because he had a habit of opening his mouth and closing it while pouring the coffee. He said he was reminded of the fish in his aquarium every time he saw the waiter.

So often, we confuse humour with superficiality and make judgments. Initially, I thought he was too until one incident served to remind me that he wasn't. We had just stepped out of the Indian Coffee House when I lost my step. The twisted ankle didn't take very long to heal because he had been caring enough to rush me to a doctor. For the three days that I couldn't walk, he would pick me up from the guesthouse and carry me down the flight of stairs.

When he carried me, I couldn't help but notice the bulge of his biceps and the smell of him. It would drive my senses wild. The proximity to him during those moments wanted me to slip and twist my other ankle. I was brought up in a very conservative home that didn't allow women to think this way but when I was with him, he would arouse me. It would make me fantasize about us making love. Often at night, alone in the confines of my room, I would imagine that we were on a private beach where he made love to me under the open skies. In the mornings, I would chide myself for being promiscuous.

Maybe, it was this confusion that didn't let me express myself. Despite our free flowing conversations, we never broached the subject. I was sure that he did feel something for me, but he never expressed it, and that took away my courage to express myself. It was a relationship, maybe even a courtship but it didn't have a name – just a little beyond friendship and a little short of love.

Today, in about two hours when my train left, it would be over. Like it had ended five years ago. He had promised to drop me to the train station but there was still no sign of him. I leaned over the balcony of the guest house, to see if there was any sign of him. There wasn't; nor was there any sound of his motorcycle.

I went back inside from the balcony and looked at the suitcases that I had packed. I had a lot more luggage than what I had come to Delhi with. I questioned myself if I was right in not asking for the office cab. It would be quite a challenge to balance the large suitcase on the bike as it rode through the ruthless traffic.

A sharp honk from a white Maruti broke the silence of the otherwise still afternoon. When I saw him, he was half outside the car window trying to grab my attention. I had seen the car once before when a torrential squall had forced him to drive into the Radisson instead of riding the bike.

I struggled with the heavy suitcase and somehow managed to reach the car. He loaded the suitcase into the boot and looked at his watch. He had lost time on the way which meant that we would have to rush to catch the train. He wasn't chivalrous enough to open the door for me so I did it myself. We women, tend to over expect.

I sat in the uncomfortable front seat and stole a look at him. I wished there was no rush to get to the railway station. Maybe, in these last moments, we could confess that we loved each other. In that instant, I wanted to kiss him – smack, on the lips. In a car with no air conditioning, the hot summer afternoon felt even warmer. A small bead of sweat rolled down his cheek. I was a little jealous of the sweat; at least it could touch him. I looked at him longingly until he turned his head towards me. I looked down, unsure, if I should listen to my heart. It had been forcing me to tell him that I loved him.

I looked up to see him but his eyes were focused on the road ahead. I fought myself again – my heart longing to express myself and the brain continually reminding me that I might be rejected. The fears of the past that my foster parents had instilled in my psyche were too deep seated. I wasn't sure if I could cope up with another bout of rejection. I chose to stay quiet.

In the brutal midsummer heat of that Delhi afternoon, not many dared to venture out. The streets were empty and moments later we were at Connaught Place. We took a turn off the outer circle to drive down the straight road that leads to the chaotic railway station. Despite our fears, we had made good time. There was still about half an hour for the train to leave when he dropped me on the porch of the New Delhi railway station.

"I'll park the car and come; just wait here," he said and drove away. He had barely travelled ten metres before being stuck in a traffic snarl.

I waited for over ten minutes but there was no sign of him. I looked anxiously at the watch. I still had twenty more minutes. I continued to brave the random men who would come by and ask "Taxi? Madam Taxi?"

Another ten minutes later there was still no sign of him. I made the decision to start walking inside. I gave another futile glance in the direction from where he was expected. He was nowhere to be seen. I continued to lug the large suitcase behind me.

The train was already stationed at the platform – the gates of the train thronged with activity. Unpunctual travellers like me struggled to board the train. I stole another look in the direction of the entrance but he still wasn't there. Hesitatingly and unwillingly, I boarded the train and made the four hour journey back to reality.

Isn't this also a reality that I continue to sit on the porch? It has been a while that Shipra and her family went back home. I look at the moth that is an exception. Even in the brutal cold, it continues to fly around the lamp. I ignore it and go inside to the warmth of a soup that Laxman has boiling in a pot. I sometimes wonder how life would have been if I had told Aditya about my feelings. I think when I stopped short of telling him the first time, I was foolish. When I stopped myself the second time, I was a blunderer.

Aditya

It is ten o'clock when I wake up to Divya's phone call. I couldn't sleep last night. I think it must be my lying that keeps me awake these days. I have heard about a clear conscience letting you sleep comfortably. When I couldn't sleep until two last night, I went out for a run. I hadn't done that for very long. To add to the adrenaline rush, two well-meaning stray dogs had started chasing me. I cut short my run and came back home. I slept at about three which naturally made me wake up so late.

'There's a bachelorette at a farmhouse in Chhatarpur and they need three or four people – do you have any references?' she asks me.

"References?" I ask her. I am still groggy. I am still trying to comprehend what she is trying to ask.

"Yes, any other gigolos that would be interested. Even if they are freshers," she replies.

"Let me see," I say and hang up.

I don't know what part of the conversation rings a bell. Maybe, it is the word fresher that lightens a lamp somewhere in my head. There was a time when I was a fresher. Way back in 1999 when I had just joined Citibank as a Management Trainee and had met Radhika at the induction. We went out to a lot of places those days because I didn't know where else I could take her. The only other option was to take her home to the bachelor pad that I had in Sheikh Sarai that I shared with friends. Two of them were still searching for a job; only Bhatoliya and I had been lucky enough to find jobs off campus. It was a relief because the allowance that I received from my parents would sometimes fail to cover my expenses. My father's business, despite his hard work, refused to gain the glory of his father's business. Towards the last few days of the training, I remember looking at the calendar. I guess it would have been the twentieth of May in 1999. I had heard that the salary got credited into the bank account on the twenty fifth which meant that there would be five more days of scavenging.

I looked forward to payday when my first real earnings would end the drought of living in debt. It was just natural that my thoughts would veer to what I would do when my first salary would come through. I owed a lot of people; the most to my parents.

I had decided that I would buy both of them a gift from my first salary as a small token of appreciation. They had made so many sacrifices for my education. Eventually, I didn't. Instead, I bought a silver chain for Radhika.

I wished I could buy diamonds, but they were too expensive; my heart settled for gold but even at the turn of the last century, gold was difficult to buy. Silver was affordable (read cheap). I settled for a silver chain, waiting for the perfect time to present it to her. Yet, that afternoon when she was leaving for Chandigarh, destiny stepped in to kill my dream.

I reached home, a little flustered and very upset with myself for waiting until the last minute. I wished the jeep in front of me hadn't caused the traffic jam. I wished that the parking attendant hadn't taken an eternity to write the car number. I wished that I had run towards the departing train and had been able to give her the present that I had chosen for her. I wished that I could have told her that I loved her.

It was an expensive gift, especially in the light of the disappointing first salary that Citibank had paid me. The salary offer that had seemed so good on paper had disappeared faster than a bolt of lightning from my newly opened bank account.

I pulled my weary self out of the car and crashed out on the mattress that lay on the floor of the apartment. I was in remorse of not seeing the smile on her face or the sparkle of surprise in her eyes.

I was in love. I had discovered that. It wasn't an emotion that had come naturally. I didn't wake up one day and say to myself "You're in love, boy" but it was gradual, subtle and steady. When I woke up each morning, the first picture that crossed my mind was hers. The first signs of love manifested themselves in a pasted smile on my face. It, stubbornly, refused to go away. In the training, I was suspected of being cheeky because of that smile. The trainers paid special attention to me; they thought that I was mocking them. They would throw questions at me just when I was lost in her thoughts.

I would dream that we were on the summit of an isolated mountain. I would be standing behind her, looking down into the valley, when her hair brushed my nose. That citrusy smell of her hair would arouse me. I would run my hand up her arm, feeling the softness of her when the damn trainer would break my thoughts.

It was in the evenings, on our dates that I wasn't able to stop myself. When she laughed at some of my poorest jokes, I felt humorous. When she laughed, she looked even more beautiful.

Laughing boisterously, we would often be stared at by the middle-aged people that thronged the Indian Coffee House. They would come and go but we continued to sit there for hours. It was just that hours of her company weren't enough. I would often wonder how I could have really long conversations with her when I wouldn't be able to talk to my friends for more than a short while. I had known Bhatoliya for years now, but even he couldn't hold my attention as much as her. If that wasn't love, then maybe love didn't exist. In the numerous meetings that we had, I was sure that she loved me too. Her eyes gave her away. Yet, she wouldn't say anything. I waited until I was convinced that I would have to make the first move in expressing what I felt for her.

Even then, there was apprehension – I had just started out my career, my salary was inadequate, and I wanted to build my career. I was only a Management Trainee. The brain gave me a million reasons why I shouldn't express what I felt for her and many more why this wasn't the most opportune time to fall in love.

I fixed myself a stiff drink, unhappy at what I wasn't able to do, but happy that I could savour the delight of being in love, without the responsibilities or the commitments of being in a relationship.

My work at Citibank had started in earnest; the reforms made to the Indian economy were less than a decade old. Banking in India was beginning to look beyond the nationalized, state-run banks. ICICI, HDFC and some other private banks were only beginning to find their bearings in the urban landscape. In this setting, Citibank stood tall – an icon of how banking should be done. I joined in as a relationship manager, interacting with some of the wealthiest people in Delhi, who were clients. I would meet them regularly, presenting new products and being responsible for sales of these products. After all, the branch manager would regularly pull up people who didn't have sales figures against their names. Most appointments were scheduled over the weekends; my learning was that wealthy people worked for the money on the weekdays and made important choices about making the money work for them over the weekend.

The fallout of these meetings was that I could not make a trip back home to meet Radhika. Occasionally, we would speak over the phone. In those times, we didn't have a phone at home; so, long distance telephone calls were made from a public call office. There was little privacy, notwithstanding the high expense that it would rake up. Meanwhile, the silver chain continued to tarnish in my cupboard, waiting for its rightful owner to wear it around her neck.

Radhika

"I'll buy the material myself," I say, "Quote me your price for labour."

I am haggling with the contractor, Why? I do not know. Maybe, the upbringing that I had and the economics of those times has made me into what I am today. There will be so much less trouble in just outsourcing the entire renovation work to the contractor but my small town upbringing refuses to let go. Even if he does overcharge, I can afford it. Even if he fleeces me, I can afford it. Even if he cheats me, I can afford it. Yet, letting go is so difficult.

"One lac for the entire thing," Sudhir, the contractor replies.

Sudhir is one of Laxman's finds. When I told Laxman that we need to start the renovation of the house, his resourcefulness introduced me to Sudhir, a middle-aged, dark man. His generosity with mustard oil makes his dark, dyed hair shine. This is his second visit to my home. On his first visit, it had taken more than a few hours to rid the house of the strong odour of mustard oil. He already took the measurements and came back today to give me a quotation. I am already wondering if I should have this conversation out in the lawn.

"That's too high," I say. I know that it isn't.

"No, Madam. Not at all," he almost cries.

"Okay, but I won't pay you if the workmanship is poor," I am unforgiving in trying to steal a bargain.

"Don't give me a rupee; give me to the police, if you find me wanting. You won't find a reason to complain." Either Sudhir is very desperate or wants to make a career in theatrics.

"When can you start work?" I ask him.

"Today, but when will you have the material available?" he asks me.

I have no clue. I don't even know where the hardware stores are and I have volunteered to buy the material. Sometimes, I am not sure if I know Delhi. I have spent time in this city, I have stayed in the suburbs, yet, it remains alien.

"Give me your number, I'll call you," I say. I will not let Sudhir take wind that I am going to struggle with the bargain that I have just hit.

Laxman is versatile and it is hardly a wonder that Vimal had employed him. He takes care of the house; he doubles up as a cook and can also drive. He is a virtual 'Man Friday'- capable enough to carry off the entire load and even then have time to find a contractor. He can almost be perfect if he stops smoking. I am sure that he's in the kitchen garden where we haven't seen a radish grow. I think it's because of all the stubs in the ground that vegetables refuse to grow. Sure enough, I find him there.

"Laxman, where are the hardware stores? We need to buy the material," I say.

"Kotla Mubarakpur," he replies, referring to the maze of streets that lie hidden between two very posh colonies of South Delhi. You can find anything from a rubber band to a steel cable there.

"Get the car out; let's go shopping for the material," I say.

I walk back inside to gather the list that Sudhir left for me. Laxman is almost becoming Ghanshyam. He has scurried off in the direction of the car. Back inside, I am picking up the list off the coffee table when Laxman comes back and says, "Kotla is going to be closed today. It's Monday," he says.

"Is there no other place where we can buy the hardware?" I ask him. I want to get this chore off my back. I remember the days in Lucknow when it took ages to complete the renovation. I know that the sooner the work starts, the sooner it will end. I want to get the renovation off my list before I give serious thought to what I need to pursue.

"There are some shops in Sant Nagar; we could go there, but they'll be a little more expensive," he says. I think he makes that comment on purpose. I am widely being recognized as a miser. I take heart that Vimal has set very high benchmarks.

"That's fine, get the car out," I say.

He backs out an old Honda Accord. It is a second hand car that Vimal had kept in Delhi. He thought that it would be cheaper than hiring a taxi. His trips were very infrequent, but even then, he did some calculation to prove that a second hand car is cheaper than hiring a taxi. I think he bought it for the same amount as a six pack of beer. It doesn't surprise me when I look at the moth-ridden back seat. I am thankful that in his will, he was considerate to give me enough money to renovate the house and buy a car. I am not sure what car I should buy. Everything comes at huge discounts in these days of recession. The automobile industry is in as bad a shape as banking was. It needs to be changed but it is lower down on my priority list. I sit on the back seat as Laxman drives out.

We exit the colony and leave behind the sleepy guard at the gate. Laxman drives onto Khel Gaon Marg and takes a left near Siri Fort. We enter Greater Kailash 1; I love the market in M-Block. There was a time when I would come here and shop for clothes. You know, the clothes that you can wear on a weekend. It has been such a long time that I haven't worn those sorts of clothes. I don't know why but I suddenly get that heady feeling. I had yearned for freedom and I finally have it. Maybe, it is time to live up my life. We go past the busy M-Block market until Laxman parks opposite a small plywood store in Sant Nagar.

It is almost evening by the time I am through with the shopping list. Laxman makes a U-turn and we start to travel back on the same route. It's the rush hour and the traffic is slower. I wonder why the traffic isn't lighter when so many people don't have jobs to come back from.

It takes us about thirty minutes to enter Greater Kailash and we are somewhere in the vicinity of the M-Block market. Laxman honks at the car in front of him. It braked suddenly because the car in front of it braked as suddenly. We are at a complete stop, yet again.

I hate the winters because it makes me pee so frequently. My bladder is on the verge of bursting. I am stuck in a traffic jam but I must go. I ask Laxman to park somewhere. I am in front of the rows of houses that have been converted into shops. There's a coffee shop and a saloon. Instinctively, I enter the saloon.

Aditya

Those days, I would often wonder why the world's largest bank could not afford to give me a salary that would help me buy a car. How could they let the face of their bank travel to meet a client drenched to the skin? And worse still – why couldn't I have chosen Chandigarh as my first posting? At least, I would have been closer to Radhika.

I stood at the traffic signal braving the rain en route to a meeting with a potential client. I said to myself, "There has to be a light at the end of this tunnel; you are doing this to make a career. You are doing this so that you get a promotion. You are doing this to have a better life."

There are some people who don't need motivation and there are some who need a reason to do well. I fell into the second category. I had to have a reason why I wanted to be successful and that reason was Radhika. Despite having not made a trip to Chandigarh or having expressed myself, I continued to build a fantasy world around me. Unknowingly, I justified each of my actions with "I was doing it for us".

I squeaked through the lobby of the office of my client. The leather shoes were squirting water from my sodden socks. A Vice President of an Insurance firm had given me a late afternoon appointment and I had accepted without expecting the rain to fall as furiously as it did. Maybe, it was my physical state and the sympathy that arose of it, that made him give me a cheque of three lacs for his investment account. The bank would get two percent of that amount, about half a month's salary for me. If I were to believe my boss, I was doing well. "On course," he would say, without implying what the course really was and where it would eventually lead me.

In the bargain, he owned me. I spoke to him about taking a few days off to go back and meet Radhika in Chandigarh.

"The bank's policy doesn't allow any leaves in the first six months, unless it's for a dire medical or personal emergency." I had half a mind to fictitiously kill a few relatives to create a personal emergency; after all, there were so many. And then, the tiny voice in my head would say, "You're doing it for us."

A famous writer once said, "Absence is to love, what wind is to fire; it extinguishes the little and enkindles the great." If it had been infatuation, this was the perfect opportunity for it to die down.

After all, it had been over two months since the incident at the train station. The monsoons had come. We seldom spoke because I was hesitant in calling her home. Her parents were orthodox and too many phone calls from a male *friend* were frowned upon. Why else would she call me up from a PCO, with the background chatter of a few hundred people, taking away the pleasure? I wished that I had been able to gift her a mobile phone instead of the worthless silver chain that I had bought – at least it would keep us in touch.

It was a Friday evening in late July when we finally spoke. It was a chance occurrence when I was at my desk and answered the phone.

"Good Evening. Citibank. This is Aditya Sharma. How can I help you?" I said into the receiver, thinking it to be a call from a client.

"Hey," she said.

I looked around to see who else might be able to eavesdrop on my conversation with her. Thankfully, there weren't many people around. "Hi! How are you?" I was happy to hear her voice.

"I am coming to Delhi," she said excitedly.

"When?" I asked, more excited than when I had seen my first porn movie.

"Next Thursday. There's a training scheduled in Delhi," she said.

"Wow! For how long?" I asked.

"Two days. But I'll see if I can extend it over the weekend."

I almost said, "I love you" at the end of the conversation, but it would be so much better to say that in person – at least for the first time.

I was excited, happy and expectant. The evening refused to give way to the night. The five days that lay between now and meeting her were unbearable. I lay awake until past midnight, knowing that Saturday was a working day at the bank. I tossed and turned, replaying in my mind a thousand times over – how and what I would say to her. I imagined us in the finest restaurant, where she was dressed in the peach sari and I was dressed in a tuxedo.

In the light of the solitary candle on the table, I would hold her hand and tell her how much I loved her and what she meant to me, and justify why I had taken so long to say what I was saying. At some point, after I paid the bill and before we made love, I slept.

The next morning, I cancelled a meeting with a stingy client to take the silver chain to the jeweller. The humidity in the air had tarnished the silver beyond the two-and-a-half months that it had existed.

Radhika

When I walk out the door of the beauty parlour, I see Laxman standing in the distance. I wave to him but he doesn't wave back. I cross the street and go to the parked car where Laxman stands smoking a *beedi*. I am almost in front of him but he still doesn't recognize me. I am not sure that a haircut can change me so much. I could've easily walked out of the parlour once I had used the wash, but I didn't. I got rid of my tresses. It's quite a fashionable cut – it's left me feeling like the rats ate my hair. It's that uneven. Even before the hairdresser chopped off the first tresses, I was unsure. Now, I am upset. I sit in the car thinking that I am overdoing this freedom thing.

It's almost January by the time that I am able to get rid of Sudhir and his workers. I have struggled to be lost in my thoughts while the workers hammered nails. I have been able to buy a new car though. It's a brand new white Honda Accord. It isn't by accident that I got stuck with the same car. The year-end discount on that model was the highest. I don't spend too much and most of the allowance that the trust gives me is sitting in the bank account. Even then, I'm stingy. I've saved from the budget of the car with absolutely no recollection of what I will do with the savings. It's the darned piggy bank from my childhood that's making me do this. I wish I could change.

I don't know if it's because of the workers moving out or that I have most items struck off the to-do list, but the days seem longer. They're also duller than before. I still sit in the winter sun on the porch for hours together. There is nothing that fills my days except the pigeons. Ehsaan must have died but I have new favourites. Even then, I feel that I am living a worthless, lazy life that bores me and questions my very existence.

Often, my thoughts veer towards having an occupation. I wish I can have a job, like I used to before I married Vimal. He had insisted that I leave my job right after I married him. I don't need the money but it'll give me a routine. I'll be doing something better than reminiscing and brooding about a love that I had lost. It is magical how some people can remain etched in your memory.

Laxman brings in the morning papers for me and my first reaction is, "Where's the rest of it?"

The paper has thinned. Not many companies advertise and I have heard that people are losing their jobs. Yet, I am immune. I wonder if I didn't have the luxury of my marriage, would I have kept my job. Maybe, some things just happen for the best. My marriage was a nightmare; I had foolishly rushed into it. But it has left me with the comfort of not having to work.

Shipra and I meet often. She is the only saving grace from my dull routine. There are times when I feel that I am bogging her down. She has responsibilities, unlike me, in bringing up the twins. I never had children. Sometimes, I think I should've had them; they'd give me a purpose in life. Vimal was happy with Meera and I didn't want children. Maybe, I did but I didn't want them fathered by Vimal.

It is one of those days that I've driven to Delhi Cantonment to meet Shipra. She brings in the tea and even before she's had a chance to pour it, I say, "I feel like I'm wasting my life". It is an honest confession. I think realization is the first step to change.

"Honestly, you are," she says.

She reconfirms what I know already. It's not difficult for anyone to make that out.

"It feels like I have no purpose in life. It feels like I am just a rudderless boat that's floating around," I say.

"I don't know if I can comment on that, but you must do something," she says.

"What? I mean there are no jobs. What can a thirty-two-year-old woman do?" I ask her.

When one starts feeling that at thirty-two years you are not capable of doing anything, it's about time to see a psychiatrist. Somewhere within, I always feel like I'm fifty. Why can't I break out of this mindset? I often ask myself this question but never get a perfect answer. Even my trendy new haircut doesn't help me feel young.

"Lots. As long as you believe in it," she says.

Long after the meeting is over, I keep thinking about what I really believe in. I mean, I am the perfect case of someone who doesn't need a financial motive. I can do stuff that people only dream of. Everyone else is so caught up in food, water and shelter. Maybe, I can do something for charity. Volunteer?

I am hit by inspiration. I log on to the Internet to come up with a few options for myself. I will speak to a few NGOs tomorrow morning to find out what I can do to help them.

Time is usually more precious than money. Maybe, I can volunteer to help them in whatever they were doing.

When I look at the causes of these NGOs, they all seem noble. None of them are worth ignoring. It isn't by accident that I choose to go with NGOs that support education as a cause. I remember my first day in YPS when I had been hesitant introducing myself because I wasn't able to speak in English. Maybe, I can make a difference to someone's life as Ms Kapoor had influenced mine. Determinedly, I put some phone numbers on a notepad promising myself that I will call them up the next day.

The next morning I am back in the dumps. The familiar laziness that prevents me from going out for a walk is with me again. Maybe I am just destined to be sitting on a chair on the porch of a large house. Maybe, I am only fit to have pigeons for a muse.

It is past eleven that I break my inertia. I pick up the phone to dial a number that I have saved. The number belongs to a NGO that helps underprivileged children study. I am a little shy when I say, "I'd like to volunteer my time for something noble."

"You are most welcome," the woman on the line replies.

"So, how do we start?" I ask her.

"Can you come over and meet us?" she asks.

I note down the address that the lady gives me. It is an address in East of Kailash. I can wait for lunch but I don't want my familiar lazy self overtaking me. I call out to Laxman to pull out the car.

I wonder why I hadn't chosen something flashier than the Accord. I could've afforded to buy a BMW but it has to be a deep-seated wish to become one with the people that I interact with. Shipra drives a Zen and I fail miserably in doing that either. The Accord is about four segments ahead of her, still.

Laxman drives through almost the same route that we had driven when we went to the hardware store in Sant Nagar. I cross a neon board that I had seen a few days earlier. I am tempted to go down and smack the hairdresser. My hair have grown but they still look like the pigeon's nest.

We reach the address that is our destination. Shiksha, the NGO, is housed in a basement and I take the few steps down to reach it. I ring the bell and wait at the door until a lady opens the door for me. She is almost as tall as me and I can't stop admiring the necklace that she wears around her neck. It is a pure gold necklace that has fine diamonds studded into it.

My perception of people who work at NGOs is very different. I expected to see someone wearing a cotton *kurta* and jeans. I turn around to see the board again, as if to confirm that I really am at the place that I intended to be.

She extends her hand to me and I shake it. I introduce myself and she recognizes me from our telephonic conversation an hour ago. She introduces herself as Sneha and says that she is the founder of the NGO. She asks me to accompany me to her office and I can't help admire the office. It is too richly decorated for it to be for a non-profit cause.

Aditya

On Friday morning, the day after she had to come to Delhi for the training, the alarm clock rang. I begged it to let me sleep. It rang again; I ignored it again. It gave up on me. I overslept, until I woke up at nine, late for a meeting. I cursed myself for having overslept. I ran into the bathroom. I was on fire: leaping up from the shit pot to reach out for the razor; the shave foam already on my face, while I had multitasked. It was already 9:45 by the time I turned the key in the motorcycle. Thankfully, it wasn't raining today and it would save me ten minutes. There was something about this city that the traffic would snarl up the moment it saw the clouds.

I was halfway to the meeting when I realized that I forgot the silver chain. It stubbornly refused to leave the confines of my cupboard. The grand rehearsals in my mind of this evening's event were on the brink of doom. I had booked a table at the Bukhara to play out my fantasy. I could turn back and fetch it but that would mean a month's hard work in prepping the clients go in vain. Not for the first time that morning, I cursed myself.

I wish I could've slept on time yesterday. I could blame the caffeine in the coffee, but then insomnia was beginning to be such a habit. There had once been a time that I would sleep even before my head touched the pillow, but nowadays, her thoughts would keep me awake until the wee hours of the night.

The meeting was the success that I expected it to be. I walked out with a thirty lac cheque to open a Citigold savings account and the promise of subsequent investments into an investment portfolio. Either I was lucky, or I was damn good at my work. "On course" had better change into a destination than being the journey it was.

There were back to back meetings lined up that day and it was already six when I looked at my watch. I could risk a trip back home, but in the unpredictable snarl of the peak hour traffic, I could lose as much as two hours. It didn't make sense, so I cleared out my inbox and went thrice to the men's room to adjust my necktie while she was in training. Each time I went to the men's room, I took a detour walking past the training room to see if the training had ended prematurely. It hadn't, so I continued to kill time, making small talk with the only friend that I had in office –Deepika. She was another management trainee who worked with me and she would cover for me in case there were clashing appointments. We had trained together and become good friends over the course of the three months that we had known each other.

We were still chatting when Radhika walked in. She looked at me and then Deepika, a little suspiciously.

"Hey! How've you been?" Deepika asked.

"Very well, and you?" she said.

Why was she ignoring me?

"Perfect, but late. I have a date with my boyfriend. I need to rush," Deepika said as she hit the shutdown button on her machine, putting to rest all doubts that may have crept into Radhika's mind.

"Are you ready to go?" I asked.

"Yes, but isn't it too early for dinner? Where are we going?" she asked in return.

"I was thinking about the Bukhara," I replied.

The Bukhara was the fine dining restaurant at the Maurya Sheraton. It served Indian Mughlai and was renowned for the skill of the chefs. The dinner would cost me two weeks of salary and I thanked Citibank for giving me a credit card that I could swipe.

We went to the Indian Coffee House again and sipped on coffee. The waiters almost knew us by name now. Having killed enough time, we started off for one of the finest five star hotels, on the back of a motorcycle.

This was the scene that I had enacted so often in my mind and it was as if the commute had been blacked out. I would've liked to be stepping out of a chauffeur-driven Mercedes but then the credit limit on my card wouldn't even be able to afford another motorcycle. I wished that I had had a head start on her in terms of years and that I could afford more. These were my salad days, when I was barely making ends meet. I consoled myself – one day, I will drive her in a Mercedes. We reached the Bukhara and we stood out even though we were dressed formally. She wore a grey business suit but still stuck out in the crowd of rich, extravagant sari-clad damsels that thronged the Bukhara.

"It is obviously not extempore. Why couldn't you just tell me?" she said. The maître d' had looked up the reservation list when I stated my name. He took us to a table by the window and lit the candle that sat on the table.

"What'll you drink?" I asked scanning the wine list. The prices were obnoxious. I changed the many pages on the wine list to get to the section that said "Mock-tails". One would've thought that something without alcohol would be a little cheaper, but not here.

"A fresh lime soda," she replied, obviously thinking the same way.

"No alcohol for you?" I asked her.

"I don't drink," she lied.

It was difficult to be Punjabi and not drink, even though her parents were orthodox.

"You liar, I remember you telling me about your antics on your cousin's wedding," I said, smirking.

We ordered our drinks and the alcohol in the wine relaxed her. Her business suit didn't seem as out of place after the first drink. I sipped on my single malt that cost me a bomb and a half. I was obviously going overboard with this whole dinner thing. I would've been happy to speak to her even at the *dhaba* near Tolstoy Lane but you know how women are. They want a candle light dinner and romance when someone proposes.

"A repeat for both of us," I said, without bothering to ask her if she wanted another one.

"I'll pass. Why are we here, Aditya?" she asked me.

"For a dinner. Just go ahead, we'll have a repeat," I said to the waiter.

"But why did we have to come to such an expensive place; all that matters is your company," she said. Obviously, this girl wasn't the same.

"I wanted to talk to you about something," I said without elaborating.

"Well, so did I. But why does it mean burning up money?" she asked me.

"Because this is a good setting," I said. I just couldn't gather the courage to tell her without some more alcohol in my system.

"Can't we just drink somewhere else?" she asked me.

"We could go to another place – a discotheque?" I asked her. I was disappointed that she didn't like the place.

"I'd rather go somewhere quieter where we can talk. I really need to talk to you about something important," she said.

I looked at my watch. It was about nine-thirty. The waiter arrived with the drinks.

"Places are going to be closed by the time we get out of here. We could go to my place, if you're fine with that," I said.

We had our drink as quickly as we could and paid the bill. I had my credit card out before her and she threw a tantrum.

"You mind if I buy some more alcohol on the way?" I asked her.

"Of course not, get some for me too," she said.

We stopped at Kailash colony where I ordered chicken *tikkas* at Saleem's and ran in the direction of the wine shop to fetch alcohol. She was still waiting at Saleem's when I returned with a bottle of whiskey and another nip of vodka, just as our order was being wrapped up.

My apartment was a typical flat that the Delhi Development Authority is so notorious of building – shabby on the outside and uglier on the inside. The walls had unsmooth plaster, the floor bereft of tiles or stone and the fittings cheap. My roommates were either sleeping or away and we tiptoed into my room. I brought two glasses from the kitchen – thick, cheap glasses that were meant for water; a sharp contrast to the crystal that we had left behind at the Bukhara.

A few drinks later, we were relaxed, sitting on the single bed in my room, devouring the delicious chicken *tikkas* and enjoying the alcohol when the power went away. It wasn't uncommon to lose power when it started drizzling. It sounded like it was going to rain if you heard the thunder in the distance. I went to the kitchen and returned with a candle. In the light of the candle, we dug into the chicken *tikkas*. That was the most imperfect candle light dinner that I ever had.

Radhika

It doesn't take long for me to realize that this is all a sham. I came to Shiksha, the NGO, to volunteer my time for something noble. I didn't know that it is a con that someone is running under the garb of a NGO. The signs were always there but it takes me time to understand them. Sneha, the lady that runs the NGO is quite unashamed about the fact that most grants that come her way are siphoned off to maintain the luxurious office and acquire the diamond necklace that hangs around her neck.

"This is business," she says.

I wonder why she doesn't open a private school instead of stealing from donors. I am happy that I have discovered this in my first meeting. I walk out in a huff, upset with the greed that has pervaded our society. It is not that I think of myself as a saint but this isn't something that I can agree with.

I walk up the stairs to see Laxman smoking a *beedi*. I don't know why I vent my frustration on him.

"Stop smoking. Let's go," I call out to him.

"Yes, Madam," he says and opens the door for me.

I sit inside, still fuming about my meeting. I don't know if it is really Sneha that has brought about this angry streak in me or if it is the lost promise of a vocation. On the way to East of Kailash, I was dreaming that I will finally have something to fill my days. Now, that promise has evaporated. It is my destiny to sit on the porch with pigeons for company. I am a middle-aged woman who can't get anything right.

Sometimes, help comes from the most unexpected quarters. Laxman isn't the sorts to want to have a conversation with you but today he is singing like a canary.

"Why did we come here?" he asks me.

Normally, I won't answer this question. It is none of his business. He is a driver and it is best that I ignore him, but I find myself saying, "I wanted to work with them to educate underprivileged children."

"Why do you have to work with them when you can do it yourself?" he asks me.

"What do you mean?" I ask him. I think to myself that I am not going to start a NGO.

"Look around you. There are so many underprivileged children in our neighbourhood. You don't need a NGO to help someone," he says.

So many times, we are unable to see everything that exists in front of us. There are underprivileged children in every neighbourhood. Who hasn't seen a labourer's child with his nose running, while the mother carries brick loads on her head? Who hasn't seen the maid's children neglected when the maid is washing dishes? They are always there, but somehow, we don't see them.

I am silent for the most part of the journey back home thinking about the difference that I can make to people's lives that I am in touch with. Even in Lucknow, I would do charity but that charity would be in the form of money. It would be in the form of a donation to one of these charitable organizations like Shiksha. After what I have seen today, I am not sure if this is the right way to contribute to charity.

As we pull into the gates of my house, I tell Laxman, "I am willing to help these kids. See if you can get them over."

Laxman serves me lunch before venturing out in the afternoon. He returns in the evening with three kids. He tells me that they are our *dhobi*'s children. They go to the government school but need help. I know all about Government-run schools; I studied in one.

As a first task, I help them with the homework. It is a little strange to look at algebra after all these years. Algebra is almost like riding a bicycle. No matter how long ago you rode it, it just comes back automatically. It is almost dark by the time the children leave. Although, I sit on the porch of the house in the rocking chair, I don't feel that bad.

I am a little more cheerful this evening when I go inside. I don't know why but I have a feeling of indescribable contentment. It can be because I have done something that gives my self-esteem a boost. It can be as simple as finding something worthwhile to do.

Later that evening, I call up Shipra. I want to tell her that I believed and I did.

"I finally did something worthwhile," I say.

"What?" she asks me.

"I taught a few children," I say excitedly.

"I told you. You can do it as long as you believe in it," she says.

In a strange way, today's events are a huge change even though it is such a simple thing. I have been so accustomed to being a rich man's wife that I have started feeling worthless. Although, it doesn't show, I lost my confidence. It wasn't that

I was always confident but the last few years have dented me some more. I had lost belief that I was young.

When I go to bed that evening, I don't feel that old. I don't see myself as a piteous thirty-two-year-old widow. There is a life ahead of me and I will make the most of it.

Aditya

Sitting in the candlelight, I wanted to start off the conversation, but I still didn't know how. For all the rehearsals in my brain, I was still inhibited. I was on my fifth drink and knowing my capacity to drink, I knew that I should do it now, rather than later. I didn't want to sleep before I got this off my chest.

The air in the room was heavy; a combination of the humidity in the air, the smoke of my cigarettes and the heaviness of expectancy. Even after spending hours this evening, we hadn't been able to break our shyness and bring forth our thoughts. The flickering candle created our alter egos on the rough walls of the room. The candle died devoid of fuel to sustain it.

It was that catalyst that I was waiting for. We both spoke simultaneously sitting in the pitch dark. Only a faint light from the street light below created a silhouette of her form.

"I wanted to talk to you…" we both said.

"You go first," she said.

"I just wanted to tell you something…" I hesitated. "I hope that even if you find it inappropriate, it will not impact our friendship…"

"I promise it won't," she said a little too eagerly.

"I am in love with you," I felt the burden being lifted off my chest. It was probably not the ideal setting or the most eloquent prose to express it. Even then, I had said what I had been endeavouring to do for a long time. I looked in her direction through the dim light that strained in through the cheap floral curtains, half expecting a blow to come flying.

Instead, she said, "What took you so long?"

I didn't answer but reached out for her hand. Her hand was cooler than mine and I held it, caressed it. She put her other hand on my hand, as an affirmation that she understood. We sat there for an eternity in the silence and darkness. The only sounds were of our breath and the rain on the window pane. I pulled her towards me until her head rested on my shoulder. We embraced each other; our bodies spoke to each other- her cool skin against my warm body. She clung onto me, pulling my shirt, as if she was trying to make up for the years that we had been together, and yet, been so far away.

I snuggled into her neck, feeling the smoothness of her skin on my face. We were both longing to move forward but a little unsure of how the other would react. Our lips met, our breaths heavy with alcohol. The sweet-sour taste of the lemon mixer mixed with the peaty flavour of my whiskey. The sensuousness of her moist lips pervaded my senses; I pulled on her lower lip, she didn't resist. Emboldened, my tongue entered her mouth; unhurriedly exploring every corner of her mouth. Her tongue had similar ambitions, she responded. We kissed, deeply and for the longest time, attempting to stop, but in vain. It was an alien feeling; neither of us had experienced this before and our naivety was telling.

She didn't stop me when I put my hand on her breast, instead she cupped my hand. She approved. I wasn't sure if it was the alcohol in our blood or the humidity in the air that made us lose our inhibitions and our middle-class values. The rain continued its monotonous thump on the window. Our clothes came off – my shirt, her jacket, my vest, her blouse – until we were naked. Our hands explored each other's bodies, while our lips were locked. My tongue travelled down her neck until I reached her breast. I pulled off her bra, exposing her mounds of flesh. My tongue continued to explore, forming imaginary, concentric circles around her nipples. The maelstrom was pulling us in and both of us were willing to explore its depths. My hand reached down to feel her; she was wet. She held me and helped me enter her. It was nothing like anything I had imagined or seen. Ever since adolescence, I had dreamt of being here and yet, I was such a novice. It was hurting her. I tried to be gentle but the animal inside me wouldn't let me be. We were gyrating in a rhythm; the thunderclaps drowned our moans. The occasional bolt of lightning revealed our nakedness as the rain continued to fall, a little faster than before, until it was a downpour. Then it stopped.

The power came back. The sudden light blinded our eyes as we lay together, spent. I turned off the light, preferring the darkness.

"I love you," I said.

"I love you too," she said, and we embraced each other. We were like two lost travellers in the desert who had just chanced upon an oasis.

We made love again, until the first rays of the sun defied the clouds. She didn't bother going back to the guest house and I didn't bother going to office. We only stepped out for food in the afternoon and for coffee in the evening, before being back in bed, gaining a little more experience, being a little more experimental and loving every moment of the investigation.

Too soon, it was Sunday afternoon. The train schedule made us make our way to the train station, stopping at her guest house en route. She returned in fifteen minutes, dressed in a long red skirt and a white t-shirt that made her body look more luscious than ever. Around her neck, she wore a thin silver chain, with a small pearl pendant that her lover had gifted her.

Radhika

As I lie in bed that evening, I can't help feeling satisfied. It was always so apparent that I could have helped the neighbourhood children. It was a mistake to have not started earlier on this task. The word mistake always makes me reach out to the silver chain around my neck. The chain is thin but the emotions that it brings to me are always the same. They always remind me of the first mistake that I had made. It had been my decision that had probably ruined my life, forever.

It was exactly two weeks after I had lost my virginity to Aditya that I was in bed with another man. I was a veritable log as he had sex with me. If he had made love to the exhaust pipe of his Audi A8, it would've been more gratifying for him. I just lay there, not even bothering to emote. Not even attempting to feign interest. Not even attempting to fulfil the duties of a wife.

In the past two weeks, I had ruined my life and probably, Aditya's too. On the Monday that followed the memorable weekend in Delhi, my mother said, "Try and come back early; there are some guests coming home for tea."

I had been more worried about her experienced eyes making out that I had lost my virginity two days ago. I just nodded my head as I left the house for work. Little had I suspected that the guests were my to-be husband and his parents. It was only when I returned back from work at five that my mother insisted that I change into a sari.

"Why do I need to wear a sari?" I asked

"They're coming to see you," she replied.

While I had successfully rejected most responses to the matrimonial listing, this one would've probably come through in the four days that I had been away. I was only twenty-two and my parents may have waited if it hadn't been for an astrologer making a prediction.

Pundit Pratigya Pal was a slimy, hateful man. I had developed an intense dislike for him over the years. There used to be a time when I was embarrassed in his presence. His lustful eyes would shift conveniently down to my bosom. In May, after I had come back from the induction in Delhi, he had made a pronouncement

"You're going to get married this year," he said.

The better part of the year was still ahead of me, but then, except in my fantasies where I would be married to Aditya, I had never even imagined that marriage could be a reality.

I frowned, "How can that be? I have no intention of getting married, not just yet."

"*Beti*, when Mercury and Venus align, no one can stop it. Any time after July, you should see yourself married. Start looking for a boy," he said to my father.

I had dismissed the thoughts back then, but today they were back to haunt me. In fact, the recent spate of these matrimonial responses had me a little worried. I had wanted to speak to Aditya about it while in Delhi, but as things turned out, I couldn't.

"Mamma, who is this guy? I don't want to get married," I pleaded, half wanting to tell her about the weekend affair with Aditya.

"Everyone has to get married, sooner or later," she replied.

"What is the hurry? I am only twenty-two," I said.

"I was nineteen when I got married," she said.

"That doesn't mean that I have to," I said.

"Girl, now you listen to me. We never even thought that we would've had to get you married. When you were adopted by your uncle, we thought our responsibility was over. As things have turned out, we need to get you married and the sooner we can take care of our responsibility, the better it is. So now, go and change and be on your best behaviour."

I should've rebelled. I should have taken the next train to Delhi to be with Aditya, but for some incomprehensible reason, I didn't. Instead, I changed into a sari to meet with a prospective groom. I purposely ruined my make-up – wore the lipstick outside my lip line; smudged the mascara so that I resembled a cross between a raccoon and a monkey and draped the sari as inelegantly as I could, hoping that he would reject me on at least one of these grounds.

Abhinav Chandra was an engineer form IIT, who had done an MBA from IIM (A) and now worked in a multinational bank in New York. With those confused credentials, he needed an Indian trophy wife and would have easily attracted a few in the US, given his six figure dollar salary, if it weren't for his parents. It was unfathomable to think that people, both me and him, with our educational backgrounds could be coerced into an arranged marriage. His annual three week vacation was being dedicated to finding a wife that would appease his parents. A week had gone by already and he was probably a little desperate.

I sat there while he admired me. I was unsmiling and put on the most unpleasant expression that I could, but he didn't reject me. I suspected that he was probably suffering from cataract. Thankfully, my parents didn't say a 'yes' immediately. His parents did say that since a lot had to be done, they would expect an answer by Tuesday.

"What do you think?" my mother asked, after they left.

I had to tell her that I was in love with someone else. I had to tell her that I could not get married to him. I still didn't know if I had the courage to say it, especially in light of the conversation earlier that evening. Then, I wasn't even willing to play martyr to my parents.

"Mamma, I love someone else," I said, drawing out all the courage that I had from the deepest recesses of my soul.

Her voice suddenly changed to a hoarse whisper, as if she had just heard me confessing a sin. "Who is he? Don't let your father hear about this."

I didn't know what would happen if my father did hear of this. This was completely ridiculous.

"Aditya Sharma, he works in Citibank Delhi," I said.

"How much does he earn?" she asked me.

"I guess about the same as me," I assumed that the bank would hire all management trainees at the same pay scale. I had never bothered to find out.

"Which is what? Fifteen thousand?" she asked.

"I guess so," I said.

"Girl, get real. Fifteen thousand in today's date and time doesn't count for anything. How will he support you? And how old is he?" she asked me.

"Twenty-two," I replied.

"I don't even believe I am having this conversation with you. You are being so immature."

It was ironic that she said what she had. I was immature to be in love and yet, mature enough to be married.

"But, I love him," I cried.

"You haven't seen life, because you've got everything on a platter. Your father would drive a taxi all day and for half the night to make ends meet. I used to stitch clothes for the neighbours so that you could have new clothes to wear. Here, you're getting a rich, educated, well-settled guy and you want to get married to a young, immature pauper? And this guy that you love, even if he does marry you, what are you doing to him? When does he get a chance to grow when you weigh him down with your responsibility? I am saying yes on your behalf and this is it."

Having delivered her sermon, she walked out of the room.

I was still not convinced and tears rolled down my cheeks. I was crying for the brutality of the situation and the lack of time to make a decision. I had to talk to Aditya. I somehow had to speak to him. I grabbed my purse and entered the drawing room where the entire family sat beaming. They had obviously been communicated that I had agreed to marry.

I was about to exit the front door, when my mother called out to my brother to accompany me wherever I was going.

We reached the PCO; I asked him to wait outside. Desperately, I dialled the number. No one answered. I prayed and dialled again with the same result. Dejectedly, I came back home and retired to my room. The tears refused to stop flowing.

Aditya

The phone rings, breaking me out of my day dream. It is Divya again, asking me if I have found any references. I wonder why she is being so pushy but I realize that it has been over two hours that I have just sat on the bed and thought back to the time that I had first made love to a woman.

"I'll call back," I say. It is obvious that I don't have any ready references, but I think about Birendra.

He is in the same situation that I was in when I had chosen to take up this profession. It isn't by choice, and it isn't ideal; but heck, it pays. It pays the bills and it lets me keep a little bit of my dignity alive; I am not begging.

I leave to go to the barber's shop to get a haircut. At another time, I wouldn't have cared for the hair that are just beginning to peek over my ear, but now it is imperative that I keep myself in ship shape. I am a product – it is important that the product is packaged well, and so, I have unwillingly visited the barber shop.

The snip of the scissors is mechanical, as the barber ponders over which hair to cut and to what length. Meanwhile, I am deep in thought, contemplating if I should lift the burden of my soul and speak to Birendra about my profession. There is no doubt that he will be left aghast given the lies that I have been telling him. The barber's razor works on my neck, scraping off the small hair that the scissors can't incise.

I weigh the pros and cons of discussing it with him – it may mean an estrangement; he may probably ask me to leave his home. Even if he does, my life will go on as it had over the years after college. Yes, he is a good friend but will losing him change my life?

On the other hand, he is without a job and any help that he can get would be welcome; the help can be as small as sharing the rent on the apartment that we are now sharing.

The barber removes the cloth that covers me, dusting off the dry, cut hairs that have fallen onto it.

"Sir, shave?" he asks.

"No, I'll go home and do it myself," I say.

He makes a mockery of dusting off the short hair that have stuck onto my shirt with the bristled brush.

"Eighty Rupees," he says, announcing that his chore is over. Talk about recession-proof professions, and the barber is at the top of the pack.

I pay him with a hundred rupee note and don't wait for him to produce the change. I walk out of his shop and cover the short distance to our apartment. I am still unsure if I have the courage to tell Bhatoliya. He is not the lady on the train, a complete stranger, who I can openly tell what I do.

"Aren't you late for work?" he asks me as he opens the door.

"I have to go a little late today," I reply.

"Good job you have there; it gives you a lot of flexibility. I hope you're forwarding them my resume."

This is the perfect opportunity to come clean. And, I do.

"I want to confess something, but only if you make me a cup of coffee and promise not to judge me on the basis of what I tell you," I say.

He is enthusiastic about the coffee and moves to the small kitchenette. It is an open kitchen and while I sit in the living room, we can still have eye contact.

"Of course," he says, keeping a saucepan full of water to boil. He nods at me to signal that I can start.

"Do you want to wait until the coffee is made?" I am eager to get the secret off my chest but there is a risk of never getting that cup of coffee that he is making.

"Shoot, it's only going to take two minutes to fix up the coffee," he says. He adds the milk into the water.

"My confession is that I don't work for Aztec software," I say.

He looks up for a moment to look me in the eye. It is a stare that states that he is upset that I have misled him. He turns around and puts the coffee powder into the mugs on the counter behind him.

"In fact, I don't work a job," I say.

He takes the saucepan off the fire and turns off the gas. I am not sure if the contents of the saucepan are boiling or he is upset enough to refuse me the coffee.

"I work as a male prostitute, a gigolo. I entertain wealthy, middle-aged women," my voice is wavering. I have let the cat out of the bag. I have committed myself to a point of no return.

He hands me a cup of coffee and takes the other one himself. His eyes don't meet mine. It is difficult to judge his reaction. Finally, after an eternity, he says, "Why are you telling me this today?"

There are three reasons: one, Divya's phone call has been a catalyst; two, that I think that he will be able to appreciate my predicament, now that he is also jobless; and three, I am sick of leading a false life. I am lying through my teeth and even if it means moving out of the apartment, I want to be honest.

"I wasn't sure you'd be willing to accept it and I am sick of leading a false life. I don't want to keep telling you that my boss called me on a weekend," I say honestly.

"It must be exciting," he says. For the first time since the disclosure, he is looking into my eyes, and I know the comment isn't sarcastic. It is genuine.

"Well, yes and no," I don't care to explain.

"How did you get into it?" he asks.

His enthusiasm is unexpected. I recount the events of the last two months, leading up from the fateful night at the Sipper to the phone call this morning. I ask him the question, "Interested?"

"Yes, but I'm a virgin," he replies back.

I smile, breaking into a grin which turns into a chortle. I am still wondering what has caused it; the burden off my chest, the enrolment of Birendra as a gigolo, or the fact that a thirty-two-year-old man is still a virgin.

I call up Divya to tell her that I have a 'reference'.

Radhika

I left for work the next morning, tempted to take the bus to Delhi as I crossed the bus terminus in Sector 17. I knew that Abhinav's parents wanted his bride to go with him, which meant that whatever was to happen would happen in a jiffy. For the hundredth time since last evening, I prayed to God. I wasn't very religious but I did believe in a super being. In my helplessness, the super being was being given faces; he was being cast in stone idols. He was my last hope if ever my dream of being married to Aditya was to become a reality. There was no God.

My swollen eyes invited a lot of stares. Roshni was seated next to me in the office and asked, "Is everything all right?"

I nodded, knowing that my voice would give me away. From my desk phone, I dialled his number. Finally, he answered.

I spoke in a low voice, "There's a guy who came to see me yesterday…my parents found him…NRI…wants to marry me," I said into the phone receiver, sobbing and incoherently stitching together a tale for him.

"I don't know what to do…parents don't understand… forcing me…I love you," I continued.

There was a long silence at the other end, until he spoke in a hushed voice, "Don't worry, I'll find a solution. I'll call back."

I waited for him to call back; each minute seemed like an eternity. I didn't log on to the Y2K call; my problems were more immediate than something that could potentially happen at the end of the year. I weighed my options while desperately trying to hide behind the conspicuous desk that I sat on.

There was a truth in what my mother had stated yesterday. He was too young to be weighed down by my responsibility. With our salaries, assuming that Citibank was willing to give me a transfer, we would barely pay the rent of a small apartment in Delhi. Yes, things would improve sometime later, but did he really deserve the stress? Eloping with him was an option, but was it really the best option, for him?

There were too many questions; the answers were few and even then, there wasn't a perfect answer. I knew that eloping would be a one-way road. I would never be accepted back into the family. I wondered if I had the courage to burn my roots in the hope of reaching the sun? I dwelled and cried and waited for that elusive phone call.

He finally called back, "Do you want to elope?"

"I am not sure," I replied honestly.

"I am ready, but you need to be sure," he said.

"How will it happen? How will we manage?" the practicality that was so ingrained in me was coming to the fore. The same practicality that had forced us to go home from Bukhara and drink out of the thick glasses instead of crystal.

"It'll all work out; trust me," he said reassuringly, but I could hear the quiver in his voice and the hesitation behind the brave façade that he displayed.

"Let me think about it. I'll call you in the evening. Be home," I said and replaced the receiver. I took out another tissue from the half-empty box. I needed to think about the most important decision of my life and this was definitely not the place to do it. I walked into my boss' office and told him that I was sick and going home. My ragged appearance and swollen eyes didn't make him think I was lying. I took a rickshaw to Shanti Kunj, a large park in the middle of the city, where I could be alone and think about my conundrum.

Sitting on a bench in the heat and humidity of that July afternoon for almost two hours, I had made my decision. The problem was that I still wasn't sure if it was the right decision, for me or for him.

Two weeks later, in New York, seven thousand miles away from Aditya, lying lifelessly on the water bed under Abhinav, I was convinced that I had made the worst decision of my life. It had taken less than two weeks to confirm my worst fears, that my decision had been incorrect. The crux of my decision had been Aditya's career and his life, without giving any thought to what he and I wanted. I had tried to play the sacrificial lamb; the one who gives its life to appease the Gods. It had to be a fool's choice to give up love but then I wasn't sure if a woman who had been given up by her parents twice should understand love.

Everything happened so quickly: my parents had already communicated to Abhinav's parents that I was ready. That evening, they came and did a small ceremony to formalize the wedding and firm up the plans. The wedding would happen on Friday, less than three days later. It was to be a registered marriage given the paucity of time. Mercury and Venus had aligned and Pundit Pratigya Pal had made another correct prediction.

I had promised to call Aditya that evening, but there was no way that I could either step out or use the phone in the house. It wasn't until after dinner, after Abhinav and his family had left that I got an opportunity to make the phone call. It wasn't even complete before I heard commotion behind me and hung up. My mother looked at me suspiciously but didn't say anything. Perhaps, she was afraid of my father's wrath more than I was.

I wished I had got an opportunity to speak to him, in person, on why I had made the decision. I wished that there was a chance to explain my stance and an opportunity for him to convince me that I had made the wrong decision. Given the timelines, there was a slim chance of that meeting coming true. In the absence of anyone I could talk to, I continued to cry in the confines of my bedroom. Another sleepless night later, I resembled a zombie. The swollen eyes told my story out aloud and I dreaded walking into the office the next day, to hand over my resignation.

"Why are you leaving? I think you'll be very successful, if you continue here," my boss said.

"I am getting married," I replied.

"Congratulations! When?"

"Day after tomorrow."

He was visibly taken aback, but even then, he agreed. He was widely known to be prejudiced and biased against women in his team. And I had done nothing to change his perception. I didn't even have time to do my exit formalities. I just handed in my laptop and my identity card, and said that I would try and hand in my clearance forms at the Delhi office. A career was the least that I was losing.

We were grossly under prepared and if Chandigarh had been as large as Delhi, there wasn't a chance that we'd have been able to complete as much as we did over the course of the next two days. It was to be a registered wedding – to facilitate the visa processing that would need to happen after the wedding. It was a godsend for the *lehenga* that I had dreamt of wearing on my wedding would never be ready at such a short notice.

It had been over forty-eight hours that I had even slept a wink. Involuntarily, my eyes closed and I was dreaming that I was getting married. Aditya straddled a white horse, dressed up traditionally in a *sherwani*. Just as he was getting off, the horse buckled and ran away. Hours later, as the many onlookers waited, the horse returned. The rider was different – Abhinav. It was a rude joke. It wasn't meant to be, but it was happening right here in my life. It would have been so much better if it had just been a dream that I could snap out of.

The registrar of marriages looked at me suspiciously; the swollen, red eyes told a story that he could fathom.

"Are you doing this of your own free will?" he asked.

My parents looked at each other and exchanged guilty glances. I just signed on the dotted line, as an acceptance of my fate. In less than two weeks, I would realize my folly.

It was the July of 1999 when I had committed the mistake of my life. I can never forget it, no matter how much I try. Even nine years later, as I lie in my bed, I can't help wondering how foolish I had been to be coerced into making a decision that I still regret. Sometimes, our actions and our decisions are so dangerous that we can't undo them, no matter how hard we try.

I look at the watch that lies on my bedside. It is past two o'clock. It is time that I sleep, hoping that another night will take away my pain and ease my guilt.

Aditya

There is something about today that I keep remembering the past. While I have enrolled Bhatoliya earlier this morning, I find myself using the afternoon to reminisce. I don't know why but my thoughts veer towards Radhika.

I remembered the time when she had gone away from Delhi after our escapade. I had a pasted smile in the Monday meeting at work, unable to erase the memories of the weekend. It wasn't just the sex; it was the lightness of having been able to tell her. It was an inexplicable feeling, when dreams were to be turned into reality. I knew that I had to marry her and to make it a reality, I needed a promotion. The management trainee program ended on the last day of March in 2000, almost a year from the date of my joining the bank. If my performance was worthy, I would be promoted as an Assistant Manager. The starting salary in that grade was 4 lacs a year; add another 4 lacs of her income and it would provide a comfortable living for us. The math had been done after I dropped her at the train station. There were eight months for *us* to be us.

I felt a sudden rush of adrenaline and I forgot where I was sitting. "Eight months," I said out aloud. Ten pairs of eyes turned their attention towards me, questioning me on my irrelevant, nebulous outburst in the middle of the meeting.

As red as a beetroot, I excused myself from the meeting room. I would have to be more careful; the next eight months were critical. In my mind, I was drawing out plans for us – She would need to get a transfer or I could go to Chandigarh. But then, my forte was sales and if I were to believe her experience with the clients she had dealt with, there wasn't too much scope to grow.

There was still time to go; the finer modalities could be worked out later. I would also have to talk to my parents. Their approval was important, but they were fairly broad-minded. I didn't expect any hassles on that front. After all, I was their only child. Why would they object? I hoped that her parents wouldn't create a fuss. She had always been a little cautious whenever their subject came up. She would try and change the topic if it ever deviated in their direction as if there was something painful about that relationship that was best kept under wraps.

Bhatoliya was turning twenty-three and all of us were going on a drinking binge at a new pub that had opened in Vasant Vihar. The clouds threatened to burst again and I didn't want to be caught in the downpour. I called Bhatoliya, he was about to leave office, and would probably take the same amount of time to make it to the pub. I left the office and reached the pub. Only the four of us were there – the band of friends who shared the apartment. The other two had finally found jobs, albeit having compromised on the salary.

"Did she go back?" Bhatoliya asked curiously

They had all been introduced to Radhika while she had been in Delhi. Surprisingly, they had all disappeared for the most part of the day-and-a-half that she had been around, giving us our privacy.

"Yes, yesterday," I said.

"So?" he said, raising his eyebrows.

"So what?" I asked.

"So, now you won't even tell us?" he was as inquisitive as a dog, whose playing ball disappears down a rabbit hole.

"Tell you what?" I asked.

"For example - Who is she? What's going on between the two of you? What're your plans?"

"And why might I tell you?" I asked him.

"I must know because I love you. I'm pregnant with your child and I don't want you to jilt me for her," he said. The others burst out laughing.

"She's Radhika, knew her from school. She works with Citi now and I am going to ditch you for her, you bitch."

We cheered for the beers that arrived just in time. Bhatoliya paid the bill but cried for the rest of the month. Little did I know that life would change tomorrow. The happiness and the cheer would get drowned for a very long time to come.

Radhika

Ibarely slept for three hours last night. Even in the morning, I can't help feeling a little melancholic. Thinking about Aditya always makes me sad. I look at the watch; it is past ten and I get up from the bed that hasn't given me the refuge from his memories. I skip breakfast and have barely had lunch when Laxman brings four more children from the neighbourhood. All of them are children of maids and servants whose parents can't afford to spend money or time on something as frivolous as education.

I am not doing so badly. Within two days, I have been able to garner seven children for my make-shift school. The children fill my time and I feel happiness in giving of me. That happiness leads me to believe that I can live a life again. I wonder what people like me do; people who are young and without a partner. I don't know anybody in my age group who is single.

After the children have left for the day, I tell Laxman that I don't want to eat at home. I log onto the Internet and am looking for a restaurant when a pop-up comes up. It is an advertisement for a single's dating site. I wonder if I should enrol myself. It might help me find people who are my age and single. It is just that they will be from a different gender.

I stop my thoughts from getting ahead of me. I am pretty sure that I am not ready for anything which mildly resembles a relationship. I need company but I'll be happier spending time with the same sex. Sometimes, I wish Shipra isn't always so busy. I wish that I had friends besides her. I don't know where to start.

Even as a child I had few friends, but now, I find myself in an absolute dearth. I wish I had some hobbies that I could pursue. I wish my mother wasn't such a disaster that she didn't let a hobby develop. It was much later in life that Ms Kapoor introduced me to reading. I used to read but Vimal thought it was a waste of time. It isn't for nothing that I wanted my freedom. I had lost much more than I had gained from that marriage. I didn't expect to hear from Meera and I haven't since I moved to Delhi. It's left me with no family and no friends. It is so easy for me to break into my piteous avatar.

Since I am planning to eat out today, I wonder if I can just go to the Gulmohar Park club that is walking distance from my house. Maybe I can find some neighbours there who are willing to entertain me. It's still only January and the weather remains cold. My outings out on the porch have decreased recently because the fog doesn't let the sun through. So, I prefer to sit beside a heater. I am brave to dress up in a dark blue sari that will not keep me very warm. I want to look worth entertaining. I look at my reflection in the mirror and I pass the test. That's when I decide to walk the hundred metres to the club.

I go there but find it almost empty. The few people who are here are snobbish. I guess it's almost fashionable to be a snob. You know, you aren't considered high society enough if you talk to someone. I think this problem is everywhere, but south Delhi takes the cake.

I am getting accustomed to see my best-laid plans to socialize, fail. I don't know why but no one wants to speak to each other. Either the neighbours are caught behind the very high walls of their house or in their snobbery at the club. I am very hesitant in walking up to someone and introducing myself. I think I am foolish to expect that someone will come and ask me if I'm lonely and want company. Sometimes, I wish I hadn't given up drinking. Alcohol makes you lose your inhibitions. I just have a cup of soup before I am back to the drear.

I am dejected and wondering if listing myself on the singles dating site is a bad idea. Even then, I am determined that I will end my loneliness. I pick up the newspapers to see what is running. I make a note of the events on in the city. Maybe, a visit to the theatre will help.

The next morning, as I am hoping to get a reservation for the show at Siri Fort, the phone rings. It is Shipra, "What's going on?" she asks me.

"Still looking for something to do and someone to do it with," I say.

"Why don't you come over this evening? We're going to the DSOI tonight," she says.

After the children have left in the evening, I dress up in another one of those saris that I possess but rarely wear. It is a maroon and black south silk. I call out to Laxman, who brings out the car and we make our way to Dhaula Kuan where the Defence Officers Service Institute is located. I meet Shipra at the gate and we go inside to the bar where the Colonel sits with one of his cronies.

He introduces himself as Colonel Raghav Khanna. In a lot of ways, he reminds me of Aditya. He is tall, fair and athletic. I have to stop myself from doing this. Why do I always draw comparisons with him whenever I meet anyone? I tell myself that it is about time that I get over my past. There is enough hurt that my heart has already seen.

Raghav is a decorated officer who has earned his stripes in the Kargil war of 1999. What was it about that year that so much had happened?

He is a bachelor and it is probably intentional that Shipra has made my acquaintance with him. He is funny too, when he speaks of the tribulations of being in the armed forces. I enjoy his company but still can't stop myself from comparing him to Aditya.

We exchange numbers and promise to stay in touch. As we drive back to Gulmohar Park, I can't help wondering if finally my life is going to change for the better. Already, the strength in my makeshift school has gone up to seven. I have to tell Laxman to stop because we are running out of space on the porch and yet, the large house has so much space that can be utilized for a noble cause.

I look at the watch, it's past eleven. I wish I had picked up a book on the way in to DSOI. I hate the soap operas that play on television but I guess I'll go home and see a rerun. By now, I am convinced that freedom isn't the great thing that I had made it out to be.

Aditya

When she said she wasn't sure about eloping, I couldn't help wondering if she loved me. She said she loved me two days ago. Why had the love evaporated, so suddenly, to not be able to take a step in the direction of us being together? My heart refused to believe that she could be materialistic, but my brain would continue to remind me that there was no other reason. Finally, after hours of waiting at the PCO, she called.

"Hi," I whispered. There was no need to be as quiet as I was but just the solemnity of the situation demanded it

"Let me go, Aditya. This is our destiny," she said.

Only the weak blame destiny.

"I can't. How can you even think about it?" I felt cheated. I wish I knew why she was doing this to me.

"You've got a career to make. You're too young to be married," she said.

"Don't worry about me. Don't blame your failure to make the right decision on me," I was livid. My frustration was manifesting itself in anger. A part of me knew that this could be the last time I was talking to her and so to be gentle, to leave happy memories of myself with her. Why wasn't I breaking out of this goddamned nightmare?

"I am making the right decision; you'll understand this in time. I just want you to know that I loved you like I've never loved anyone. But, not all lovers meet."

There was a commotion behind her, voices that were getting louder. Suddenly and without warning, she hung up.

I punched my hand into the wall and small chunks of plaster dropped onto the floor. My hand was as numb as my mind.

The conversation left me a little confused when she said that marriage would ruin my career. Most successful people that I knew were married. I was convinced that she was misleading me.

In any case, it was unreal; this couldn't be happening to me. This was not me. I couldn't be hearing the love of my life telling me that she was getting married to someone else. The male ego was so seriously dented that it hurt much more than the self-inflicted bruises on the knuckles of my hand.

Alcohol was always my refuge. When I was happy, I drank and when I wasn't, I drank a little more. I went back home and drank straight from the bottle that day, inspired by the story of a jilted lover. I drank until the last drop of alcohol was drained from the house and I slept in the balcony. I woke up the next morning when a fly entered my open mouth. Severely dehydrated, my head throbbed. Despite that, I still remembered the conversation from last night. I was tempted to jump off the balcony and leave behind a suicide note that would blame her for my death. I didn't have the courage to do that either.

Somehow, I made my way into work. Deepika saw me and my droopy shoulders

What's wrong?" she asked.

My eyes welled up with tears and I turned my head away

from her. I didn't want her to know that the six-foot tall hunk, the best salesman in the team was crying like a wimp.

"Do you want to go out for coffee?" she asked.

I nodded my head and stepped into the pantry behind her. We went downstairs, into the compound below the branch, where most smokers would light up. I couldn't hold myself back anymore. I cried like a child, inconsolably, grieving for my loss. She tried to console me and asked me what had happened. I told her every little detail of it. She heard me and finally said, "Let the bird free. If she's yours, she'll come back".

Retrospect is such a wonderful thing. In hindsight, I would've never taken her advice seriously.

It took me three days to assimilate and understand myself. A long time in the context of what was happening. After work on Friday, I travelled by night to Chandigarh. I intended to call in sick on Saturday morning. Although it would sound a little dubious since I had done the same thing last weekend, I was prepared to take some risks.

I got off at the bus station and took a rickshaw, the most popular means of public transport in Chandigarh, to the Sector 9 branch. It was still nine and I waited for her, chain smoking cigarette after cigarette to calm my nerves. The adrenaline was pumping despite the uncomfortable journey.

It was about five minutes before ten that I saw Roshni enter, the girl with us in training. Still, there was no sign of her. I waited another five minutes but she wasn't there. The security guard had opened the doors; customers who wanted to make important transactions on the short working day thronged the bank. Working through the crowd, I reached Roshni. She gave me a smile, recognizing me instantly.

"Hi" she said and extended her hand.

"Hi! Where's Radhika?" I asked, coming straight to the

point.

"She got married yesterday. Wednesday was her last working day."

I knew it was going to happen but I didn't know that it would happen in three days.

"Are you sure?" I asked her.

"Of course, that's what she said."

I had been looking for a faint glimmer of hope, a tiny thread of optimism that I could weave into a rope. And, it was all lost. I had lost.

Dejected and dismal, I returned back to Delhi on the next bus. I didn't even bother to meet my parents. I would've been unable to hold back the tears and that would mean a lot of explaining. I just wanted to be alone. Alone to introspect, why I was being subjected to this agony? I tried to make sense of the situation, but in vain.

She loved me, I was sure of that. Why does someone get married to someone other than the one you love? Money? Was it just because I wasn't an NRI and didn't earn in dollars? Looks? Was he Brad Pitt, a picture-perfect representation of the male form? What did he have that I so desperately lacked that she chose him over me? I did not know and now, there was no way of knowing.

When I went back to the office on Monday morning, I felt naked. I didn't know why I felt that everyone knew my story. I felt that everyone was mocking me; they were calling me a loser. A failure, whose girlfriend got married to someone else. I hunched and slipped further down in my seat to hide my nudity.

At that moment, I had no interest in being in that room. I had no interest in sales figures and sales targets. I had no interest in being a star salesman. I had no interest in getting promoted. There was no motivation; she had left me without an objective to pursue.

My manager turned his attention towards me and gave me the sales targets that he expected me to achieve over the next week. The targets were stiff and I would've taken them on as a challenge. Only if that little voice in my head didn't keep repeating, "There are no us".

The meeting ended and my manager asked me to stay back and gave me a chiding for absenting myself for the last two weekends. He didn't bother to find out that I had found love and lost love, a week apart. All he cared was for me to bring in the revenue, as reward for the small salary they gave me. The salary that was so small, that it didn't even make me worthy of being seen as a suitor.

I had no business being in the office on Wednesday. There were scores of potential clients that needed to be convinced, yet, I was there. Fortunately, I was there when Radhika came out of the Human Resources room, accompanied by a man, who could pass off for a mouse. Looking at him, I knew that it had to be the money. She saw me and wasn't sure how she should react. I saw her and was equally unsure.

She introduced her husband and the mouse shook my hand. He had a feeble grip, and yet, had been strong enough to defeat me.

She asked him to leave under the pretext of using the rest room.

"I'll meet you downstairs," she said and he was gone.

There was just enough time for us to exchange a few words in the unlikely setting of the elevator lobby. She looked unhappy, her eyes said it all. They were redder than I had ever seen them.

"Why, Radhika. Why?" I implored.

"I wish I could explain…" she was looking at my shoes unable to meet my eyes. If ever there was an expression of guilt, this was it.

"Then tell me, what was wrong with me? Why couldn't we have eloped?"

"What had to happen has happened. There's no point in discussing it anymore. Just forget me. Hate me, if you must."

Those were her last words as she entered the elevator and left, as she had on that last day of school. She went away. Far far away.

"What time do we have to leave?" Bhatoliya asks me.

"What time is it?" I ask.

"Five-thirty," he says.

I have spent an entire day remembering her.

Radhika

When I first met Colonel Raghav Khanna, I had compared him to Aditya. A few meetings later, I know that he can never be Aditya. He is more like my first husband Abhinav Chandra.

Abhinav was a gentleman. I had been able to ascertain that when he let me sleep on the first night of my marriage. I was visibly uncomfortable with him in the hotel room that we had retired to, after the marriage had been solemnized at the registrar's office. There were no sexual overtures until now, when his animal instincts took over and he had sex with me. It was only natural. I was his wife and it's an unsaid law that a marriage needs to be consummated by physicality.

He had been patient for a while, waiting for me to open up. He realized that we were two strangers until a week ago and it would take a little time for me to get used to him. The problem was that he was nothing that I had ever imagined my husband to be. Ever since adolescence, I had a formed a mould of my husband and that mould fit just one man – Aditya. Despite Abhinav's best qualities, he was the round peg trying to fit a square hole. He was failing miserably. And I was failing miserably in being able to break the mould.

We moved to New York, a couple of days ahead of his annual leave being over. A honeymoon would be out of question until the next year.

He worked at the Bank of America, the branch manager of the Wall Street branch. The apartment was a short walk away from his office. The studio apartment had been bought by him a year-and-a-half ago, without envisaging that he would ever be married. It was just too small, but then Manhattan was expensive.

"People work for forty years and can't afford to buy an apartment in Manhattan. I've done it in four," he had said when I had remarked about the size.

There was no falsity in that statement, although it sounded a little pompous. Whatever the apartment lacked in size, it made up for in the view. The large bay windows overlooked the Hudson River. At the peak of summer, the sail boats in the river were a magnificent sight. Over the first weekend, before he joined work, he took me out around the block to introduce me to my surroundings. He walked me into the 7-11 convenience stores and the grocery just off West Street, just in case I needed anything urgently. He wanted to take me sightseeing but instead I chose to clean up the apartment. It had been used as a bachelor pad for too long. The closets had never been cleaned and didn't have space enough for my clothes. I hated living out of a suitcase.

New York overawed me – the skyscrapers, in some strange, inconceivable way reminded me of Solan. They were towering and humbling structures not unlike the Himalayas. It was man's attempt to challenge nature, although they could only build it with concrete, steel and glass. The twin towers, the most mammoth manifestation of that challenge, still towered over the New York skyline.

On my first Monday in New York, Abhinav went to work and I stepped out of the house, alone. It was brave of me. Until a few months ago, I hadn't even ventured out into New Delhi alone. I was attempting to explore a city that I had only seen in pictures and read about in novels. In the first few minutes, I was shouted at by at least two people and had been nearly run over once. I felt like that migrant labourer that had been employed last year to renovate our house – miserably out of place. I wished for the umpteenth time that a familiar rickshaw puller would come by and I could just hop on and see the city.

I returned home and waited for Abhinav to return. I flipped through channels on TV that couldn't hold my attention. There was hardly anything else to do in the apartment. I wished I hadn't gone overboard in cleaning it over the weekend; it would've left me with a few chores for the weekdays. Bored and lonely, I wondered if this was the life that destiny had forsaken me to. And why even blame destiny when it was my own decision. I sat beside the bay window, admiring the New Yorkers in frolic, the quintessential grasshoppers, the ones who sang the summer away. Very often and inevitably, my thoughts veered towards the past, the thoughts of Aditya and all that had happened between us. Suddenly, the future would start looking as dark as the clouds on the horizon.

Aditya

We ride up to the farmhouse on a motorbike that Birendra has borrowed from his neighbours. It is a 100 cc Hero Honda, which buckles under our combined weight, notwithstanding that one of us only weighs fifty-five kilos. We must be a funny sight – two men, dressed in dark business suits and neckties, riding on a flimsy bike. We are wearing helmets lest we be caught breaking the law on a lesser offence.

When I had spoken to Divya and confirmed that I did have a reference, I had chosen to hide Birendra's sexual status and his weight, lest she object.

"Thank God! I knew I could count on you," she said, as if I was a recruitment specialist who had just filled a long open position.

We reach Chhatarpur and take directions from the security guards that perch on chairs, outside each mammoth gate. It is difficult to find the address in the maze of narrow streets that lead through rows of similar farmhouses. One of the security guards confirms that we are at the right place.

The farmhouse is a two acre sprawling expanse of green with a diminutive five bedroom house in the middle. I make a call to Divya, who confirms that she is at the venue to coordinate the event. She meets us at the gate minutes after we have parked the motorcycle. The security guard is interested in us and continues to hover about.

She walks out alone and hugs me, a warm hug that means that I have saved her skin. In the dark recesses of this profession, the pimp has to be reliable. If I didn't have the courage to speak to Birendra, she may have been deemed unreliable. She turns her attention towards Birendra, and gazes at him from toe to head. It is an uncomfortably slow scrutiny that mentally undresses him. She stops momentarily at the unmentionables. He is blushing; he isn't used to being treated like a potato.

"Thin, very thin," she surmises the two-minute gaze.

I choose to ignore her comments; this is the best I can manage in the circumstances. If she doesn't like him, she can let him go back on his borrowed motorcycle. I can take a ride on the Metro to get back home tomorrow morning.

"But, he'll do. Does he have any experience?" she asks me. She doesn't direct her question at Birendra. Am I his pimp?

"No, but neither did I when I started," I say. In saying so, I put to rest any further interrogation on the subject.

She looks at the time on her Rolex. I am certain that it is the commissions that she is making that have made her afford this watch. It is eight o'clock, still too early for a party that will run all night.

"You might have to striptease, are you ready for that?" she asks both of us. Her eyes move from Birendra to me and back to him.

I have a sudden sense of revulsion. I want to tell her to fuck off. I want to slap her across her face. I want to tell her where she belongs. I then think about a conversation with my wife when I was jobless and I choose the lesser of the two evils.

"Yes," I reply instinctively.

She construes that as a collective agreement and doesn't wait for Birendra to respond.

"Well, just go in there naturally, as you would be attending a normal party. Let the drinks be served and we'll take the entire thing impromptu. My guess is that you won't need to strip, the ladies get wild after a few drinks," she says and walks away.

Birendra looks at me. He is baffled and excited. "Is this real?"

"Yes, my friend, this is as real as it can be," I say.

We smoke on the porch and wait for the ladies to arrive. When they do arrive, they arrive in droves. They step out of their shiny black, chauffeur-driven cars. They are dressed in Gucci dresses and Jimmy Choo shoes. Each one is trying to outdo the other with the make-up on their faces. They've become replicas of each other in wearing the most fashionable clothes. They are unshelled eggs of the same size and shape; you can't tell one from the other. I wonder why the recession hasn't impacted them when it has turned us into objects of lust.

The party starts. We drink and make conversation with the ladies. It is all small talk which starts with the weather and progressively gets dirtier as the drinks flow.

Birendra's shirt is ripped off and he looks at me helplessly. Another woman, whose name I don't care to remember smooches me.

It is about six in the morning, when the early morning joggers are just venturing out of their homes. Two men, with crumpled and torn three piece suits, reeking of alcohol, make their way back home on a delicate motorcycle. The motorcycle buckles a little more, for there is the additional weight of the wads of currency notes in our pockets.

Radhika

I saw the strip turning pink. Now, when I thought that the worst was behind me, it couldn't be true. Now, when I thought that I might, somehow, get over Aditya, the nightmare reappeared. Now, this was the only other horror yet to unfold and it was happening now.

My menstrual cycle was usually more accurate than the Mayan calendar. When I missed the date, I figured that it could be a miscalculation. I re-counted the days; so much had happened in the past month that it wasn't difficult to have been mistaken. But I wasn't. Three days later, I was worried. Today, as I compared the pink strip of the home pregnancy test with the legend on the box, my worst fears were coming true. The fastest sperm had met my egg. It would've probably been a little better if I had just known who that sperm belonged to.

I sat on the commode and held my head in my hands, in resignation of my foolishness, of my imprudence and of my fate. It's sometimes strange when you look at the mirror and see the reflection of a stranger – a person whose actions and decisions are so extremely contrary to yours. Yet, I was that stranger who could explain but not convince you why she made the decisions that she had.

I sobbed uncontrollably which involuntarily turned into a howl. In all the things that were out of sync, the only thing that worked in my favour was the absence of Abhinav. He was at work and it would've been difficult to explain why I was crying when I had discovered that I was pregnant. Motherhood was meant to be a pleasant experience; it was meant to make a woman complete but now, when I had discovered that I was pregnant, there was only misery.

The two men in my life were as different as chalk and cheese. One, a little over six feet, fair and handsome; the other, dark, five feet seven and a veritable mouse in comparison. It wouldn't require a DNA expert to figure out my infidelity. This was a possibility that I hadn't even explored while making the decision to marry Abhinav. I must have been a sinner in my past life, a wretch, who was being made to pay for the sins in this birth.

It had to be Karma; why else was I enduring this? I knew that I would have to get an abortion because there, simply, was no other way. It was better to do it now than to have Abhinav stare at someone else's child after nine months. If the child was born, it would only complicate matters a little more than what they already were.

Involuntary tears would well up in my eyes and roll down my cheeks. Even long after my affair with the commode ended, the tears didn't stop and neither did the agony. I spent the day in anguish, waiting for Abhinav to come home.

The truth was that I didn't even know him. I didn't even know how he would react if he found out what I was suspecting. Would I still be married or would I have lost two men in the space of two weeks? I was livid with myself, for my foolishness, for not having used contraceptives and for not having taken this eventuality into perspective when I had made my decision to marry Abhinav.

A large part of me wanted to come clean, to have the courage to walk up to Abhinav and say that I wasn't sure if he was my unborn child's father. I longed for the strength and the courage to be able to tell him the truth. Even in the short time that Abhinav and I had been together, I had been able to gauge that he was extremely egoistical. He would never be able to understand that his wife had an affair previously, forgive her and move on. I shuddered at the sheer thought of being truthful. It was just not an option. Where would it lead but to a divorce?

It would give me nine months of a breather, until the truth came out in the open. Wouldn't everything work out perfectly if the foetus that had once been my egg was fertilized with Abhinav's sperm? What if the child turned out like Aditya?

These random thoughts tore me until the best option was to not have the child. I would have to handle this with tact. I could not sound unexcited or unenthusiastic lest Abhinav suspect me. I hated myself and detested the situation that had turned me into a manipulative vamp. A woman, that was plotting the murder of an unborn child, based on a suspicion that it had been fathered illegitimately.

Abhinav came home that evening, carrying with him a box of authentic Chinese food. It was completely different than what I had ever had in Delhi, Chandigarh or Solan. It was as if the Chinese had forgotten to grow chillies. The food was bland and distasteful to my spice hungry palate. I waited until the dishes were done and just when he was about to switch on the TV, I finally blurted out, "Abhinav, I'm pregnant."

It didn't sound like anything that I had rehearsed over the course of the day.

"What?" he said.

I didn't understand if the 'what' expressed surprise, shock, excitement or indifference.

"I'm expecting," I said, hoping that he wouldn't catch the quiver in my voice.

"That's great news," he said beaming. My task of being able to sell him an abortion would be a little more difficult. He was only twenty-seven, and who wants fatherhood at that age? I certainly wasn't ready for motherhood at twenty-two.

"I am not sure if I want to have the child," I said.

I saw his expression change. It was as if I had dropped a bombshell on him or had committed a cardinal sin.

"I want this child," he said and walked away.

It was a demand. It was an order. It was a diktat that couldn't be challenged. He didn't even want to understand my reasons for not wanting the child. For the first time in the two weeks of marriage, I felt that I had misjudged Abhinav. I wasn't sure if he was a gentleman that I thought he was.

I tried to raise the subject a couple of times later, with the usual rejection. He would simply walk away, leaving me fuming at not being heard. Slowly, I was beginning to reconcile that this child would be a reality. It would come into this world.

I thought about calling Abhinav in office to tell him that I had slipped in the bathroom. I would tell him that I had had a miscarriage but instead go to the obstetrician and get an abortion. If I had been a little more courageous, I might have tried it. I wasn't. I must have been at the back of the line when God gave the virtue of courage to all his children.

Three months later, I knew that the child was now a certainty; especially when I had crossed the important threshold of the first trimester. Neither had I been able to convince Abhinav, nor had I been able to gather the courage to get an abortion done on my own. I had resigned to the fact that if doom was inevitable, it would have to be endured.

Through those three months, Abhinav had had enough of me; I could make out from the long sighs and the expressions of exasperation that he gave me. He was probably ruing his fool hardiness of rushing into a marriage with a stranger. When he sighed and let out deep breaths, he would remain polite. I wondered if I hadn't been pregnant, how it would've been. Would he have vented his anger on me? Would he tell me that I had ruined his life and mine?

After all, from his perspective, he could have done without me. Physically, I had graduated from being a log in bed to being a corpse. Mentally, he was years ahead of me. When we spoke, it was as if we were on two diametrically opposite tangents. Emotionally, there was no gratification for him. I still lay strangled in the cobwebs of my heart.

Several times I had imagined Abhinav to be Aditya when he would want to have sex with me. I would switch off the lights, so that he wouldn't see my face as I shut my eyes and let myself be sucked into an illusion. When he touched me there, I would try and imagine that it was Aditya's hands; when he kissed me, I would try and imagine that they were Adi's lips. Yet, when I wrapped my arms around his frail body, the illusion would snap. Why hadn't I rejected him on grounds of his looks?

The hormones weren't helping, sending me into bouts of extreme happiness and extreme melancholy a few moments apart. There were days when I would shout at him, not knowing why, then suddenly be over polite in a matter of minutes. I didn't know if I could just blame the hormones when it could have been the stress of not knowing whose baby I was mothering. Maybe, the stress had brought me to this point of insanity and irrationality.

My pregnancy was turning out to be very far from pleasant. Each passing day brought me a little closer to the day when I would be found out. I didn't have a way to know whose child I was mothering but a woman's instinct told me that it was Aditya's. In my mind, I would imagine how the child would look like when it was born. I wanted him to be a clone of Aditya but I knew that it would only serve to alienate me from Abhinav.

Abhinav backed out the Audi from the basement parking spot and turned on the heat. It was November, the pleasant but short summer had ended and the evenings and mornings were chilly. There was some talk of a blizzard next week and that had started a mad rush to buy overcoats. The malls were flooded, in anticipation of the winter and the holiday season that it would bring with it. We crossed the malls as we drove to the New York Downtown Hospital which was a fair distance away. It was the day of the monthly meeting with the obstetrician. It wasn't that there were no better obstetricians or hospitals near our apartment but I realized that Americans are a slave to their insurance companies. His insurance only allowed him to visit this particular hospital.

I wasn't complaining about the distance because Dr Jill Fonda was my obstetrician – a matronly, middle-aged, Caucasian lady in her mid-forties – whose face would cheer me up. She checked the blood pressure reading on the digital monitor and looked directly into my eyes. I wondered if the blood pressure machine knew what I was going through. She asked Abhinav to wait outside and even before he was out of the room, asked me, "Is there something that's bothering you?"

I wondered if I should tell her, like a good patient should, but I didn't. Instead, I shook my head like Indians do, which can so easily be mistaken for a nod.

She again took a reading of the blood pressure and then said, "Your blood pressure is a border line high. Reduce your salt intake and calm yourself. At any moment that you have any discomfort, call me SOS."

She called Abhinav and explained my situation. I didn't know if that disclosure elongated Abhinav's sighs a little more. His dreams of a healthy child were being jeopardized by me and worse still, he had no option but to remain calm, patient and docile.

As fall turned to winter, the hormones were beginning to be innocuous; the mood swings were slightly better and I could hear his sighs abating. The only problem was that as each day passed, I was getting a little more anxious about what would happen. The stress was unavoidable and involuntary. I wished I had a friend who I could talk to. Anyone, who would just hear me, even if they didn't have a solution to offer. Just someone who could help me get this cancerous secret out of my system.

Aditya

I wake up to the sounds of the rooster. The old watch that sits on the crooked coffee table next to the couch is letting out a shrill sound, faintly resembling a rooster. It is four in the afternoon; I rub my eyes and make my way to the bathroom past the feeble form of Birendra Singh Bhatoliya.

Bhatoliya is bucking in his dreams, making love to the woman in the red skirt, the one who had ripped off his shirt. I push him, careful to avoid the flagpole that stands conspicuously through his boxer shorts. He wakes up beaming, a smile that reeks of sexual fulfilment.

"Wow" (pause), "wow" (pause), "wow". A man with a limited vocabulary explains what he is feeling.

I remember the morning after I had made love to Radhika and smile. I dress and am about to go into the kitchen when I think I will complete a chore that I do twice a week. It is more out of compulsion than any other emotion. My wife is still my wife, even though there is hardly any contact between us, except these intentional phone calls. I often wonder if she feels the same way. My emotions are dead and buried.

"Hello," I say into the cheap Motorola handset.

"Hi! How are you?" she asks. I am thankful that cell phones

display names; it saves us both the trouble of delving into our memory to recognize the voice.

"Fine and you?" I ask.

Our conversation is the conversation between strangers; formal and measured.

"I am fine. Any plans to come and visit me?" she asks.

"I won't get leave, but will try to come the soonest I can. Why don't you come?" I ask her.

I hear the sigh of relief despite the crackling phone line.

"I will try; work's pretty busy. Traffic cops. Bye," she says and hangs up.

Either she is driving a lot or lying a lot. The first thing the CIA teaches a new recruit is to never believe in coincidence. It can't be a coincidence that every time I call, she is driving.

Bhatoliya is still languishing with his memories of the night before. I am doing it for money, but he has found passion.

"How much did that woman charge?" he asks referring to Divya.

"Twenty five percent," I reply.

"That's cheating. How come we do all the hard work and she just skims off the top?" he asks.

"You wouldn't even have known that there was a party on if she hadn't called me," I reply.

"Even then, it's an obnoxious commission," he says.

I agree but between the two of us, we earned fifty thousand last night, net of the commission. A huge amount for a single night's work. People who don't have any other source of income can't complain.

"I agree. Get dressed, I am hungry," I say, choosing to change the topic.

It is almost half past five in the evening that we leave the house. I can't help thinking that it is a remarkably awkward time to find breakfast. We take a rickshaw to the Jwalaheri market, and have chicken Momo's and Indian style Chow-Mein from the Chinese van that doesn't move. The Chicken Chow Mein is smothered in soya and chilli sauce. I tell the cook to start using *sambhar masala* in the Chow Mein; he can easily pass it off as South Indian Vermicelli.

It is dark by the time we return to the cigarette shop at the corner of the street that leads up to our apartment. It is almost the end of January and there is still a nip in the evening air. Bhatoliya lights up a cigarette and looks at me. He says, "Aditya, What's the plan now?" I can't really say why he lays special impetus on the 'now'.

"I guess, go back home and sleep or read, in the absence of a TV," I say nonchalantly.

"Ever wondered why I never bought a TV?" he asks.

"Several times. Why?" I ask.

"I have a dream…" he starts. He has a faraway look in his eyes and sounds like Gandhi when he first envisioned India's Independence, "…that someday I can have my own business; a day when I don't need to sell toothpaste to make a living; a day when I don't have to suck up to a bastard to get a promotion."

"What business?" I cut short the elucidation of his dream.

"Anything that doesn't involve me selling toothpaste," he proudly proclaims, as if he has narrowed down his options considerably.

"So, what's that got to do with the TV?" I ask.

"I've chosen to give up some material things like a TV to achieve that dream," he says. This guy is on the verge of insanity and needs help.

"And what have you achieved in doing so?" I ask, reasoning with him to check if he actually is mentally imbalanced.

"I have the capital for starting a business," he says.

"What business?" I ask, repeating my question to hopefully get a more favourable answer than his last response.

"A Massage parlour," he says. His eyes are gleaming with excitement. In that moment, he is a four-year-old child who gets a shiny red bicycle on his birthday.

Radhika

It was the ninth month of my pregnancy and the monthly visit to the doctor was scheduled at eleven that morning. Abhinav had taken half-a-day off and was in the bathroom when the phone rang. I wished to ignore while I sat snugly on the lazy boy rocking chair. Maybe, I'd just let the call go into voicemail. I hardly got any calls and it was too much of an effort to get up from the comfort of the well-cushioned chair.

On instinct, I answered the phone. I instantly knew that it was Aditya. We had spoken too often on the phone for me to not recognize his voice. My heart skipped a beat. He had found my number.

"Hello," I said.

"I...I...I just wanted to tell you that I got promoted," Aditya said.

"Congratulations," I said. I was so happy for him. I was happy that he had achieved what he aspired for.

"I love you…," he said and his voice trailed off.

As if it were pre-planned, the door to the bathroom unlatched at exactly the same moment. The small studio apartment could hardly afford any privacy and even though there were a billion things I wanted to say, Abhinav's presence only made me say, "I don't know what to say".

"Say, I love you too," he implored, begging me to say what he wanted to hear.

Abhinav was almost behind me when I said, "I have to go, bye," and hung up.

"Who was it?" Abhinav asked.

"Aditya," I replied, almost whispering through my choked throat.

"Who's that?" he asked.

His eyes narrowed suspiciously, watching me when I lumbered back to the softness of the lazy boy. I could feel his gaze on my back. I sat down hoping that he wouldn't carry on this interrogation. His eyes hadn't left me for a moment. He raised his brows, as if to repeat his question.

"A friend; you met him," I said dishonestly. It was difficult for me to keep a straight face. I could feel the muscles of my face tighten.

"When did I meet him?" he asked. He just stood there, with only a towel covering his thin, slimy body.

"At Citibank Delhi, remember?" I was struggling to keep up this conversation. I wanted to break down and tell him that Aditya was the love of my life, and just like now, you – Abhinav Chandra – had intruded my life to take me away from him.

"Oh! That fair, tall guy?" he asked.

I just nodded and turned my face away to look out at the boats on the Hudson. They had returned with the spring.

"Does he call often?" he asked.

I wish he did but I shook my head and turned away to face the window. I knew that my eyes would give me away.

"Are you sure you're not doing anything that you're not supposed to do?" he said.

My patience broke down. I had had enough of this nonsense. Yes, I did not love him and yes, I hadn't told him the entire truth and yes, I had a past. But in the nine odd months that we had been married, I had never cheated on him. I had Aditya's number memorized and I could have made phone calls when I wanted to but I had never ever done it. And despite being the dutiful wife, he was suspecting me! I did something that was extremely uncharacteristic.

"What do you mean by that?" I asked, a trifle louder than I should have.

"Nothing," he said in an attempt to avoid a conflict.

"Abhinav Chandra, explain that last question. Don't fucking nothing me," I shouted.

He was visibly taken aback, for he had always seen me as a docile, peaceful doormat that would try her best to avoid conflict. And here, right now, that stereotype was shattering with my loud pitch. He tried to avoid the question again, but I wouldn't let go.

"I want a fucking answer right now." I was shouting loud enough for the neighbours to hear us.

"Calm down. I just wanted to check," he said, visibly on the defensive.

"Check what? Do you doubt my fidelity?" Maybe I was over reacting, but the rush of adrenaline and the months of misery that I had undergone and kept within myself came to the fore.

"I never said that," he replied meekly.

"You son of a bitch! What then did you mean by your statement?" I said, livid and angry.

I think he took offence to his mother being called a bitch and he lost his temper.

"You have no interest in sex; you just lie there like a corpse. I know you don't love me. Then why am I wrong in suspecting that you're having an affair with someone else?" he shouted back.

The volley of abuses continued until I felt a blow on my cheek. It was surprisingly hard for a man of that shape and size. In that instant, I understood why the Americans had bombed Hiroshima and Nagasaki to end the Second World War. Sometimes, harsh methods bring about a peace, and my peace started or ended when I slipped into nothingness – a black hole that I travelled through. There was nothing else but darkness in that tunnel. Not even a light at the end of that tunnel. Just when I was getting accustomed to the darkness, a flash of light revealed that I was a little girl on my third birthday. Another flash – I was in Solan. Another flash – I was in Chandigarh at YPS. Another flash – I was in bed with Aditya and then there was darkness again.

The darkness broke with a blinding light on my face and then there was a calm – I was floating. Maybe, I was dead. Maybe, this was heaven. Maybe, God had chosen to relinquish my wretched life. Everything here was white – the people, the walls and even the sky. And then the whiteness gave way too, to people who were dressed in blue, a pale blue; a familiar blue of the uniform of the hospital – they looked like doctors and nurses. I was still alive. Abhinav's contemptuous face came into my line of vision and that confirmed it – this was hell.

Dr Jill Fonda looked at me and smiled but she didn't look happy. My mother-in-law was there too. When had she come? Was I still dreaming; maybe hallucinating? What was going on? My hands were numb, almost porous from the multiple injections that had been thrust into the vein to draw blood. On instinct, my thoughts moved to the baby and despite the numbness, I could feel the void in my belly. It had to be out. Who did it look like? Was it Aditya's? Where was he? Or was it a she? There was no crib and there was no howling. There were no answers. A mother's instinct took over. I tried to leap out of bed in search of the infant, but the body doesn't work on instinct, it works on strength and I was devoid of it.

I looked back at Jill hoping that she would tell me; she would explain what had transpired since my argument with Abhinav. Instead, she pushed another syringe into the intravenous drip that brought about another bout of floatation. Another dark alley, that became white and then blue to wake up into the darkness of Abhinav's soul.

I didn't know what date it was but it seemed like a beautiful spring morning. The tree outside the window of my room in the hospital was beginning to get back its leaves. Very similar to my situation, as I was beginning to regain strength. Jill was there and today, she wasn't pushing a syringe. She was willing to brave my questions; to answer them despite the complications of postpartum depression. There was no one else in the room – no Abhinav, no mother in law.

My mouth was dry, parched from the pipe that had been pushed down the oesophagus. My tongue was sore and I could barely rake out the words. But in garbled gibberish, I asked Jill, "What happened doc? What happened to the kid?"

"Your blood pressure shot up. It causes a complication that we doctors call Eclampsia. It's a situation where the baby has to be delivered speedily through a caesarean. Your husband got you here but it was just a little too late. We couldn't save the child."

She was compassionate, holding my hand as she spoke to me. A mother who knew what I had been robbed of. I sobbed, slowly at first, progressively increasing in intensity until it was a cry. My child had died. Irrespective of whose sperm it was, the egg was mine. No matter how it had been conceived and who his father was, I was his mother.

"Was it a girl or a boy?" I asked. Abhinav had let it be a secret, specifically requesting the sonographer to not let me know.

"A boy. Very fair and tall too, given that it was premature," she replied.

The mouse had killed Aditya's child and I had killed my own. I grieved in silence. I mourned everything. I just lay on the hospital bed staring at the ceiling and questioning the God who had written my destiny. The One who had robbed me of everything – of parents who I had thought were my own, of love that I thought was forever, and now, of motherhood.

At some point, Abhinav entered the room with his mother, but they didn't perturb me. I looked at him and there was only contempt in his eyes. There wasn't a hint of compassion for what I was going through. To his mind, I had robbed him of his child. I wish I could tell him that it was never his. Maybe, he knew already.

I didn't know it then, but I had spent five days in the hospital and I was discharged. We reached back home, the three of us to the confines of the studio apartment. The air that hung over the apartment was heavy. It stank of the unsaid story of a terminated pregnancy.

It remained like that until a couple of days later Abhinav broached the topic, "I think we should look at separating for some time. I am not sure if this is going to work out."

Hadn't I known all along that this relationship was never going to be the same again? We would never ever be able to erase the memories of what had transpired. There was no regret; why even regret the end of something that I had built on a foundation of deceit.

He booked my tickets for two weeks later when the airfares came down. Always mindful of expense, Abhinav was living up to his reputation, even if it meant tolerating me for the extra two weeks. I don't know why but I sent an e-mail to Aditya after this conversation.

Aditya

I lie in bed that night thinking about where my life is going. I have not only degraded myself but now, I have also involved Bhatoliya into this nefarious profession. I am feeling a little lost because I don't know where this will end. It reminds me of the time when Radhika had left me and gotten married. I felt lost those days, rudderless and demotivated.

Those days, I would often tell myself, "She left you. She doesn't deserve you". It didn't make things easier. I learnt that repeatedly stating the truth does not make you believe that it is true. It had been over three months that she'd been married and I was still having trouble standing on my two feet. She had left me with an indelible void when she had married the mouse. Despite my musings, the hole refused to fill. I thought that I would be able to get over her, but I didn't. I had even attempted to start off a conversation and flirt with another woman. All in the hope that if I could delude my brain, the heart would also be deceived. I tried, in vain, to get over her.

At work, my promotion didn't seem like the certainty that it had been a few months ago. It was early November, which meant that there were only five months left for the promotion and two months to bring in the results that would get translated into figures on the income statement. My boss had attempted to threaten me, coax me, cajole me, motivate me, demean me and yet, the slumbering salesman inside me refused to wake up. It was almost like I was hell bent on ruining my career.

Perceptions are formed when people are ignorant or know half the truth. The truth was that I was too emotionally hurt to be able to work without feeling naked. I felt that everyone I met knew my story. When you are self-piteous, you don't love yourself. When you don't love yourself, you can definitely not love your work. When you can't love your work, there is no way you can work with passion. Client after client rejected my sales pitch and the products of the bank. Actually, they rejected me.

Each rejection made me a little more self-piteous, a little more complaining and a lot grumpier. My manager only knew the half-truth, so his *perception* of me was that I had a bad attitude. I needed a Guru, a spiritual healer that could get me out of the mess that I was in. I had weird thoughts, of leaving the job to go to Rishikesh; maybe even to the higher reaches of the Himalayas in search of this anonymous healer.

Bhatoliya was the only other person, besides Deepika, who knew what had happened. He was the only person who I had been able to tell. Even as a child, I would sometimes be fearful of stating the truth. This time, the fear of being ridiculed was much larger than the fear of telling the truth.

Bhatoliya had been patient, letting me wallow in the mud of my grief for over three months now. He refused to encourage me, and refused to demean me and just heard out everything that I had to say. Not once did he pass a judgment on either one of us, never telling me what I should have done or what she should not have done. He knew that I was struggling to keep my job and I was struggling to come to terms with my loss, but he didn't utter a word. Not until today.

He entered after work, looking a little distraught, and I asked him, "What's wrong?"

"Just work. I don't have anything else that makes me happy or unhappy," he said.

"My work sucks too. I haven't sold an investment plan in nearly a month," I said.

I was attracted to grief. Anyone else's grief would bring out my own.

"Let me refresh your memory," he said, "It's been over three months that you've sold one."

I almost began to counter his statement but I hadn't sold as much as a savings account, let alone an investment account. My last sale had been made to the lawyer, just before Radhika's news had struck me. Bhatoliya was right.

"And it's about time you broke out of your misery, because the world doesn't care. It doesn't care if you loved her or if she loved you. Your company definitely doesn't care a fuck. They pay you a salary and they expect you to bring in the money. Three months is a lot of salary that needs to be paid off," he said.

They were harsh word, but they were true. They were severely practical words that brought me crashing down from my search of the Guru and the Himalayas.

"I can't get over her," I almost cried.

"You can't fucking get over her until you fucking stop sounding like a fucking wimp," he shouted, louder than my cry, "Goddamn it! You're twenty fucking three years old fucker and you have a fucking life ahead of you, son of a bitch."

He continued, "And the next time I see you here when I get home, I will fucking blow your head off. Go do some fucking sales calls."

I thought some of those 'fucking' words didn't fucking fit in, but it was from the heart – loud and clear. I suddenly wished that Bhatoliya hadn't had a bad day at work. I wished that the inertia that had so engulfed me over the past few months wouldn't break. It was a change that I was beginning to get used to. I was beginning to enjoy seeing myself as the scapegoat and the underdog. Either it was that lecture or another incident that marked my turning point, but it came.

The next day, I walked into work a little confused. One part of me trying to improve after Bhatoliya's hiding; another refusing to leave the quicksand of inertia.

My manager summoned me into his room and handed me a letter. I read the contents of the letter, unbelievingly. It hurt to be even thought of in that way, but I had been put on a Performance Improvement Plan – a rare compliment given to some of the most incompetent that the bank had ever hired. I was being told that I was one of them. A ruder shock than when she had left me and ruder than when Bhatoliya had given me the verbal whiplash. I was ashamed. Period.

I realized that the resurrection of a broken career is more difficult than making a career. I was finding this out the hard way. When you are on top, you get to cherry pick. When you are on top, you can afford to cancel some meetings. When you are on top, you get credit for meeting clients that were sold on the product in any case. I was nowhere near the top. In fact, I was the only one, amongst the hundred MTs hired last year and the ninety-nine that still remained, to have been given a performance improvement letter.

I looked down at my diary – the leather bound organizer that had been my faithful servant on the field. The one that would help me keep a track of my appointments. Today's page was empty. I turned the page, it was empty, too. Another, and then another; all I saw were blank pages. No appointments lined up. It was apparent why I had been given that letter. In a business where one in ten leads actually materialized, I was looking at no meetings and it wasn't surprising that I had no sales against my name in the last three months.

I went back to the pages from three months ago, a week before 29 July, when she had been married. I looked at the sea of black – scrambled up logs of meeting, follow-up lists on what I would need to do to convince the clients. I flipped over the pages, slowly and the black marks on the pages reduced until I reached today's date. The page was empty. I had a sudden urge to go back to my self-piteous avatar. The one that said, "Isn't my life empty, too?"

I fought it like an addict on his way to recovery fights the urge for drugs. I wanted my glory back. I wanted back everything, and that included her. I wanted her back. I would get her back. I did not know how, but I just had to be better prepared when she did come back. I had to be seen as an able suitor and again, an irrational, unrealistic, impractical voice in my head said, "you have to do it for us".

I picked up the phone and started making phone calls. I didn't know where to start. I didn't have any half-baked leads and there was no one willing to drop a free lunch in my kitty. I started with people who had rejected me in the past three months, the people who had thought that I and the bank's products were unworthy. They were the most difficult to convince and the most difficult to get appointments from.

Driven by belief, I spoke to them, begged them and coerced them to grant me another meeting.

I ran into more rejections and little success but I was adamant. The first cheque that finally broke through the darkness was for a meagre sum of twenty thousand, but it broke the drought. It was like the first drop of the first monsoon shower that bestows life to the parched earth.

By the end of November, I had three sales – just enough to be able to get a tick mark on my performance improvement plan. December was marginally better with about seven sales. My peak had been twenty sales in June and I was still severely short of that figure. Somehow, I didn't feel as naked. When I spoke to a client, I didn't talk to him as if I had left my clothes at the laundry. I was on my way, a little slowly, but fast enough to have my manager stall the performance improvement plan. It would still not guarantee me a promotion though.

The Y2K issue turned out to be a non-issue and while most of the world partied, ushering in a new year, a new decade, a new century and a new millennium, the technicians heaved a sigh of relief. I didn't have anyone to party with: Bhatoliya had gone back to Himachal for a few days, the other two, Sameer and Kunal had taken their respective girlfriends out.

I sat out in the balcony, alone, thinking about how life would have been different if she hadn't left me. For one, I wouldn't be here alone with a bottle of whiskey for company.

On the positive side, the New Year's Eve is a great time to introspect and plan, especially when you have nothing else to do. I sat on the balcony, thinking how wonderfully the year had begun – the job offer from Citibank, our training where I had met Radhika and the romantic times that we had spent.

I wondered what might have happened if July hadn't come the past year. It may have stopped the turning point: her marriage, the heartbreak that followed it and the dip in my performance.

The year had been a see-saw. I prayed that I had hit the ground, the lowest point of the veritable see-saw. I prayed that the next year would be better.

Through the inebriated recesses of my brain, I gave my sober self a challenge for next year: Go get a promotion, and go get her back!

The problem was that I still didn't know how to get her back. At the back of my mind, I knew that I would somehow have to woo her back, but I could barely afford a train ticket to Chandigarh, let alone buy an airplane ticket to court her. Hell, I was so poor that I couldn't even afford to make a call; long distance international was exorbitantly expensive for my flimsy pocket. That I didn't even have her number was inconsequential. In the absence of an alternative, I would just have to wait. Until then, I would just need to strengthen my credentials and awaken the salesman that had chosen to die.

The whiskey brought about an exothermic reaction. Despite the severe chill and fog, my body was warm. Sometimes, the cool wind would bring about goose bumps on my naked arms. Very similar to that evening in July when we had first made love.

That moment had to be the highlight of the year gone by; not because of the sex, but because it had bonded me to her. It had made us one. It had brought about a union that a million candle light dinners would have never achieved.

It was almost yesterday that she had whispered sweet nothings into my ear. It was almost an eternity since I had felt her fingers through my hair. It had only been yesterday that her smooth skin had brushed against my hairy torso. It had been ages ago when I was inside her.

The frivolous people of Delhi weren't romantic and they had no place for a jilted lover to relive the moments of his love. They broke the calm with loud fireworks forcing me to abandon my thoughts and return to bed – alone, except for her thoughts that refused to betray me.

Radhika

I am pretty much back to square one. The few feigned dates with Colonel Raghav Khanna have fizzled out. They continued until I understood that I was only a muse for him. Despite Shipra's best efforts at helping me get hooked up, I am not being very successful at my social life.

The school, as I now call it, has over fifteen students who come at various times of the day. I am amazed by them. They are resilient. They are courageous. They come from backgrounds that don't allow them to pursue education but they are determined to defy their situation.

Their defiance gives me a courage that I didn't know I possessed. I have converted the den into a school and have put up five benches and a blackboard to help them. As a child, I had a problem in speaking English and so, I make it a point to converse with these kids in English. They were hesitant at first, but are beginning to learn, like I had at Ms Kapoor's residence.

Given my non-existent social life, it is a good thing that I have the children, or else I might have become a nut case by now. I wonder if I should enrol for a course or two in education; I think I have found my passion.

Even when I was working with Citibank, it had never been more than a job. It had never excited me enough to be passionate about it. With education, I can safely say that I am passionate. It isn't so much about mathematics or science or English. It is about what a teacher can contribute for the overall development of the child. It gives me an indescribable pleasure.

Shipra is still worried about me. She still tries to make me meet some people: eligible bachelors who are broad minded enough to marry a woman who has had two marriages previously. Somehow, I have reconciled to the fact that I can live my life without a man. Yet, sometimes, I feel horny and crave for physical intimacy. Maybe, if I had been fifty, I would have survived without these cravings. Sometimes, I still fantasize about Aditya. Despite having been in bed with three men at different points in time, I crave for Aditya's touch. The other two were only compromises.

The season has changed; it is February and the newspapers are still not thicker. They continue to be as thin as they were three months ago when I had moved here. Even today, the papers carry bad news. I wonder how it must feel to be laid off. The newspapers are so unemotional about these things. I wonder how people who are going through this ordeal are faring when I am sitting in the confines of my lavish house and sipping on cups of hot tea.

The phone rings and I half expect Shipra to be on the line, but it isn't her.

It is my brother; my biological brother who is making a call from Chandigarh. "Papa passed away," he says. Under normal circumstances, the passing of a parent would've left me crying inconsolably, but I wasn't attached to him. After all, how much had I known him? Yes, he had provided me with a roof over my head after my foster father had abandoned me, but it was really only out of a sense of duty.

I think duty begets duty. You can't expect affection if you've only done something out of a sense of duty. It is out of a sense of duty that I go back to Chandigarh for his cremation. Chandigarh has changed from what I had known it to be. It's not that ghost town from the nineties. I wonder if I can meet Ms Kapoor while I am in town. I take directions to the cremation ground from a guy on a scooter. He's trying to peer down my cleavage and I roll up the window. The rickshaw puller is poorer but he's still more civilized than the guy on the scooter.

Laxman is tired; he's driven a lot today. I tell him to have something to eat while I walk into the cremation ground. I find about three funeral groups who are burning their dead. Everyone seems unfamiliar but I see my mother, Sudha. She's crying like she was on the day that she sent me away to Solan. I am tempted to go and console her like I had on that day. I don't. There is so much that has happened between then and now that stops me. Perhaps, if she hadn't said yes to Abhinav's proposal, I may have forgiven her. There is howling all around. Everyone is around: my foster father, his wife, their children. My brothers, their wives that I don't know and everyone else seem to be crying. I try to join in but not a tear rolls down. There is no sadness. It feels like I have lived my share of sadness in this lifetime.

I look at my foster father and he can't see me in the eye. I have never met him since that Saturday when he dropped me to Chandigarh. His guilt refuses to let him look in my direction. I want to go and scratch his face. Maybe, that way, we'll both be scarred.

We leave the cremation grounds and while everyone goes back home, I don't. I will go to the hotel that I have booked for myself. Even at the sombre hour of his death, I can't relate to them. I have hardly been in touch with them over the years and they haven't made any attempts to bridge the distance. The one to have passed away could have been a stranger; it certainly doesn't feel like he was my father.

My mind tells me to return to Delhi the same day, but for some reason, I stay. It is a welcome change from my drab routine and I think it might help me relive a few memories of the place that I have grown up in.

I check into the hotel in Sector 35 and flip through a few channels on TV; there is nothing interesting enough to hold my attention. It is only five o'clock and I decide to take a walk. Maybe, I can do in the evenings what I don't do in the mornings. Sector 35 is a busy commercial area that doesn't provide a lot of open space. Even though there is a park nearby, I think it would be better if I go to a more scenic place; maybe the lake or the rose garden.

I call Laxman to bring out the car. As he drives through the maze of Chandigarh, I can't help noticing that it is busy. Almost all the roundabouts now have traffic signals that snarl the traffic. There had once been a time that you could cross Chandigarh diametrically within fifteen minutes; but today, I have barely been able to cross over into Sector 22. At this rate, the sunlight will fade before I reach my destination.

I ask Laxman to take a detour. I struggle to remember the ways that I had once known like the back of my hand. Laxman has never been to Chandigarh before and he thinks that it is a driver's nightmare. It is probably the rush hour traffic that makes our progress so slow. We are now on a road parallel to the one that we have been travelling on where the traffic was a little lighter. We cross Sector 22 and are on the dividing road between Sector 16 and Sector 17. On the left, there is an abandoned cricket stadium. Instinctively, I ask Laxman to park the car where ever he can find a spot. I cross over the cycle track and go through the gate to an abandoned cricket stadium that no one really uses.

Aditya

The January of 2000 began a little precariously. I had made only one sale in the first ten days. Like most organizations and human beings, my boss too had a New Year resolution. In the first weekly meeting of the year, my boss had made it amply clear that he expected a less than unambitious, twenty-five percent growth over last year's figures and that too, at ten percent lower cost. I was amazed at how greedy people could get.

In any case, the mathematics, when translated into the real world meant that the bottom ten percent of the ten-member team would be axed and the rest were expected to deliver twenty-five percent higher sales. I looked around the room at the bunch of aspiring folks sitting in the meeting, hoping that I wasn't the softest target. Yes, there was Deepika, who would never go above the fifth rank but would never fall below the seventh. Yes, there was Bakshi, the guy from Fore School, who had been at the bottom of the sales chart last month. But I was the most consistent. I was the poorest performer in the team for the last few months and so, was the prime candidate to accomplish my boss' goal of reducing costs. In a company, where you look as good or as bad as your last month's performance, I was downright ugly. It was imperative that the salesman rise from the dead.

It wasn't that I didn't have leads, but they just hadn't materialized yet. It wasn't abnormal for the first few days of the New Year to be slow, but ten days with a single sale to my name had me in a state more gruesome than anxious. My fortunes turned on the eleventh, almost miraculously.

Rishi Prabhu was the head of finance at a BPO. The BPO was a new entity on the corporate landscape. As I delved deeper on what people did inside a BPO, I realized that it was hardly anything more than a call centre. It could've been a fad but India's newest industry was taking India by storm. It was a guzzler of human capital and it already had a few hundred thousand people employed.

My meeting with Rishi had been planned a few weeks ago, when a regular client had given me his reference. While I waited for him at the reception of the plush office, a crowd of yuppies entered, wearing low-hanging jeans and talking amongst themselves in feigned, accented English. They were probably my age. I looked at their attire and then at the neck tie that was almost strangling me.

If I got fired, I could become one of them. I could give up the neck-tie and come to work in a T-shirt with the middle finger embossed on it. Maybe, I could also have a caption written below the middle finger that proudly proclaimed "Up Yours". I wouldn't be out of place for sure.

At that very precise moment, Rishi called me into his office. I was pretty sure that he had liked my sales pitch, but even more than that he loved the investment account that didn't make him walk into a branch. He signed up for a Citi gold account, and promised to spread the word around.

I didn't realize that his idea of spreading the word around was to get me the salary accounts of the entire organization. Rishi turned out to be the stroke of luck that had eluded me for so long.

Over the next three months, until 31 March, the day of my promotion review, I had opened two thousand salary and over five hundred investment accounts that had a combined net asset value of over five crores. It was a record of sorts; it was the highest that any management trainee had ever achieved in the near hundred year history of the bank in India. Even though it left Rajat, my manager, a little red-faced for having given me a performance improvement letter, he was magnanimous in his adulation of my achievement.

That I would get promoted was expected but what I hadn't expected was the award – The CEO's award for being best in class. When the new cards got printed, they read:

Aditya Sharma

Assistant Manager.

It was one of my proudest moments as I admired the ink on the small piece of paper that proclaimed my new identity.

The moment was also my loneliest. The award and the promotion were a means to an end but that end had so ridiculously been snatched away from me. The improved salary didn't mean anything, not without Radhika. Even now I was no closer to achieving her than I was a few weeks ago.

I had the goal of wooing her back, but needed a starting point. My first instinct was to go back to Chandigarh, and try to get an address, a phone number or a clue that may lead me to her. In that very moment, my mind replayed the events of the last time that I had seen her. She had walked out of the Human Resources room. Chances were, that they might have a forwarding address or phone number for her.

I cursed myself for not having the common sense to explore this avenue for the past few months. Maybe, I was going senile at twenty-three.

I casually walked in to the HR room where Smriti, the friendly HR generalist sat. I didn't waste too much time in the niceties, "I need Radhika Kapila's number in the US, I lost it. Would you please pull up her file?" I said it in the most casual, matter-of-fact way, and the charm that had helped me bring in a few hundred clients last year, worked on her. Luckily, she had it. It had to be the stars and their astrological confluence that made me feel lucky these days.

I made a phone call that I had been yearning to make for the last eight months that she had been away from me.

After the phone call, I realized that she had changed. The Radhika I knew would have jumped with joy. The Radhika I knew would've asked a million questions. This wasn't her. This was an alter ego, an impostor who had taken on her voice. Perhaps I had been stranded in my love of her while she had moved on. She didn't love me anymore. I was her past that she had been able to bury, and I had stubbornly clung onto.

I still had the receiver in my hand when I sank down to the floor. I couldn't believe what I had just heard. I didn't know why the stars that had made me feel so lucky earlier this morning, refused to make me feel lucky in this instance.

I cried. Unashamedly, I cried. Not so much for her loss or her refusal to be with me, but for my own foolishness. I cried for being a romantic. I cried for not being a realist. I cried because it hurt. I cried because I wasn't born a few years earlier. I cried because I hadn't been well-settled when she had married someone else. I cried because she didn't love me. I cried until I howled. I howled until the neighbours came to check on me. I drank until I could stop howling. I slept when I couldn't drink anymore.

When the alcohol wore off, I could think straight again. In a way, I was happy that I had made the phone call. Although, the result wasn't as expected, it told me where I stood. At least, I knew that beyond the realms of fantasy there was a bitter, realistic world that existed and it existed without her. I forced myself to come to terms with living my life without her. She had been the rope of hope that I had clung on to; the rope that had for so long threatened to fray and give away. And today, it had finally done so.

I fell hard and it hurt. I looked at myself in the mirror as I shaved; that time of the day when I would introspect. I asked myself, "What don't you have today?"

I was young, good-looking and had a great career ahead of me. I was making good money, at least enough to satisfy my needs and occasionally, even my greed. Everything that I should have at twenty-three years of age, with only one exception, Radhika. Then, hadn't I survived without her for over eight months? And why couldn't those eight months become a year or two, even a few? I consoled myself as best as I could. I put the aftershave on. It stung on my face as did the bitter reality that I would need to move on.

Maybe, I would find another girl, someone I could love, someone I could marry and live with, like how Radhika was doing with her husband, the mouse.

I vowed to myself that whatever happened, I wouldn't let the next one get away; at least not for being poor.

In my new role as an Assistant Manager, I was responsible for selling credit cards. The profitable business line was Citibank's focus and already over two hundred of their best people had been given roles within the cards organization. The middle class citizens of India that had been so averse to living a debt-ridden life were being teased into tasting the forbidden fruit. About eight thousand people were earning a living out of cranking phone calls and making field visits to potential customers, to get them hooked onto the narcotic-like debt instrument.

It was a change away from selling investment accounts but then there were so many other changes underway at home. First, Bhatoliya moved when his office relocated to Noida, a suburb, where the rentals were far cheaper. He chose to relocate to Noida into an apartment closer to his office. Kunal chose to marry – he found himself a nurse from Kerela who worked in the gulf. It seemed like the best thing for him to do, given that he was stagnating in his job. *Stagnating,* although he had worked for less than a year. That left the expenses of the apartment to be shared between Sameer and me. Sameer buckled first; his salary couldn't afford him the luxury of having a room to himself. He decided to move in with his maternal uncle, until he could find something more affordable. I was just plain lucky that Citibank moved its main offices from Connaught Place to Gurgaon, for the same reason that had made Bhatoliya's company move. We gave up the apartment that had seen us through from college, until we had found jobs and until now, when we were growing.

The swanky new office of Citibank was spread across five floors of a fancy office complex. It was in stark contrast to the crumbling office in Connaught Place. It even boasted of a coffee shop in the lobby from where you could buy real coffee. Real coffee, that is not to be confused with the muck that the vending machine throws up into a glass. I moved with the office to Gurgaon. The suburb was cheaper than Delhi but even then it took a lot to fit an apartment into my budget. Finally, after two complete weekends spent with brokers, I finally had a place. I signed a year's lease on a two-bedroom apartment which was roughly ten kilometres from my office, but the distance didn't worry me. The first thing that I had done after I had received my promotion letter was to encash a soft loan that Citibank offered as a perquisite. The cash had then been exchanged for a shiny, second hand Maruti 800 that seemed like a bargain. The car was a milestone: it was the first asset that I had ever acquired.

On the silent drive to work, I would look at the vacant passenger seat and wish that there was someone sitting beside me. A nameless, faceless person who would love me and I could love in return and *marry*. I roved the deepest realms of my mind to have a face that would fit this character. It would turn out to be Radhika's face and then I would clinically, surgically, intentionally give the face a cosmetic surgery so that it didn't resemble her any more.

Life was moving at a frantic pace. All this had happened in less than thirty days of that fateful phone call. I was beginning to feel that I could live my life without her. Beginning to feel that we were never meant to be. Beginning to understand that not all love stories have a happy end, when a random e-mail changed my life, again.

Radhika

I have no business being in an abandoned cricket stadium but I am here, led by my memories of the past. I remember when I had come back from the States, Aditya had met me at the airport and asked me to meet him here. It was an extraordinary choice of location because there were places in Chandigarh where lovers would date and there were places where acquaintances and friends could meet. A cricket stadium that was lonely, except for the few gardeners, is probably ideal for a meeting between people who had once loved each other.

I sat on the wooden stands, where many a cricket lover had admired the proceedings in the past; today, there was no one. It was just me, the gardeners and the few children in the distance. Aditya was still not there and I almost began to doubt that I had heard him correctly. I hoped that this was the place where he had expected me to meet. I searched the stadium, craning my neck to see his form appearing out of the long shadows that covered the ground and the stands. Almost out of nowhere, I saw his familiar form making his way down from the grandstand.

It was still warm, and in the company of the gardeners we restrained ourselves from giving each other a bear hug. It could've been mistaken for a business meeting if it weren't for our refusal to leave each other's hand. The touch of skin created a longing that we had both craved for in the time that we had been away from each other. Yet, morality didn't allow me to hold on for any longer. Despite my hate for my husband, I was still married.

"How've you been?" he asked.

"Not the best that I've ever been," I said.

"What happened?" he asked.

If it had been one thing that had happened it would have taken a little time, but it was dark by the time I finished recounting my tale. All that had happened in the space of the last nine months – my leaving Aditya, my reasons for doing so, my marriage, the pregnancy, the seizures and then the separation, until now that I was talking to him. It could have been considered strange that I was sharing all this with the same man that I had let down because of my foolishness. I don't know why, but I didn't tell him that it was his child.

He was empathetic as he listened to every detail. He stared into the horizon and looked at the setting sun without commenting, without telling me I was wrong. I wondered if I might've pulled out his hair, cursed him or kicked him in the knees if I were in his shoes. Would I still be here talking to a woman that had left him and gone? I admired his patience.

He finally broke his silence, "What now?"

I wasn't sure, a feeling that I had by now been accustomed to. When Abhinav had suggested we separate, I had looked at it as the best option available. It would let me go back to familiarity and be around people I knew. But I had expected too much from my family. I had come back expecting them to support me through this ordeal, but instead, I was condoned.

This morning's conversation with my mother had been frustrating. When I narrated the incidents of the past nine months, putting special impetus on the part when he had hit me, I had expected sympathy. Instead, she was unsupportive. She thought my grounds of separation were flimsy and urged me to reconcile. "These things happen; you can't just leave him and come," she said.

Now, without their support and without another means of a livelihood, I would need to resolve my dispute with Abhinav. Knowing him, it would be the death of the little self-respect that I still possessed. I'd have to go back to him begging to take me back. Even if he did agree, it would be a life of degradation. In that moment, the only surety was that I wouldn't go back to him.

My only other option was to restart my career. Assuming that I did find a job, it would make me financially independent to take my own decisions. I had been hustled into a decision and the experience taught me a lesson on how wrong decisions can change your life.

"I am not sure. I want to find a job. I am certain that I don't want to go back," I said, summarizing my thoughts out aloud.

Aditya looked at me with those deep, dark brown eyes that had made me fall in love with him six years ago in school. He took my hand between his; the giant palms dwarfed my hands. In that instant, he was the father-figure that I didn't have, in spite of calling two men father. He pressed my hand softly, as if to say that he would help. He remained silent and I did too. I just savoured his company and his touch.

The sun had set and the moon was shining, but it was still warm; the heat of the May sun had left a warm breeze to hit our face. We continued to sit there, knowing that we should've gone home like the gardeners and the kids. There was a solace in that place that made me think why my love story couldn't be ordinary. A story where a boy and girl fall in love, get married and live happily ever after. A story in which there was no villain. A story in which *I* wasn't the villain.

On the plane back from New York, I hadn't slept. I had thought a lot about what I should tell Aditya. I wasn't sure if he would be interested in knowing what I had gone through. I didn't know if I should be completely truthful when I spoke to him.

I knew that he loved me, or at least loved me until a month ago when he had called. I simplified my conundrum and searched for a friend that I could talk to, but I really only had one, and that was him. He was the only one that I could bank upon to help me. I knew that I was the cause of his heartbreak. Yet, he was the only one who would understand me. Even after I had told him, I felt guilty about burdening him with my troubles. I was broken and confused – emotionally, mentally and physically.

"Send me your resume; let me see what I can do," he said and stood up.

We walked out of the cricket stadium taking the longer route through Shanti Kunj, the same place where I had made the decision of leaving him. I couldn't help but wonder how life would've been if I hadn't chosen to leave him. We walked on the trail that would see many a jogger in the morning. At this hour, it was desolate. We reached the bridge built over the stream that runs through the park. The bridge was still the same as it had been ten months ago, but a lot of water had flown under it.

At home, I was being treated like a stranger. It was almost akin to the day that I had come from Solan to live with them. They didn't say anything, nor did they demean me. Maybe, that was the problem. If they had cursed me, it would have sounded better than the pall of gloom that engulfed the house. I yearned to get out of the house, to break away from the accusing eyes of everyone at home. Those five days before I got a call from Citibank were unbearable. I knew Aditya would have arranged that call.

Citibank didn't even bother taking an interview; they just said that I could pick up from where I had left. They were extremely gracious, given the circumstances and the notice that I had given on my separation with them. There was just one condition – the Citibank branch in Chandigarh wasn't profitable enough to pay my salary and hence, they would require me to move to Delhi.

It was a Godsend, given the accusing stares that I had been getting from the family ever since my return. To be fair, I was an exception in the family; male or female, not one person had come close to separating from their spouse. Even if you traced back four generations on either side of the family, there still wasn't. So, I had the dubious distinction of being the only woman who hadn't been able to adjust to a life with her husband.

I waited until that evening before I spoke to my mother just as she was folding the freshly laundered clothes, "I've got a job in Delhi. I will be moving over there."

"You're ruining your life. I am telling you, go back to America, and reconcile with Abhinav. These small things happen in marriages, but you shouldn't let it bother you," she said.

I wasn't going to fall for it, not this time. I had listened to her once before and I had hated it. I fought with myself to not be impolite and chose only to say, "Mom, I'm not going back. Forget it!"

In less than three days' time, I was on a train to Delhi, armed with almost everything that I'd need to start life afresh. I realized that it was going to be a little awkward to be a management trainee when most people of my vintage were Assistant Managers. I compared it to being in New York, where anonymous sail boats and a ruthless, unlovable man had been my only company; suddenly, the awkwardness left me.

The morning I entered the new offices of Citibank, Aditya stood there waiting for me. He beamed at me like a child who had done his parents proud.

"Thank you," I said. I couldn't help but say that, although the words were too small for the favour that he had done me. I wondered what would have happened if Aditya hadn't been there. I would have been forced out of the house and sent back to the States. Nowadays, I couldn't be sure about anything.

Even though my salary was small, it would at least help me stand on my own feet. And it wouldn't have been possible without Aditya.

"I'll meet you after work. There's a coffee shop close by. It's not as good as the Indian Coffee house, but should do," he said and entered the elevator.

I nodded and went about my work. The work on the first day in an organization is really only about filling in forms, and Citibank wasn't very different. I met Deepika when I was filling in the forms and she obviously knew my story, for she put an arm on my shoulder and squeezed it. I sometimes disliked these gestures of sympathy; breaking up a marriage was common, but in our psyches it was still a stigma.

I was assigned to credit, the function that dealt with underwriting and risk. It was such a welcome change from sitting in the bay window. I had brought up the topic of starting work with Abhinav once, but he had curtly reminded me, "Who's going to hire you when you're pregnant?" He was right but that had left me bored and jaded. I yearned to do something meaningful with my life and here was the perfect opportunity.

I was told that I could use the guest house for three weeks after which I would need to move out. I met a few people that day and found out that rents were steep, even in a suburb like Gurgaon. By the sounds of it, I wouldn't be able to afford a place of my own. I would need to share an apartment, which in itself was alien. It might not have sounded so strange if I had stayed in a hostel in school or college.

Aditya was standing at the same spot that I had seen him this morning. He led me to the car in the parking lot.

"Yours?" I asked him.

"Yes, Ma'am," he said.

"Very happy for you," I said as he opened the door for me to sit.

We drove down a short distance until we reached Barista, a relatively new coffee shop that had opened up in Gurgaon. At some point between the coffee being ordered and the coffee being served, I asked him, "Adi, How much are you paying in rent?"

"Seven grand" he replied.

My heart sank as I did a mental calculation; it would be over fifty percent of my take home salary.

As if he had read my thoughts, he said, "I have a spare bedroom that you could use."

I shook my head. At heart, I was still that middle class girl that couldn't be seen in a live-in relationship. It was a wee bit too scandalous given that I was still married.

"Never mind. We'll figure something out," he said.

It wasn't really very difficult to find a place that I loved. It only took a week to find a four bed apartment on the second floor of a house that a group of three girls had taken on rent. They were looking for a fourth roommate and I was looking for a place that was clean and affordable. Without a moment's hesitation, I took up the offer and moved over the weekend. Aditya put my belongings in the trunk of the car and that was all that it took.

I wondered where I would be if it weren't for Aditya. He was doing it out of love; I could see in his eyes the same passion that had existed earlier. But a large part of me was dead; I needed time. I needed time to break away from the mess that I had created. I wish I had a time machine that I could turn back a year and undo the decision. I had to constantly remind myself that I was still married to keep myself from hugging him and kissing him passionately as I once did. I couldn't be sailing in two boats.

I unpacked the suitcase and as I put the final set of clothes into the closet, I fell on the bed. Lying on the bed, I looked up at the monotonous whirring of the ceiling fan and heaved a sigh of relief. It had all worked out. Well, almost. Three weeks after moving back from the States, I had a job and a home to go back to. With those essentials in place, I wanted to move forward.

It had been such a long time that I had felt that I could achieve something and be happy. I had almost lost hope that this day could ever be a reality. I felt like the bird that had just escaped from its cage and was ready to fly. Fly it would, if it weren't for that feeble string of a failed marriage that still shackled it. Maybe, now, was a good time to cut those shackles.

Aditya

We have our bags packed – it has taken exactly thirty-three days from that fateful day at Jwalaheri to have come to this point. When Birendra had proposed, I had disposed, until I finally came around to the consensus that we could open up a massage parlour. It makes practical sense. I am spending a large sum of money in hotels and guest houses, and a massage parlour will be a great front for the business that we are in.

Bhatoliya is excited and somewhere, very deep inside me, I am too. I have never imagined myself doing this. It is by a quirk of destiny that I have not only entered the world's oldest profession but am now looking at ways to legalize it.

We have used a broker to negotiate the lease on a three bedroom apartment on the ground floor house in the posh neighbourhood of Greater Kailash 1. The house is a short walk away from the busy M-block market. It is nestled amongst the many houses that have been converted into commercial complexes to satisfy the never-ending need of retail space. In the vicinity is the branch of a multinational bank, a constant reminder of how my life has degraded. The plush office of the bank that I had once inhabited has given way to an under construction massage parlour.

Bhatoliya is leading the charge at the site of the renovation. He has spent the better part of his life's savings on his dream parlour. He chooses a tacky, ludicrous name for the project – "HappyEndingz Massage Parlour". I beg him to be a little more discreet, to avoid the attention of the authorities and to give it a slightly more suave feel, but he is adamant. My learning in life is that whoever has the money calls the shots. Given that my investment into the project has been minimal, I have suppressed my rebellion. The parlour has been designed such that the drawing room serves as a reception and waiting area; the two bedrooms that have attached bathrooms are massage rooms designed to entertain patrons and the one large room at the back has been partitioned into two rooms, serving as our living quarters.

It has been painstaking work to get the entire thing completed in record time, and now, only the finishing touches remain. The carpenters, having created the partition, are making the beds; while the painters are polishing the newly-created reception desk. Above the din of the hammer hitting the nail, my cell phone rings. It is one of those rare occasions that my wife has found the time to call me. Not wanting to let go of this momentous event, I answer the phone.

"Hello," I say. The carpenter drives the nail home, bringing a brief moment of silence

"Hi, how are you?" She sounds surprisingly happy in her demeanour today.

"Very well. How are you?" I reply trying to sound as chirpy.

The carpenter starts hammering another nail.

"Good! What's that noise in the background?" she asks.

It is an unanticipated question. I can tell her the truth; this is a perfect opportunity to come clean. It will mean a failed marriage, but then it has failed already. After an eternity, I say, "Just some carpenters working at the new house."

"New house? Where are you moving?" she asks me.

"Greater Kailash," I reply, knowing that it will ring some bells. An unemployed man, who within three months of moving to Delhi, in a job that doesn't pay enough to send anything back home to his wife, is shifting to a place that commands an exorbitant rent.

"Greater Kailash? Who's paying the rent?" The surprise in her voice is apparent.

"Bhatoliya. His company got him this place," my voice is quivering. Despite the noise of the carpenters hammer, I know that she is certain that I am lying. It will not take a genius to figure out that at the peak of the recession, no company is willing to expend a dime.

"The reason why I called is that your provident fund came through. I want to send the cheque across to you, so just message me your address," her voice is a lot colder now than when the conversation began.

"I'll do that," I say.

"Bye," she hangs up. The traffic cops in Chandigarh are on leave.

The provident fund is good news; a few years' worth of deductions from salary, held hostage by the government, are finally being returned reluctantly. I didn't see the money when I had needed it the most. If I had that money then, I wouldn't be here today. If I had the money then, Bhatoliya would most certainly not be here today. If I had the money then, I would have been writing a different story. I text her the new address. There is an appointment later this evening and I go into the bathroom to look worth the few thousand rupees that my patron will pay me.

Radhika

I was still undressing on that Saturday evening when Abhinav called on the cheap Nokia handset that could sometimes be called a cell phone. It vibrated aggressively, until it was almost ready to fall off the table. I pulled my nightie down in time to answer it. It was a US number and I immediately knew that it was him.

His voice was muffled, sounding as far away as he was and I barely made out the words.

"Yes," I said dryly.

"Abhinav here. What have you thought?" he asked.

I fiddled with my hair. Even as a child, it was my response to nerves. I remembered when my foster mother had to oil my hair to get rid of the knots in my hair after the board exams.

"About what?" I asked, knowing exactly what he wanted me to think about.

"About our relationship. Are you coming back?" he asked. This was the attitude that I hated about him. The tone of the question was demanding, as if he were my Lord and Master.

"No, I haven't thought about it," I replied untruthfully.

"I am coming to India next month. We can do the

formalities in case you think that you don't want to come back," he said.

"I'll let you know," I said and hung up.

That I would never go back to him was a certainty, then why hadn't I said so? It could be a sense of insecurity that prevented me from stating it.

The truth remained that I would gladly jump off the eleventh floor of DLF square than go back to him. It was important that I speak to Abhinav and clarify, but even before that, I needed to speak to Aditya. I called him; it was about ten and it had been less than half an hour that he had dropped me back home after a delectable meal of Kebabs at the Jama Masjid. Jama Masjid was Delhi's hot spot for all foods that had once walked on four legs. We had followed up the meal with a cup apiece of coffee to wash down the layer of fat that clung onto our tongues. I had a feeling that Aditya might think of me as crazy, but even then, I hit the green button on my cell phone.

"Coffee?" I said into the phone even before he had had a chance to say hello.

"Too much caffeine for one day. Tea, my place. I'll pick you up," he said.

I heard the honk from his car downstairs; I hadn't bothered to change when he had said we were meeting at his place but instead just wrapped a stole around me as I rushed down the flight of stairs. I didn't explain why I wanted to meet him so urgently again, until we were at his place.

Robin, his man Friday opened the door for us and we stepped inside. I requested Robin to brew us some tea. He looked at me, as if I were insane, but why blame him? It was July and the monsoons were back, bringing with them the uncomfortable humidity. As if the sweat wasn't enough, I had asked him to brew tea, when most sane people would be happy to have a frappe. Surprisingly, the weather outside was better than within. Aditya didn't own an AC, not that I did, and it just made sense to go out.

"Let's go upstairs, it's much better up on the terrace," I said.

We climbed the dimly-lit flight of stairs to the terrace with tea cups in our hand. I wasn't sure how to bring up the topic. That I would someday have to bring up this topic was a certainty and yet, I was so unprepared. Abhinav's phone call had been such a catalyst that I still had no inkling of what I was going to say to him. I just waited for inspiration to strike me, but before that I had called out to Robin to make us another round of tea. Out of nowhere, I told him about the phone call.

"Are you sure about this?" he asked me.

"I am. I can't even fathom going back to him" I said.

"Then, tell him that," he said.

"I will, but that's not the reason why I called you," I said.

He looked at me, puzzled. He had become my advisor and my agony aunt, so when I didn't want advice, he must have been bewildered.

"I called you to ask you if you still love me enough to forgive me and take me back," I said.

I should have said this a long time ago, but something within me stopped me. Maybe it's just difficult to accept that you are wrong, even when you have known that yourself, all along.

In contrast, he didn't hesitate, "I do, and I was always here. Only you went away."

"I know and that's why I am asking you if you're sure," I moved a little closer to him.

He pulled me closer until we were touching each other. He put his arm around my waist. Somewhere, in the background I thought I heard Mozart's symphony. It had to be my imagination. Why else did I see candles when the terrace had been dark when we had come here?

We broke the hug when Robin came and gave us two cups of tea. It didn't take long before we were kissing each other. The moonlight and the clouds played in heaven as we played on that terrace. One moment it would be dark and suddenly there would be light. It reminded us of our lives, of the moments that we had spent together and the moments that we had been away. The crickets in the wastelands broke the silence of the beautiful night. When the first drizzle started, we were forced to go down. Robin had slept in the study that he used as his bedroom and I made another cup of tea.

Even before we had finished it, he had me in another embrace. We were almost plastered to each other. It wasn't long before we were kissing. He put his hand on my breast and that's when I stopped him. It took a lot out of me to stop my lust, to give into the whirlpool and go down with the flow. Yet, I did. It still wasn't right.

It was raining at dawn when he dropped me and I slipped into the house. I hit the bed and fantasized about him making love to me. What was it about July? Wasn't it a sodden evening in July that I had given him my all. I slept and dreamt – happy dreams of us together. It had taken such an eternity to come to this place.

Aditya

The massage parlour isn't busy enough today to not let me reminisce about Radhika. I don't know why my thoughts veer towards her. I have been thinking about her a lot lately. Maybe I crave for her in the company of these women. Yes, there is Shazia, the rich Muslim girl who wants to take me home to her fanatic dad, so that she can marry me. Yes, there is Jaya, the thirty-two-year-old divorcee, who often uses my services and sometimes only pays me to talk to her. Despite them, I am lonely. I long for a partner like the one I had many moons ago; I long for Radhika.

I remember when I had got the e-mail from her I couldn't help thinking that God was a sadist. God had to be an evil villain who took pleasure in seeing his people writhe. When I had longed for her she hadn't been there and when I was hell bent on forgetting her, the e-mail said that she was coming back.

I remembered when I had waited for an eternity at the airport for the update on the leaderboard to change from "On Time" to "Landed". It took another hour or so for her to emerge out of the terminal, dressed in denim dungarees and a red t-shirt. I wondered if it was just an illusion created by the dungaree or if she had really gained more weight. She came closer; she had gained weight. When we neared the exit, she said, "My parents are going to be outside. When can we meet? I am going to Chandigarh directly."

"I'll see you tomorrow at the Sector 16 stadium. 5 p.m. Get some rest," I said.

I rushed back home, showered, threw in a couple of clothes into a small duffel bag and rushed out. It was about 1 a.m., not the best time to gallivant on a notorious, unsafe highway in an unsafe car, but it was imperative that I meet her. My curiosity had the better of me. I wanted to understand why she was back and if I had a reason to dream again. I drove at break neck speed, completing the journey in record time. Michael Schumacher would've been proud of me that night as I drove on under the night sky, not even stopping to give my burgeoning bladder a breather. I wondered if Maruti would appoint me as a brand ambassador for being able to cover that distance, in that time, in *that* car.

After my meeting with her, I realized that she needed help. If I had never been romantically involved with her, and if she were just a colleague who had been a great friend, I would've helped her. When I saw her that evening, she was a faint shadow of herself. The skin that had once glowed was jaded. The eyes that had once twinkled were almost lifeless. They weren't smiling even on the few occasions that she managed a smile on her stressed face. I had wanted her back and yes, I still did, but not this shadow. I wanted the Radhika that would come in my dreams, the one that I fell in love with.

On Monday morning, I made my way to the office a little earlier than usual. I waited on the mezzanine floor of DLF Square, a floor that was designated for people who worked in Human Resources. Deepika, after graduating from the training program, chose to take a posting in Human Resources. She felt that it was her kind of work because it didn't come with insane targets and a mad rush to meet them. She had barely entered the door when I led her to the Nescafe counter in the lobby.

"Remember Radhika?"

"Of course. Why wouldn't I?" she said emptying the contents of the sachet into her cup of coffee.

"She's back," I said. My lips curled up in an involuntary smile that had become a part of me ever since that e-mail had arrived.

"What're you saying?" she said. She was surprised. When she had put forth the idea of the bird returning if you left it free, she had never envisaged it coming true.

"Yes! The marriage didn't quite work out," I said careful not to give her any details.

She shrugged her shoulders and for the lack of a better response said, "Shit happens."

I nodded in response as if I completely understood what she meant.

"She's looking for a job. Can you help?" I asked her.

Deepika was managing recruitments within Citibank and although she was relegated to hire staff rather than managers, she was an insider. "I'll try," she said, which meant that she could do it. Deepika was a master at underplaying her abilities.

"I'll send you her resume," I said.

We broke up on that note and went about the mundane chores that a Monday morning brings to a bank.

That day, after a two week hiatus, I went back to work with a renewed sense of vigour. There were still a lot of questions that remained unanswered about *us*, but hope is such a wonderful thing. We work, in the hope that we will get a raise. We love, in the hope that we will find a soul mate. And we earn, in the hope that we will never have to work again.

Talking of earnings, I had lost her because back then, I didn't earn enough. I lost her because I wasn't an able suitor and despite my promotion, there was still a lot to be done. If I were to be compared to an NRI who owned an apartment in Manhattan, I still had a long way to go.

I wondered how simple life would be if there was no currency. No notes made of paper or plastic that differentiated between people. Or if there had to be a currency, then why it couldn't just be love?

I imagined myself walking into a grocery to buy a loaf of bread. The pretty girl at the counter says, "That'll be two hugs and a kiss on the cheek". I laughed out aloud which made my colleagues turn around to see me. I must be naïve to imagine that love was the only thing that could run this world. I remembered my vow: I would never let the next person I loved go away. Ironically, Radhika was that next person. A large part of that vow meant that I had to be rich and I delved into the spreadsheet on my desktop that would make my employer rich. Hopefully, some of my employer's wealth would flow back to me.

Deepika's magic worked and Radhika was back in Gurgaon. Those days, I think I took my work too seriously. Maybe, the memories of the Performance Improvement Plan were too severely etched in my brain to let me relax. I was almost mechanical, blocking out any emotions of romance or love with Radhika until I was off work. It would be hard to believe how little we saw of each other even though we worked in the same office. Yet, the evenings were ours. I think that was the time when my taste buds possessed me.

We would meet in the street adjacent to DLF Square, away from the prying eyes of our colleagues. I don't know why we even bothered when the rumour mills were already abuzz with our affair. From there, we would drive to Barista and have a coffee before dinner. At least four times a week, we would go out to eat. The place could be dirty as long as the food tasted good. I think that's when Culinaire became our favourite. On the other days, I would eat at home, courtesy of the new boy who would cook and clean for me. The incentives that I had been making in selling credit cards afforded him. He was referred to me through a colleague at work and he arrived one day, unannounced, just before I was leaving for work. A Nepali, with a sharp nasal twang, he introduced himself as Govind. Govind sounded like Robin and hence, Govind was rechristened when he got employed.

Robin was such a great cook and it was a pleasure to come back home to homemade food, clean floors and a made-up bed. I wondered if my bachelorhood days were coming to an end. In the six years that I had lived away from home, life had come to a point that sleeping on clean sheets seemed to be a luxury. All in all, life was moving perfectly.

Radhika

The cricket stadium had left me weeping. I think Aditya was really my saviour back then. I stay in Chandigarh a few days longer than I should have but except for the children, I have nothing to look forward to back home. I think today is the third day since I have been here. The visit to the cricket stadium has brought back a flood of memories that refuse to leave me. I have never had the urge to go back to YPS. Except for Shipra and Aditya, I have no fond memories of that place. The only other exception is Ms Kapoor.

I don't even remember my way back to the school but the boards that the school has put up direct me to the place. The guard at the school gate has changed. The Sikh gentleman at the gates is now replaced by a Hindu. I've never been really religious. Maybe, I should have been. Maybe, it would have reduced my suffering.

The guard says that he doesn't know any Ms Kapoor. I go inside and check at the reception. They tell me that she left the school about ten years ago. I am dejected and unhappy about not meeting her when I bump into Mr Razdan, the mathematics teacher. He tells me that Ms Kapoor retired but still stays in her house in Sector 18.

243

I walk back to the car and ask Laxman to drive to Sector 18. He thinks that I am crazy. I can see it in the way he looks at me. I remember that this is his first time in Chandigarh and I give him some vague directions. Even before we reach her house, I can feel a wave of nostalgia come over me. I remember how my days were spent at this very house when I transformed from what I was to what I am. My hair were cut short then. I still sport short hair, but this is ugly, and that was elegant.

I enter her house without ringing the bell. I remember that the bell was only at the front door and not on the gate. She is basking in the sun and recognizes me immediately. She thinks my hair look good. I want to tell her to stop lying, but I don't. The respect is too deep seated for me to be impolite. I tell her that I try and emulate her and she is proud of what I am doing. In some ways, she is the mother that I have never had. She is everything that I wanted of a mother but it wasn't my luck. She has aged, must be sixty now. I think she was in her mid-forties when I last saw her. Yet, she's like that delectable aged cheese which has been in the cellar for long.

It's difficult to go back but somehow I bid her goodbye. She hugs me and kisses me on the forehead. I ask her to come to Delhi and visit me. I know that she won't when she says she will. I have nothing else to do in Chandigarh. I check out of the hotel and ask Laxman to drive me back to Delhi.

It's about nine by the time we reach Delhi and for some strange reason, Laxman takes the BRT. It is jammed as it usually is and so he goes even farther away from home. I know he is insane but he drives well. He takes me through a convoluted route that sees me crossing Greater Kailash. It's already nine-thirty and the traffic is dying down. I see the board of the Saloon but I don't hate the hair dresser anymore. Ms Kapoor has given me some positivity about my hair. I am just about to take my eyes off the board when I see a bright neon board.

It wasn't here the last time I crossed. In a cursive hand, it says "HappyEndingz Massage Parlour". It leaves nothing to imagination and I can't help wonder what the world is coming to. I reach home and sleep.

The next morning, Shipra having learnt that I have lost my father, has come over to offer her condolences.

"I'm really sorry for your loss," she says.

I don't know why I tell her everything about my childhood. Everything, that begins from being offered up for adoption to being returned. I have never shared this with anyone, except Aditya and yet, I tell her. It is as if my telling her will in some way undo my parent's follies. Often, I think that if they hadn't done what they had, I might have been a different personality. I wouldn't be this shy. I wouldn't be this person who struggles to make relationships work.

She listens patiently. I mean, that is the best that she can do. If I don't have a solution to my problems, she definitely doesn't have any. Just before she leaves, she says, "It's my anniversary next week. I'll need your help."

I can't be more elated in someone asking me for help. I wonder if I should start hiring out myself for odd chores that can help people.

"Name it," I say.

"Come over tomorrow and we'll figure it out," she says.

Shipra leaves and the children from the neighbourhood come. My *dhobi* wants to give me a discount on the ironing bill for helping his child. I politely refuse because it takes away the premise on which I am running this cause. It is a means to make myself useful. It is a means of giving back to society.

In some countries, civil punishments require a certain number of hours to be volunteered for community service. I sometimes see this activity as a penance for having jilted

Aditya. I had been coerced but it was really my weakness that I hadn't been able to stand up to my parents.

The next day, I go to Shipra's. It is her tenth anniversary and she wants to make quite an extravagant affair out of it.

"So, what do you want me to do?" I say.

"Why don't you just take over food completely?" she asks me.

"I'll do that. Are you fine with a non-vegetarian menu?" I ask her.

"Yes! I am no longer the Tamil Brahmin," she says.

It is funny how much Shipra has changed. I remember her not eating out of my tiffin box once she learnt that I was a non-vegetarian.

It is seldom that I get an opportunity to be useful and I get working in earnest. By that evening, I have a list of five caterers that we can use. I have the menu worked out; I go back to being a seven year old child at the farmer's market who loves to haggle with people for money.

I beat them down on price until they are a fraction of their initial quote. The party is to be at DSOI and I am there in the morning of that March day that is their anniversary. It is only after I think that the cooks are on schedule that I go to Shipra's home in the cantonment to change. It is warm already, so I avoid wearing silk, instead choosing chiffon. It is an elegant turquoise sari that I had once bought on a trip to Bangalore with Vimal. It has just stayed locked up in the closet until today.

When I reach the venue, the guests are already there. Shipra and the Colonel are busy entertaining their guests and I feel a little out of place. After all, they are the only people that I know there.

Aditya

I was now the proud owner of a cell phone. I dialled a number from the contacts list and waited as I heard the familiar voice of my mother answer the phone.

"How are you?" she asked.

"Fine. Just came back home," I said.

"Did you have dinner?" she asked.

This conversation was our ritual every evening and this last question could never be missed.

"Yes, just finished. The *dal* was horrible today, though" I said.

"Why don't you get married? At least you'll get good food," she said.

I didn't know if good food was a good enough reason to get married. I was just a shade under twenty-four and marriage could wait. Of course, if the marriage were to be with Radhika, then I was ready. But she wasn't. Her divorce was still not completed, though they had had a conversation.

"I will, Mom. I just need a little more time," I said.

We exchanged news about Dad; how he was getting frustrated because another shipment of garments that he had sent had been returned because of a quality issue. He was nearing fifty-three and I wished I could send some money home to ease the pressure. My financial situation was a lot better but I still didn't have any savings. My near impossible fetish for food meant an empty bank account at the end of the month. She hung up and I stepped out into the balcony for a smoke. I hated the habit; maybe if I quit it and saved the money that I blew up in smoke rings, I would be able to send money back to my parents. They had done so much for me and even after being in a job for a year and a half, I was still struggling to be a good son.

The more I thought about it, the more frustrated I became. I needed money, more money than what I earned today. More money to be able to be a good son, more money to be an able suitor and more money to drive a car better than the flimsy four wheeler I was driving today.

The more important part was to be the able suitor, and how could I be an able suitor to a woman who was already married. It wasn't long after she had met me on the terrace and asked for forgiveness that I had agreed to marry her.

I went back to work on Monday, after the amorous weekend on the terrace and looked at the sales figures on my desk. They were less than promising. My next promotion depended on the numbers being miles ahead of where they were. I had to secure a promotion in April, eight months away. I knew I was being overambitious to expect a promotion within a year, but I was committed.

I saw the promotion as a means to an end – more money, able suitor, marry Radhika. I didn't realize when I changed, but money was beginning to be a priority. I was finding ways to save a little money. I was certain that I wouldn't ask my parents to support my wedding. I would do it on my own.

Now, when the time was nearing, I realized that I wouldn't even have money to take her for a honeymoon. It gave me a sense of urgency that had made me question Robin about the kitchen expenses last week. He had looked at me strangely, wondering what had prompted that question. I had even cut down on going to Barista, choosing the Nescafe counter downstairs. It was cheaper. There was always something to talk about and really, the ambience didn't matter.

April was going to be an important month. If I did get the promotion, then I would speak to my parents about her. Maybe, it would put an end to my mother's concern regarding my marriage.

Radhika

At Shipra's party, I try to make myself unobtrusive by supervising the caterers. I think Shipra is able to see my discomfort and maybe that is the reason why she introduces me to another lady who feels almost as out of place as I am feeling.

The conversation veers towards what I do for a living and I have nothing to say. I am just a very bored widow who lives alone in Delhi. I could've chosen to tell her that I run a make shift school but I don't. I don't think she is the sorts who will appreciate it. I ask her the same and she says, "I work for an advertising agency". I learn that she is a divorcee.

I think that she is another one of those people who will come and go from my life. When I meet her at Shipra's party, I find her a little pushy and demanding. I don't like her enough to exchange phone numbers but she is insistent. I don't see too much harm in it, so I give her my number hoping that she will not call. I type the phone number first into the phone and then reach the field where I have to type in her name. Slowly, I type in the letters D-I-V-Y-A.

Divya starts calling often and then we start meeting often. It isn't my company of choice but at least she is here. So often, during our conversations, she excuses herself and makes phone calls. I wonder if they are all really related to her work at the advertising company because she speaks in such a hushed voice.

My school is beginning to do very well. When the results came out in April, almost all my students scored better than their previous result. I am overwhelmed when their parents come to see me. They thank me profusely for helping their children. Even more overwhelming are the sweets that they have brought. It has taken me a week to finish off the sweets and will take months to lose the extra weight that it has left me with.

My days are passing faster than they used to. I am not the same whining woman that had moved to Delhi six months ago. Maybe, it's because the winter is behind me. I have been able to make my life a little more useful. I know that the pigeons are feeling neglected, but even then. Sometimes, I think that it is about time that I can have a partner. I am just readier for a relationship now than when I had come from Lucknow.

I call out to Laxman to pull out the car. I am going over to meet Shipra today. Ever since I have been introduced to Divya, my trips to her house have become a little less frequent. I feel guilty that I am not being such a good friend. I feel that I have been using her when I didn't have company; but ever since I have met Divya, I have shirked away.

When I reach Shipra's house, I realize that I am not wrong in thinking this way. Shipra's house is half packed when I get there.

"Where are you going?" I ask her.

"Sidhu's being transferred again," she says.

I am hit by anxiety. I know that people in the Army get transferred very often but I have taken Shipra's presence in

Delhi for granted. I can't fathom myself being without her support.

"Where is he getting transferred?" I ask her.

"We're moving to Ranikhet," she says.

I don't know why but I break down. I don't want her to leave. She isn't just another friend. She is the only family that I have, now that my parents are estranged and I have no other family to speak of.

"Don't cry, Radhika. Look at it this way: it's only an eight hour drive out of here," she says.

"I know but I just can't drive over there like I did today," I say through my sobbing.

"Let me just get settled there and then you can come and stay with us for a few days," she says.

I am halfway back home when Divya calls to ask me if I am interested in watching a movie.

I look at the watch, it is only seven-thirty and I agree. It has to be Shipra's going away that has made me agree so suddenly. I am now left with only one friend and I can't afford to lose her. Even if she is not someone who I really like.

I ask Laxman to take a detour to Vasant Vihar. Divya said that she was already at Priya, the cinema hall at Vasant Vihar, and would arrange the tickets. Surprisingly, the place isn't bustling with activity as it used to. The restaurants are empty. The crowds at the movie halls are thin. The recession isn't leaving anyone. I wonder what those jobless people do. It is quite a dichotomy that when they had work, they would go out for entertainment and now, when they don't have work they choose to stay at home.

I find Divya in line, still waiting for the ticket counter to open up.

"Hey, you didn't take very long to get here," she says.

"I was on my way back from Shipra's when you called," I say.

"It's sad that she's leaving," Divya says.

Divya is quite a social butterfly. Sometimes, I envy her for her social skills. She always knows what everyone is up to. She already knows that Shipra is leaving, when I have only found out today. I am about to ask her how she manages to do this when her cell phone rings. She fishes into her large purse and excuses herself. I take her place in the queue while she goes out of earshot and has an animated discussion with someone on the phone. One of these days, I am going to ask her who she speaks to, I say to myself.

The movie is a disaster and we walk out even before the intermission; it was unbearable. I wonder if the recession has anything to do with that. Maybe film makers also don't have the budgets that they used to have. We have dinner at a restaurant and somehow, I gather the courage to ask her about her phone calls.

"Who do you keep talking to on the phone?" I ask her.

"Clients," she says.

"Do they have no respect for personal time?" I ask her. Her last phone call had been well past eight.

"Well, these clients are different," she says without explaining much further.

I want to probe further, but I don't do it. I don't want to seem like I am trying to pry into her life.

"I was thinking about visiting Shipra once she's settled in," I say.

"Count me in. I have wanted a change for some time now," she says.

We walk to the car park and just before we are going to part and go our separate ways, she asks me, "Do you ever feel the need to have sex?"

I am not sure that I have heard correctly.

"What?" I ask. I am a little surprised and maybe even a little offended. Divya isn't close enough to be asking that personal a question.

"I mean, you're pretty much in my situation. We don't have partners so just thought I'd ask."

I shrug my shoulders. I don't know the answer and I think it is best not to answer that question until I know for sure.

Aditya

It wasn't smooth. It wasn't rhythmic. It wasn't even passionate. It wasn't even innocent. It was everything that I had thought it would never be. We made love but there were strange thoughts that ran through my mind. Did he give her more pleasure? Was my performance good enough? Did he have an organ larger than mine?

Maybe, the questions were natural but in the labyrinth of those questions was the answer that it could never be the same again. Yes, we were together as we had intended it to be for an eternity and now that we were together, there was the burden of the past that we carried. I didn't ejaculate and I wondered if she had come. I didn't ask, instead just turned over and slept hoping that sleep would give me some answers.

Her divorce had happened a few months ago, giving us the moral high ground to be able to make love. We lay in my apartment on the same bed that we had lost our virginity on and yet, we were unable to have satisfying, gratifying sex. She put her arm around me and slept, completely ignoring my underperformance.

I woke up first and saw her form under the sheets. My hand was under the covers as my finger created imaginary images on her thigh. It was enough to wake her up. She turned her head, until I could kiss her. I kissed passionately and ran my hand up to her breast and cupped it. She let out a sigh as I gently plucked her nipple. She turned around a little more. My hand ran down her stomach, stopping momentarily on her navel. My index finger probed the depression and then the hand went on downwards until the stubble of recently shaved hair stopped the smooth slide. She opened her legs a little farther apart. My middle finger found another depression to explore, a moist depression this time. I felt my lower back stiffen as her hand moved down my back. It only took a few minutes before I was inside her, the gyrations started, a little better than before, the rhythm a little more harmonious until it finally ended on a high note.

Wasn't this Nirvana? To be in the arms of the one that you love – sweaty, tired and spent, yet happy. The human need was to copulate before social structures had denigrated it with marriage. Even now, when we weren't married, we were so together. We just lay there immersed in our thoughts searching for answers in the whirring of the ceiling fan.

I turned around and whispered into her ear, "I love you".

She whispered back, "I love you too".

I had been the industrious ant all winter and now, when spring burst through, my hard work was beginning to be recognized. My conversation with my boss had been fantastic for he had committed to promote me in April. Life was on a high. As things looked, I would be the only person amongst my peer group that would get promoted as a manager. Rightly so, given that they weren't a patch on me. I had done it; I was king – God's gift to mankind. If not, for Citibank India, I certainly was.

There was just one more thing that was pending on my plate – to marry Radhika and make her my own. That's when I made a trip back to Chandigarh to broach the subject with my parents. I didn't expect resistance, especially when they had been more eager to see me married than I was. It would just be a formality.

I entered my house through the narrow winding stairs that took me to the two bedroom house on the second floor. I couldn't but notice that the paint on the walls needed to be redone. The house needed urgent repairs. Had I been ignoring my parents while I blissfully carried on my life in Delhi with Radhika?

My father was out, but mother had been expecting me. I hugged her and touched her feet like any good son does. My father returned in the afternoon, looking harried and frustrated. His turban was soaked in sweat, even though the weather was at its best in February. I thought about bringing up her topic now, but maybe it would be better to wait until he was in a better state of mind.

"How's the job coming along?" my father asked.

"Very good, dad, spoke to my manager last week. He's promoting me in April."

"Congratulations! Good thing that you chose to work a job instead of a business. It's so much easier," he said and then embarked on telling me a tale of the woes that he was up against. The shortage of labour, the shortage of raw material, the poor quality of labour and the inspectors of the government who would constantly demand bribes on one pretext or the other.

I caught up on some sleep in the afternoon, a luxury that I could hardly afford on the short trip back home, but I was exhausted. My mother had attempted to make some of my favourite dishes and they were horrendous. I wondered how she could mess up something as simple as a salad. Her affection for salt had smothered the salad into bitterness. And yes, there was the infamous pineapple jelly that wiggles. I don't know how she managed it but Robin was a godsend. I stopped myself from critiquing her culinary skills. It would certainly spoil the mood and I didn't want anyone upset when I brought up Radhika's topic.

I didn't even know how to get to the topic but I gathered all my courage and said, "Mom, I want to marry this year."

I directed my statement towards Mom, knowing that I would find an ally in her. She had been after my life for over a year now.

"Finally, I hear you saying it. Just last week my friend was talking to me about her girl," she was so visibly elated.

Oh, no! I wanted to make it amply clear that I had found my girl. I didn't want her to find me one.

"That won't be necessary; I've found the one for me," I said

"Good going" Dad said, participating in the conversation for the first time.

"Who is she?" my mother asked.

"Radhika. Works with me in Citibank Delhi," I said.

"Hindu?" They asked in unison. I saw the expressions on their face change. Just moments ago, there had been elation and that was quickly changing into something else, something indescribable.

"Yes, but you'll love her," I replied, suddenly aware that this conversation may not be the breeze that I was expecting it to be.

"Where is she from?" my father asked.

"Chandigarh. She was with me in school too," I replied.

"What does her father do?" he asked.

Why was this important? What if she had been an orphan? Would they still care to ask?

"I think he's retired. He used to work in the gulf as a mechanic before that."

They exchanged glances and then looked at me.

"Anything else?" he asked. I wondered if there was merit in telling them that she was a divorcee. Somehow, your parents always know who you are and there was only one reason that the last question had been posed. They knew that I hadn't told them the whole truth. In some uncanny, strange way, they were able to decipher that I was withholding something.

"Yes, she's a divorcee," I said.

"Are you crazy?" my mother asked me.

She was holding her head in her hands, as if someone had just died. I ignored her posture.

"Why? What's wrong?" I asked.

"My son is telling me that he wants to marry a Hindu, a daughter of a mechanic, who was once married, now divorced," she asked me to reconfirm that she wasn't hallucinating and that she had heard what I had told her.

"Yes, Mom. I love her," I implored.

"You're too naïve. What has she done to you for you to lose your sanity?" she had tears in her eyes.

This was absurd; why would she do anything? Maybe I wasn't making my love of her clear for them to look beyond their prejudices.

"Mom! I've loved her since school," I said.

The voices were a little louder than normal, "And she loved you in return? Then, why did she marry someone else?"

They won't understand, I told myself, but still attempted it, "Because, I wasn't settled".

"So, she leaves you when you're unsettled and comes back to you when you're settled? She's using you! Can't you make out?" my father pitched in.

In a realistic, normal world, this was the truth; but they didn't know her they way I did. They didn't know our love. They wouldn't understand the depth if they continued to look at the surface.

"I don't think she is, and I am going to marry her," I replied back.

Uncharacteristically, my father, the usually boisterous Sikh, lowered his voice and said, "Now, you listen to me. You want to marry her, go ahead. But don't expect us to approve. I don't care if you love her or if she married someone else or she divorced or she is the daughter of a mechanic. Above all, she is a Hindu and I will never have a Hindu girl be married to you. They killed my father."

I walked out in a huff. The next morning, I boarded the bus back from the ISBT in Chandigarh, confused and stressed. What I had thought to be a cake walk wasn't turning out to be one.

I was a smoker; I hadn't seen the insides of a Gurudwara in over five years; I had had my hair cut when I was seven and I was referred to as Aditya Sharma. And yet, I was to believe that I was a Sikh? I was doing everything that the Sikh religion forbids and still I could not marry the girl of my dreams because my grandfather had been murdered by some fanatics posing as Hindus? This situation was ridiculous and so was my father. I wished to rebel and tell them that I would do as I pleased. Only the gratitude of having been brought up by them stopped me. If I didn't remember the sacrifices that they had made to bring me up, I would've definitely revolted. I remembered, so I chose to linger on.

I returned back to Delhi on Sunday, confused, irritated and unhappy. Had I underestimated the depth of the conversation? Had the wounds of the riots been so deep, that nearly two decades of peace hadn't been able to heal them? Just when everything was falling into place, why did this have to come up? My father was well educated, had travelled the world and was broad minded. Yes, if he had raised an objection on her being divorced and all, I would have been able to counter it. But religion? How do you counter that? I didn't have a solution and that was worse than the problem.

I was stressed – not only because of the conversation of the weekend, but also because I was committed. If I hadn't said yes to her proposal on that night on the terrace, maybe, it would have been better. Why had I not brought this subject up with my parents before I had said yes? And now, when they were against the marriage, why didn't I have the courage to stand up and rebel. Did I even love her? If I did, why were these thoughts crossing my mind?

At work, my boss had promised me a promotion but thought he had enslaved me. I was expected to be present in office at the weirdest hours – on weekends, on late night calls and early morning conversations. I toed his line; I would have to do it at least until I got the promotion letter in hand. The pain was self-inflicted. I could have easily waited another year for the promotion and the money that came with it, but I wanted it now. I wanted to be at twenty-four what others become at twenty eight. Unknowingly, the promotion, career and money that had been a means to an end were beginning to become an end. I was obsessed with money, trying to learn to earn more. Hell, I even financed Robin to open a cigarette shop by night for a share in profits. I had changed, but I was still unaware. I was selling my soul for money. Much later in life, I have realised that selling your body is better than selling your soul.

Radhika

When I get back home from the movie, I think about what Divya had asked me. I'll be honest; sometimes I do want to make love but I don't want to have sex, like she had so cruelly put it. Every time, I speak about making love, I remember Aditya. Wasn't it sometime after my divorce had been completed that he became such an animal. Initially, Aditya was hesitant and stressed when we made love but he was beginning to find his bearings and bringing me throes of pleasure. There was just one thing that we couldn't agree on – he hated contraceptives. He thought that it spoilt the spontaneity of the moment. I wish I could tell him the repercussions of not using them. Hell, even if we did conceive, we would just marry and have the child. We'd tell the child that it was a premature kid, if the dates of the marriage and his birthday ever made him suspicious.

Yes, it was just after my divorce when I had broken the shackles that I had so stupidly put around my ankles. Abhinav had met me a day before we were to meet our lawyers. He was his usual self – defiant, arrogant and uncompromising. He wanted to create a fuss about the alimony and the belongings. I was expecting a long, protracted legal battle of the lawyers to solemnize a separation but things changed, probably at the advice of his lawyers.

The Indian judicial system was slow and inefficient. Add to that cauldron the new dowry laws and the powers it bestowed on women and you have the recipe for trouble. I think Abhinav realized that he could be in more trouble than this. When he came back the next day, he was as meek as a lamb. He was back in the United States within the week of filing the decree and we were both free to marry and lead independent lives. Whoever said that two wrongs can't make a right was mistaken.

Life was near perfect again, even though Aditya was obsessed with work and money.

For the first time in my life, I was leading an independent life and making my own decisions. My trips to Chandigarh had nearly dried up. Earlier, I would visit once a month, but it had been three months now that I hadn't made a visit. Worse still, I wasn't missing it. At first, my parents had continued to pester me about going back to the States but now they had resigned. They still believed that I was ruining my life.

I just wish I knew what was going on in Aditya's mind. Why had he become so centred in the material plane? Why did everything boil down to money? I knew that he was ambitious and that was something that had made me fall in love with him. Even in YPS, when those spoilt brats would spend their vacations abroad, Aditya would try and get a summer job.

I wished that I had told him that my happiest times with him were on his motorcycle. I still remembered the times when I would ride pillion clutching onto him every time he braked. Now, he wanted a fancier car, a home of his own and a promotion. It was as if the promotion and the designation that came with it were going to be the cornerstones of his existence.

When I had just moved to Gurgaon, we would promptly meet at 6 p.m. just as the crowds left to take the bus back to

Delhi. Then, we left a little later. My work wasn't as taxing and I would while away the hours, surfing the limited Internet that was available. Now, that timeline had slipped to as late as 8 p.m. I wished I could bring this up at some time but I felt he was too obsessed to understand or appreciate what I expected. Even then, I asked him, "Why do you have to stay in office so late?"

"I have a lot of work to do," he replied back a little brusquely.

"Everyone else seems to finish up by six."

"They're working a job and I am building a career," he said.

I didn't question him again on the subject for a very long time.

Sometimes I would wonder if Aditya was really wrong in what he was doing. Didn't we all have the right to dream? Wasn't I dreaming of owning a home, of being married to Aditya and of our children?

I reached back home after work on Saturday, not really looking forward to a lonely weekend without him. He was making one of those rare visits to Chandigarh to meet his parents and I was beginning to worry about how I would be able to live the weekend without him. The weekend was our dress rehearsal of when we would marry. I would go back with him from work on Saturday evening, change and go out for a bout of drinks. We would return drunk, sloshed and uninhibited. Our passions would take us over and I would spend the night with him. On Sunday mornings, he churned out a lavish spread of bacon, ham and eggs. Robin, who hated his kitchen being taken over, would insist on brewing the coffee.

After breakfast, we would laze around in bed, reading the newspapers when he would snuggle in. It didn't take long for me to be aroused in his company and invariably we would end up making love. I had come a long way – from the village belle that I once was, to a woman, now divorced, almost living in with a man that I loved. I wondered how scandalized my parents would be if they ever came to know the truth about my sexual escapades. I laughed to myself when I pictured my mother's jaw drop. It would almost hit the ground.

It was after that weekend in Chandigarh that he changed, and worse still, he refused to speak about it. Every time I broached the topic, he would ignore it, looking through me as if I were made in a glass factory. Our love affair continued despite the waning intensity. I wanted to reignite the passions that had helped us go through thick and thin. After all, hadn't our relationship withstood the test of time and heart break? Only if he would talk to me, we could find a solution. Everything had a solution.

It was the second Saturday of March 2001, when he said, "I have work this weekend. I won't be able to go out."

I let him be, giving him the space, hoping that whatever was on his mind would auto correct. I went back home to see my roommates getting dressed. Shilpi, the girl, who worked in Max New York and the one that I was relatively close to, asked me, "Home on a Saturday evening?"

"Yes, he had work" I replied. It was an open secret that we were dating and would be marrying soon.

"What'll you do at home all alone? We are going out for a party. Want to come along?" Shilpi asked me.

I didn't have anything to do. I would probably end up lazing in front of the TV. So, I agreed to go. I was so short on my social life that I really had no notable friends. My world had just revolved around Aditya for so long. Maybe, that was what was wrong. Maybe, that was suffocating our relationship as too much familiarity does. In a life that we would spend together, it was important that we give ourselves the space to be able to create room for our own personas to blossom.

We went to Rodeo, one of the few choices of eating joints in Gurgaon. They called themselves a Tex Mex restaurant and so, you couldn't blame them for not being unique. The moment I walked into the restaurant, I felt out of place and wondered if I had been better off whiling away time at home. It probably was so, because I was alone with three couples. The others attempted to make me feel comfortable, but I concentrated on my drink. The others had a conversation going and I only had a drink. So, I drank faster than the others. I could feel myself a little tipsy and I should have stopped, but I continued, ahead of the others. The alcohol went to my head, bringing up the thoughts that were uppermost in my mind.

Why was he acting so strangely recently? Was it something that I had said or done to him to behave this way? Why couldn't it be perfect like it was earlier? Didn't he love me anymore?

I pulled out the cell phone from my purse and typed a message "I love you" and sent it.

I went back to my drink, sitting in isolation within the crowd. Two swigs later, I pulled out the cell phone again from my purse to see if the beep of an incoming message had been drowned out by the music. There was no message. He might have been busy with work. He was always busy with work. Why was he so obsessed with money? He had said that he wanted a promotion and then he would ease up. And even that was a certainty now. Why didn't he stop now and take a short breather to rejuvenate? We had enough between the two of us, for even I was going to be promoted this year. We could easily have a very comfortable living. I replaced the phone into the floundering depths of the large purse.

Two more swigs later, my drink was finished. The others were ordering the next round, so I ordered it too – my fourth.

I opened the purse again, searching for that elusive message that he had forgotten to send. It was still not there. I stepped out to make a phone call. All thoughts about giving him space had vanished, not unlike the alcohol from my glass. He didn't answer. Was he trying to avoid me? Why? What had I done to wrong him? Why didn't he love me anymore? It had to be the alcohol that threw up more questions than there were answers.

Disappointed, I went back to the table and gulped down the rum and coke that sat there in one single gulp. The conversations sounded like gibberish and I put my two bits in. I was slurring, but still, I continued to talk. I was talking about Aditya – raving about him one moment, and calling him names another, for not replying to my message. They weren't interested; they didn't know Aditya. Hell, they'd only met me once before and here I was, a stranger talking about another.

They exchanged embarrassed glances at each other. I was making a fool of myself. I could make that out but to prove my innocence, I was talking much more than I ever had. Shilpi suggested that I should go home and sleep, as politely as she could, but I had no way of going home. Aditya had been my ride for so long and so, I called him once again. This time he answered. I couldn't explain where I was and had him speak to Shilpi's boyfriend.

I was leaning on the two boys who helped me get to the parking lot when he arrived and took me away. My last recollection of the event was when he said "I love you too" in response to my "I love you".

I woke up on Sunday morning without the customary breakfast being brought out on a tray. I looked around. He was still sleeping beside me. The events of last night had left me red-faced. Why did I have to drink so much that I had lost my senses? I vowed to myself that I would quit drinking, even socially. I went to the wash and then to the kitchen. As horrible as I was with the eggs, I thought they turned out well. The yolks didn't run this time but they were still not half as good as the eggs he made.

Talking about eggs, I was due to release mine in about fourteen days which meant that I was to start bleeding today but it hadn't happened until now. I looked at the watch; it was still only nine and an entire day lay ahead of me, but the familiar pain that preceded the event had also not started. No, not again, a voice in my head reminded me. The same voice said that this was different – this was Aditya's kid and I was with Aditya.

I woke him up and presented him with the tray on which the breakfast lay. I don't know if the eggs weren't to his liking or whether he was upset about last night's episode but he wasn't his cheerful self.

"I am really sorry about last night. I was really upset about not being with you. I had a few more than I should have had," I said.

He just shook his head, ignored the tray that lay in front of him and walked away to the bathroom. I didn't even remember my conversations with him. Had I said or done something I shouldn't have? I waited for him to come out of the washroom and it took almost an eternity.

"I am sorry," I said again to rid me of my guilt.

"It's okay," he said. However, it didn't seem like it was okay.

Why had he lately started sounding so superficial? I missed the guy who spoke from his heart? The guy whose voice would implore you because it sounded so genuine. I missed the voice of the man that I had fallen in love with.

Aditya

Bang! Bang! I wake up to the sounds of someone knocking on the door. I am sweating. I realize that I am in the middle of a power cut. The AC that I can now afford has switched itself off sometime in the middle of the night, leaving me to sweat in the unbearable August humidity. Through the sleepiness of my eyes, I see the clock sitting on my bedside. The cheap rooster hasn't yet blown its trumpet, so it has to be before eight. The clock confirms my fear; it is only seven fifty-five. It is too early to have customers. Maybe, it is Bhatoliya who is knocking. Maybe, he went out for a walk and forgot to take the keys, leaving him stranded on the street.

I wear my pyjama over my boxer shorts and groggily walk to the front of the house to the source of the noise. I open the door to see Jasleen standing at the front door. She is clad in jeans and a white top and has a small overnight bag in hand. She would've taken the overnight train from Chandigarh. I am not sure why, because it has been nearly nine months that I have moved to Delhi and she hasn't had the need, desire or the inclination to see me. It is mutual; I haven't made a trip to Chandigarh either. Then, why today?

I rub my eyes, to ensure that if I am hallucinating, she disappears. She doesn't.

"What's going on?" she asks. Her mouth is in a grimace that tells me that the cat and mouse game is over. There are no hugs, no kisses, and no feigned or superficial expressions of love. It just doesn't exist.

"Nothing, just woke up," I try to brush aside the question. I hold the door open for her to enter.

"I figured that. My question is – *what's going on*?" she asks again. Women have a special talent of asking an open ended question that can be interpreted in various ways.

"What?" I ask, I still play the farce and avoid the question.

She walks into the reception area and looks around at the contents of the room. There is a small podium like desk in a corner and a couch that is seldom used, as most customers come in with prior appointments.

"What are you up to? What is this place, this Happy Endingz Massage Parlor? I want to know." She says. She plonks herself on the sofa.

"What'll you have? Water? Coffee?" I ask. I am embarrassed at having been discovered. The truth is that if I had a clue that she was coming, I would've removed the board, moved furniture and cancelled appointments. She hadn't, which leaves me with only coffee as an option to delay the moment of truth.

"Coffee, but only if you're going to come back and explain what's going on," she says. It gives me a little time to dwell on what I will say. The lack of caffeine never lets me think straight.

I walk to the kitchen and take out a saucepan and fill it with water. In the background I can hear the shrill ringing of the telephone. It is Bhatoliya's cheap Nokia handset that should have been upgraded about five years ago.

I add a dash of milk to the water, still thinking about how I can explain myself. One way is to give her another cock and bull story. In person, I am sure she will not fall for it.

The phone is answered; Bhatoliya's voice wafts through the house. In the kitchen, it's just slightly louder than a whisper. I look into the saucepan again, trying to find a solution to my conundrum. I can tell her the truth but knowing her, it would be the end of our marriage. Not that the marriage is alive in any case. The water and milk boil, starting with small bubbles at the edge of the pot which gradually move inwards until the whole thing is a cauldron. Bhatoliya is in conversation.

"Divya called. Ratna wants you at three in the afternoon, full service, our place, saying she loves the way you touch her. I need to call back and confirm. Are you in?" Bhatoliya's voice booms through the house. The saucepan almost drops from my hands.

Somehow, with shaking hands, I carry the two mugs of coffee into the reception. She is staring at me. It is a cold stare that raises the hair at the back of my neck.

"Who's Ratna?" she asks.

"A client," I can't look her in the eye.

"What do you do for her?" she asks.

"I give her a massage and…." I let the sentence trail off, leaving her to imagine the rest. Bhatoliya has given away enough already.

"And?" she asks me.

I can give her the gory details; I can tell her every sensitive part of Ratna's body that I titillate and the things that she says in return for that favour. I choose to keep quiet.

"*What's going on* Aditya?" she asks.

And so, I tell her. I tell her of my journey from being an unemployed banker, who was living off his wife's money, who was treated like manure and had a golden break of servicing rich, middle-aged women. I tell her the success story of the massage parlour that we have been able to put together and that it is more profitable than working at the bank could ever have been.

I know that I am inviting trouble. I know that this will mean the end. I speak, and I speak fearlessly, knowing that the marriage has reached a befitting end. It shouldn't have begun in the first place. And if it has to end, it is best to kill it by sudden death, than to prolong it, causing more pain than what it has already caused.

"I want a divorce," she says.

"I thought you would," I reply.

The attorneys will make some money in drawing up the paperwork. It will take time to have the decree in hand, but there is happiness at the end of the divorce. Both of us are free to go our separate ways, not that we haven't already, just that it is hidden behind the façade of the marriage. I often wonder why I had let myself be coaxed into marrying her when I should have rebelled and married the woman I had loved.

Radhika

It was on Sunday morning after my escapade at Rodeo that I wanted to tell him that I had a strong hunch that I was pregnant, but I wanted to be sure before I brought up the topic. I wondered if in his current state of mind, he would be happy to listen to me talking about missed periods.

We finished up the breakfast and stepped out of the house. There was no love making today. We reached Barista, one of those now rare occasions that we would go there. We sat there, short on conversation until I suggested that he drop me back, if he didn't want to talk. He agreed. Normally, he would've resisted, but today he didn't.

His behaviour was troubling me. He refused to tell me what happened over the weekend that changed him. It almost seemed that he was trying to avoid me. I decided that I needed to take the bull by its horns. Just as we were about to enter the car, I said, "Aditya, I need to talk to you. Can we go back inside?"

"Are you crazy? We just came out of there?" he was visibly irritated.

"Yes, but I want you to tell me what's bothering you?" I asked.

"Nothing. I don't know. Work pressure, maybe. Don't know. Can we go now?" he said, carefully hiding behind work as an excuse.

As vague as it sounded, perhaps it was best to let this conversation be. It wouldn't lead anywhere.

I was at home before lunch; an extremity by my standards. I was met by stares from the rest of the women who sat out in the living room. "I am sorry about last night," I quickly apologized. The surly expressions on their faces changed. It had been taken in good humour. I had probably only made a fool of myself, innocuous babbling that probably spoilt the mood but didn't leave memories bad enough to hold a grudge. Then why was Aditya so upset with me?

With nothing else to do, I retired to my room and read a book written by Khalil Gibran. I turned to the chapter of the book where a prophet speaks about love:

'To know the pain of too much tenderness. To be wounded by your own understanding of love; And to bleed willingly and joyfully.'

This brought me back to another painful truth. I was still not bleeding: that elusive spot had still not appeared and neither had the pain.

My periods hadn't come on Monday. I thought I'd give it another day before I used the pink strip to seal my fate. I really wanted this child. Unlike the last time, when the child had been so unwanted, this time it would be cherished. I felt that I had matured over the past couple of years and I was much better prepared for motherhood. Aditya wasn't in office on Monday, and so, I had no one to talk to about my gnawing fear.

He wasn't in office even on Tuesday. I checked with his colleague and learnt that he had had a death in the family and would be out for a couple of days. I hoped that everything was well with him. Maybe that explained his leaving in a rush and not answering my calls. I hated myself for always jumping to conclusions. I took the rickshaw back home, stopping en route at the chemist to buy a home pregnancy test.

On Wednesday morning, my hunch was confirmed that I was pregnant. I called him up, but he didn't answer. I reached the office, grumpy and upset. Even if there was a death in the family, that didn't stop him from returning my calls. I thought that he was taking me for granted; it almost made me feel like a fixture on the wall that one can so easily ignore. I saw him during the lunch break but couldn't talk.

I hated him in that moment, but loved him way too much to be upset with him for too long.

It was Wednesday evening when he picked me up on the street close to the gate; he was sombre and not his usual jovial self. Sometimes, I felt that the Aditya I fell in love with had disappeared. The man who sat beside me in the car was an impostor who had taken on the shape of my lover.

"I have something to tell you," I said.

"So do I. But you go first," he said.

"I am pregnant."

Aditya

Now that I am divorced, I feel free. It feels like the stress has been lifted from my shoulders.

It is not that the marriage had ever stopped me from doing anything, but it was like a parasite. It was there somewhere on your body or on your mind but you couldn't feel it. I wonder if I should take a break and go to the Himalayas. The Himalayas give me a peace that the city could never give.

I had last gone there when I was troubled about my relationship with Radhika. The Himalayas gave me a tranquillity to introspect and understand what I wanted to do, with my life, with her and with us. I lied to my boss that someone in my family had passed away and it would take me a couple of days to come back. Instead, I drove to Mussoorie, a hill station in the lower Himalayas that while commercialized, still had a few pockets of isolation. I didn't even bother to inform her where I was going.

I found a cheap hotel, the kinds that have a dirty bed linen and a musty smell, but that didn't bother me. I was only going to sleep in it for a night and then be gone. I had come here to understand what I wanted, and a dirty hotel room was the least of my worries.

As a child, I had visited Mussoorie often and remembered a particular place that had been etched in my memory. At day break – I drove to the Kempty Falls, about ten kilometres out of town. It was early in the tourist season and there weren't as many tourists revelling in the water. Nevertheless, I trekked up the falls, a kilometre, maybe more. The sun was out by now, shining furiously as it always does in the mountains. At a point, the entire stream that makes up the falls passes between two round boulders. One can lie across the boulders and hear the water gushing below you. I took a dip in the chilled, icy cold water and lay on the rocks questioning myself.

Why did I have to make a choice between my parents and her? Why couldn't they co-exist?

The stream gurgled on below; the tiny drops of water that had cut through rocks left me untouched. They refused to break my chain of thoughts.

One part of me wanted to rebel and marry her. It would leave me with guilt of not being a good son. I wasn't sure if my parents deserved a child for whom they had sacrificed so much. It would be obnoxious of me to forget that my mother had sold off her jewellery to buy me an education. I already struggled to be a good son and I would only give them more heartbreak.

It wasn't that I hadn't tried to reconcile. After I had come back from Chandigarh and when I thought that tempers had cooled down, I called my mother, "Mom, why don't you just meet her once?"

"What is the point? We will not be a part of any ceremony even if you want to go ahead. I will think I have no son."

Emotional blackmail is a woman's forte and she had played her part well. If she had such strong views, I shuddered at the thought of talking to my father.

My thoughts went back to Radhika. The seed that had been planted by my parents was now a weed – it was growing like a parasite, eating into the cells of the brain that dealt with love. I tried to justify her leaving, but my brain refused to understand. I don't know if I was thinking correctly or not, but my brain ruled my heart. I even thought she might be having an affair with one of those two guys at Rodeo. Despite everything that I was thinking about her, I still thought I loved her. I was torn because I was committed. I had given her my word that I would marry her.

Time passed by like the stream below. It was afternoon. I dipped into the small bag that I had carried and pulled out a packed sandwich that I had asked the hotel to put together.

Late in the evening I left, back to Delhi and its moronic grind. My decision was made.

The more I thought about it, the more the situation became clearer. I, simply, did not have the courage to rebel against my parents. I don't know what it was that made me feel like that, a deep-seated respect, compensation for their sacrifices or simply, gratitude. I would have to be the sacrificial lamb; the same sacrificial lamb that Radhika had once been.

I still loved her and I knew that I would hurt her by my decision. Jesus, hurt was an understatement, it would shatter her. I knew that she depended on me. Her relationship with her parents was almost negligible and I wasn't only her lover, I was her father figure.

Yet, I would need to do it. I would need to do it because I was weak and how can a weak man support anyone when he can barely support himself?

The third part of the equation was me: my aspirations and my ambitions. I had reconciled to the fact that my ambitions and aspirations could be sacrificed. I would still be able to sustain my career, irrespective of whether I married her or not. When this aspect moved out of the equation, the thinking was a little clearer. It was a simple choice of choosing between the parents and her. I had made my choice.

I would just need to make sure that she wasn't shattered by what I had decided. There had to be a way of manipulating the situation such that I could make it look like her decision. She would still be able to walk away with her head held high. My plan would mean that she would think of me as an asshole, a bastard, a coward and a cheat. I would have her hate me than be shattered. It was sad that my story was going to meet a tragic end.

Radhika

Ranikhet isn't quite the eight hour drive that Shipra made it out to be. We drive overnight on the broken roads. I realize that the distance that has been created between Shipra and me is going to be much more than that. It is a good thing that Divya has agreed to come with me. It gives me company for the arduous journey.

It has been over three months now that Shipra has moved away from Delhi. I have never been to this side of the country and I looked up Ranikhet as a destination. The website said that it is a cantonment town in the Kumaon Himalayas that houses the Kumaon Regiment. It promises great views of the Greater Himalayas. After making this back-breaking journey through some of the most horrendous highways in the country, I pray that the websites are right.

I don't know what it is about Divya that she doesn't feel as tired. I guess it's about one's state of mind. We are almost the same age but she has oodles of energy that doesn't make her stop talking. On the journey from Delhi, I pretty much know her entire story.

She belongs to Mangalore where her parent's still stay. She has been married once but had divorced her husband on grounds of infidelity. She's quite unashamed in stating it and it surprises me that her husband had suspected her of being adulterous.

"Was it true?" I ask her.

She nods her head unashamedly.

I can choose to remain quiet but I don't know why I ask her about the details.

"Why?" I ask her.

"He couldn't satisfy my sexual needs, so I had to look out," she says nonchalantly.

I had been in the same position with Vimal but I had never ventured out. He was much elder than me and of the six years that I had been married to him, he had spent three years in and out of hospital. Even then, I hadn't.

It's about eight in the morning when we cross the busy town of Haldwani. As we go a little further up the hills, the weather starts to improve. I grew up in the hills and I love them. I have always longed to go back to them. Sometimes, I even harbour strange thoughts about moving to the hills. I know that life is tougher here. City dwellers have difficulty adjusting here, yet, I think about buying a cottage here with all the money that I have saved. I don't want it to be the piggy bank that I left in Solan. Now that Shipra is also here, I will also have company.

Divya gets one of her strange calls again. She doesn't have the luxury to go to a secluded place, so she continues the conversation in front of me.

"Yes, Ratna," she says into the phone

Ratna must have said something when Divya says, "I'll check with him if he's free today".

There is a slight pause in the conversation. After a slight pause, she says, "Twenty thousand an hour."

In the peak of the recession, Divya is sitting on some goldmine, I think to myself. I wonder what she's dealing in that commands that rate.

She hangs up the phone and looks at me. I turn my face. I am not really interested in knowing whatever she was dealing in. She makes another call to someone and promptly calls back Ratna. I am a mute spectator. I only take in the fresh mountain air. It's the middle of August and the rains are on. July came this year too, but it wasn't the same. Laxman stops the car for some time because the rains have caused a landslide. I step out of the car to admire the green of the valley. In some strange way, it reminds me of myself on the porch. The valley is almost as green as the moss that threatened to cover me back then.

It isn't long before we are in Ranikhet. Shipra gives us directions over the phone to reach the Bungalow that the Army has given to her. We are greeted by the twins and I can't help wishing that I had a child of my own. Maybe, if things had panned out a little differently, I might have.

Aditya

We were driving when she told me that she was pregnant. I had been so certain until last night that I was going to break up with her and suddenly, this came up. My first thoughts were, why couldn't she have used oral contraceptives to prevent this? We were only twenty-four; what was the point in having kids that early? Hell, we barely had enough money to afford a priest to solemnize a wedding.

Fatherhood was a huge responsibility. I had to be someone of consequence, even before I could dream of having children. I had had a difficult childhood; there were so many times that teachers would call out to me in the middle of class and say that my father hadn't deposited the fees. It had been embarrassing and I had vowed to myself that my child would never face the same. I needed a little more security, the safety that manifests itself in a large bank account.

Secretly, I hated myself, my family and her. I wished that my life was simpler. I wished that my parents would just agree. I wished that she hadn't married. I wished I was born a Hindu or she a Sikh. I wished I were a year or two older to be able to afford the marriage and the child. Most of all, I wished I had a backbone that wasn't crumbling in the face of adversity.

I kept driving, dazed by what she had just told me. The Maruti was a bitch, rattling at every pothole that it encountered. The rattling of the plastic was disrupting my thoughts, it wasn't letting me find a solution to this conundrum. I turned around to face her, she looked steadfastly ahead. I wish she would understand that I would never be able to express myself for fear of hurting her. I would never be able to tell her that my parents loved a God that they had never seen. They loved Him more than their own son. I would never be able to tell her why I was behaving the way I had been for the past few weeks. I drove past the half constructed structures that the realtors had sold, but not bothered to construct; through the tall grasslands that the realtor's greed hadn't yet reached, until I had to take a left for her house. Instead, I drove straight to the dead end on the road. The government funding for the road had stopped abruptly and so had the contractors will. The sun was about to set over the fields of Gurgaon. The city was still caught between the agriculturists and the real estate mafia; even within the civilization, were pockets of countryside untrammelled by road rollers. I stepped out of the car, still lost in my thoughts, still not being able to make a decision. I was alone despite her presence. I stood there looking at the setting sun. She was right beside me, as lost as I was.

It was almost dark when the labourers, returning home on bicycles, gave us suspicious stares. Rightly so, when neither of us had any business in standing at the end of a road that didn't lead anywhere.

Finally, it was dark, a deep moonless dark that matched the darkest side of me. I turned towards her and said, "I am not ready. Let's get an abortion."

She didn't respond, she didn't chide me for announcing my decision. She didn't even want to know how or when. She just went and sat back in the car, a sign to say that we had reached the end of the road and we would need to turn back. I opened the creaking driver's side door of the Maruti and sat inside. I turned the key and the engine started with a meek purr. I changed the gear, backed out and drove back, first to her house and later mine. We didn't sit in the car as we normally would. I could have so easily been mistaken for a cabbie who had dropped off his fare and left.

I was certain that I had hurt her but still remained unrepentant. I wasn't ready, I justified it to myself. I was only twenty-four and had a career to make. I had to be a good son. I had to be a good husband and a good father, but how, I didn't know.

Robin opened the door and gave me one of his wisecracks through the nasal twang that had stopped bothering me. "Not today," I shouted at him and he quickly withdrew, hiding himself in the warmth of the kitchen.

The mutton was tender and juicy, but it didn't enthral my taste buds. The tea that I would have before retiring to bed felt bitter and acidic. Nothing seemed good, nothing was right. I wished I could just run away somewhere and hide. A place where there was no pressure of expectations. A place where the boss didn't want cards to be sold. Run to a place, where my parents would support my decisions. Hide out at a place where Radhika and I could be together making babies that didn't have to be aborted. A place where you didn't have to buy anything, and everything was free in return for love.

The muscles at the back of my neck screamed that they needed a pillow. They were taut with stress. My head was throbbing. I pulled out the travel kit and popped in a pill to ease the pain. The pain eased somewhat, but what could I do about the pain that I was giving to her.

Radhika

Shipra's children are playing out in the garden and I am wondering that if I had only refused to abort the child, I might have had my own. I hadn't refused. I still remember that time when I located that place that would afford us the anonymity to be able to get the abortion. I had found the place, that rotten, sick-looking nursing home that screamed of poor hygiene. If I went anywhere else, they wanted documentation, marriage certificates and what not. I reconciled that Dr Grover, the portly, round lady would abort my child.

"Why don't you want to have this child?" Dr. Grover asked.

"I need to go to the US for a few months for work and my husband and I think that it's best that I not have the child," I spoke confidently.

She looked at Aditya, who was going to give us away. His eyes were shifty. He couldn't look into the doctor's eyes and speak to her. We were supposed to be a young married couple that had accidentally conceived and were going to abort it. I was certain that the doctor hadn't bought the story but nevertheless, I just couldn't say now, "My boyfriend thinks that condoms spoil the spontaneity of sex and so we conceived".

"Your name," she asked while filling in the dossier.

"Radhika Sharma," I replied.

"Husband's name?" she asked.

"Aditya Sharma."

I let out a silent prayer that one day, this dossier that she was filling would change into a wedding card.

I had agreed, reluctantly, to have the abortion; not that he had left me with much choice. I hated myself for falling into that trap again. The trap of emotions that led through indecision until it opened up into doing something that I didn't want to do. Abhinav had been one of those traps and now, this abortion. I was so dependent on him that I couldn't assert myself. I think I should've given him an ultimatum that he marries me now.

"We'll give you general anaesthesia and do the operation. It should take two hours or so. You can go back in the afternoon, but you'll have to rest for at least twenty-four hours before you can start your normal routine. We'll need your signatures here," she said motioning to Aditya.

He was so shifty, he signed all the documents without reading a word. Even if the doctor were to believe my cock and bull story, he was a giveaway. It amazed me that he was behaving this way. It made me feel like I was the Virgin Mary who had conceived the child without his help. His attitude wasn't any better than Abhinav; he was blaming me for the child. It was as if my egg wanted to become a foetus on its own. It was his sperm that had fertilized it, then why did he disown his sperms?

I went into the operation theatre where masked men surrounded me. I thought I saw Dr Grover behind one of those masks and then there was nothing. There was cotton in my ears and the sounds were muffled. My eyes shut and I was dreaming.

I woke up to see him sitting beside my bed. He looked harried and uncomfortable in the stench that emanated from the hospital. It had to be the smell that gave me a sudden urge to puke but nothing came out. He disappeared into the bathroom and came back after five minutes, his eyes bloodshot and his face a deep crimson. He had puked the contents of his breakfast. We waited until the time that Dr Grover gave us a signal to go back home. He cleared up the bill in cash and we drove back.

Robin wasn't sure why I wasn't being able to walk by myself.

"What happened to Didi?" he asked through his nose.

We weren't sure how much to tell him and how much to hide. After all, he would be able to deduce given that he slept in the room next to ours. The creaking of the old wooden bed left no doubt what its occupants were up to.

I didn't answer, nor did Aditya. I tried to fight the sleep when I lay down on the bed, but I couldn't. He was there when I slept, hovering around me.

I don't remember how long I had slept but it was dark outside when I woke up. I moved my hand on the vacant mattress besides me. It hadn't been slept in. I was too weak to get up and switch on the lights, so I called out to Aditya.

Robin came rushing and switched on the light.

"Water," I said through my parched throat.

He came back with a bottle of water and a glass. I looked at the prescription that lay on the bedside table and withdrew a tablet that the doctor had recommended for pain. I swallowed it down with a gulp of water, waiting for it to relieve the pain that pervaded my lower abdomen.

"Where is Aditya?" I asked Robin.

"Bhaiya went to work," he replied.

Asshole.

I wanted to scream out, a cry that would relieve my frustration and my anxiety. I wish I could cry to reduce the pain of loving this man. A man, who had left me writhing in pain and gone to work. I felt like a cheap whore, degraded and mutilated.

He was back when I woke up again. His shirt wasn't crushed like it usually was when he came home from the hours of warming the soft, cushioned seat in his office. He continued to hover around and didn't once bother to ask me if the pain had lessened or how I felt when my womb had been invaded by forceps.

The tranquilizers that had been prescribed were clouding my brain, blurring my vision, but even then I attempted to think. There had been a niggling feeling that had started creeping into me that he just wanted me out of his life. Today, that feeling was a little stronger. Yet, someone inside me kept saying that I was wrong. The voice was faceless, almost like hope.

That voice wanted me to believe that all was well, that it was just a phase; a trough that we would emerge out of.

I slept again and woke up the next morning to see him by my side. I put my arm around him, gently so as to not awaken him. The medicines had worked. The pain in the lower abdomen was much better. The burning sensation was gone. I wasn't going to go to work today at the doctor's advice. It was a pity, because today was 2 April, and I was to get my letter of promotion. We had planned to celebrate our promotions very long ago and now, when that time had come, I wasn't in a state to. What is a celebration without a drink? I had vowed to myself that I wouldn't drink anymore.

He stirred up, looked at me and his expression changed. He pushed my arm away, got up and walked the five steps to go to the washroom. For the umpteenth time, I wondered what was going on in his mind. He came out and wore his clothes, still silent. He didn't even bother asking me how I was. He didn't even smile at me. He could have been a corpse that had started walking, having found a reservoir of energy.

"Why won't you speak to me?" I asked, unable to hold it any longer.

"I don't feel like it," he replied. *Feel* like it, how could you even come up with a witty retort to that?

"What's wrong? Tell me. You've never been like this," I implored him to spill out his heart.

"It's nothing. Go back to sleep," he said in a gruff tone.

"I want to speak to you at length about what is bothering you," I demanded.

"I'm getting late for work. I have to go," he said and took two steps towards the bathroom.

I waited for an eternity until he returned back from the bathroom.

"All right, but today, not tomorrow, you and I need to have a conversation," I gave him an ultimatum.

"I'll do it when I have to," he replied arrogantly

He dressed as I contemplated what to say next.

"Have I done something wrong?" I was near tears.

"No, I have," he said and walked out, not giving me a chance to even understand what he meant.

Robin gave me breakfast. I was feeling better by the afternoon, physically. Mentally, I was a wreck. Emotionally, I was an inferno.

I couldn't hold myself back. I couldn't wait until he was back from work. I just couldn't. I looked around for my cell phone, but couldn't find it. I hadn't used it since yesterday. I bent down to look under the bed and a sharp pang of pain rose through me. The cell phone lay there, I picked it up and dialled his number.

"Yes, what is it?" he replied.

Normally, I would've given him the benefit of doubt that he was busy at work, but not today.

"What did you mean when you said that you've made a mistake?" I asked him.

"In just being with you," he said.

"Why? What makes you say that?" I asked. My worst fears were being confirmed.

"I am not sure if I love you," he said.

"And you're saying that today? After so much has happened?" I said.

"What's happened?" he asked.

The divorce and the abortion weren't *happenings*? The affair, the love and the passion weren't *happenings*?

"The abortion... Didn't you think this over when we were having sex and you got me pregnant?"

"How do I know it was mine? You went around drinking with strange men. How do I even know that the child was mine?" he said.

I took the phone away from my ear, just to double check that I hadn't dialled a wrong number. It wasn't so much about feeling like a whore but being thought of as one. I was so deeply hurt that words failed me.

"I am so disgusted. I hate you," I screamed in rage.

"That's fine. It's about time you stopped using me," he said.

"Using you? I thought we were in love..." I said.

"And where was that love when you got married to someone else?" Aditya said.

Why didn't he bring this up when we had had this conversation earlier? He hadn't had any reservations about this back then. The man didn't cease to surprise me.

"I did it for you. I thought I already explained myself," I said.

"You leave me when you want to and you come back when you want to. You're only interested in my money. Outside of that, there is nothing else. I am sick of being treated like a doormat."

This conversation was over. I neither had the energy nor the willingness to explain to an uncouth, rude, insensitive man what I had felt. I hated him. It was a good thing that he wasn't near me, else I would've dug my fingernails into his face and scratched him. I wanted to kill him with a dagger – stabbing it in his chest, once for every word in this conversation. I detested him. Period.

Despite the lingering pain, I picked up the small bag that we had brought with us to the hospital and packed up everything that belonged to me in this house. I had Robin summon a rickshaw and I went home. In the sweltering heat, the sort of heat that evaporates dreams, I was burning. I had been slighted, I had been wronged and I wanted revenge.

Aditya

The banker, that I was, refuses to let me keep my eyes off the markets. I sit on the chair in the reception of the massage parlour and flip through channels looking for Bloomberg. I wonder why I continue to watch it when I have never heard anything positive on the channel. Each day, there is a little more gloom about the economy.

Today, for a change, the stock market is up 329 points from its last close. It is the strongest indication that the recession may be over. A thought crosses my mind that if I had invested in stocks, I might be a little richer today. I wonder what I would do with all the riches because it can't really buy love. I am still lost in thoughts of recession, money and love when the phone rings.

"Am I speaking to Aditya Sharma?" a suave voice says from the other end of the line.

"Yes," I say confirming it.

"My name is Saurav Dutta and I am the Human Resources Head at Axis Bank."

The name sounds Bengali but there's not a trace of an accent. I wonder if someone's playing a cruel joke on me. I am so unaccustomed to hear anything but Divya's voice on the phone.

"We got your resume from a job portal and we like your credentials. Would you be interested in an opportunity with us?" he asks me.

Instinctively, I say "Yes".

"Would it be convenient for you to come and meet us tomorrow?" he asks me.

I don't want to get my hopes too high. I don't want to believe that I can be lucky enough to make an honest living. Even in my mind, I think like a whore. I am sure there is no God, but if there is a God, this is his revenge.

"Yes, it will be," I say.

I note down the details of our appointment on a piece of paper and bid him goodbye. I still can't believe that he had called. It's been nearly two-and-a-half years of trying. The two-and-a-half years that have made me lose everything.

The next morning, I cancel an appointment and go to meet Saurav Dutta at the address that he had given me. He interviews me for the position of a Vice President. He says it is positive and that he will arrange another meeting with the Chief Operating Officer in the next few days.

I continue to wait for him to call again. Ratna, Divya, Shazia and Jaya continue to fill my days. Bhatoliya's become quite an entrepreneur and I continue to be lonely.

I often think that it must be my sins that have caught up with me. I still drink as often as I used to back then but I don't pass out. I am wiser. Even then, my slate refuses to be wiped clean.

It's on one of those days that Saurav calls me again. The COO is a busy man but has found the time to meet me. I meet him wearing the same suit that I had worn when I met Divya.

I am superstitious. I think it is lucky if I wear it. Maybe, I am not so wrong. The COO thinks I am perfect. I wish I can tell him the truth.

I step out of his office in Connaught Place and I can't help sneezing. It is spring and the pollen always gives me an allergy. Even then, I like this season because it awakens the optimist in me. I know that the flowers will bloom, even though they don't smell the same as they used to.

Three days later, I get a letter in the mail. It's an offer letter to join the bank. The recession is finally over.

Radhika

I don't know if he had miraculously had a change of heart. Just yesterday, we had had the ugly conversation and now, Aditya was calling me incessantly. I switched the phone off and continued the conversation with my boss, "What next?" I asked.

"There are plenty of roles available, if you're interested," she said.

"I want a new role, preferably a posting away from Gurgaon," I said.

The girl from Human Resources looked at me strangely. Gurgaon was the head office – it was an aspirational place to be in within the realms of the bank, and here I was declining one.

"There's an operations position, reporting to the branch manager in Lucknow that fits your grade. Would you be interested in something that mundane?" my boss asked me.

Normally, I wouldn't have been, but it was imperative. I just had to go away. There was no other option. I had to get back at him, somehow, for what he had done to me. For that, it was important that I go away. I was taking a rash decision driven by anger, I knew it. I didn't know anyone in Lucknow and that would mean a loss of familiarity. I wonder if familiarity always ends up in heartbreak.

"Yes, I'll take it," I said, sealing my fate.

The meeting ended with shallow expressions of gratitude. I still had a week to wrap up. I thought about him and a sudden sense of disgust pervaded me. I didn't know why he did this to me but another voice in my head kept asking me, "Didn't you do the same?" I justified to that voice that I had done it for him. It didn't agree with me, so I ignored it, revelling in the loathing of him.

In the evening, I didn't take the route that I normally did, instead took the bus that went to Delhi. I got myself dropped near the Delhi border and took a rickshaw back home. I sneaked in through the back door, knowing that he would come there too. I wondered if calling the cops on him was enough revenge. Maybe, I could press charges of stalking and harassment. Maybe, that would douse the fire. A small part of me still wanted him to be there and maybe that is why I went to the balcony to peek through the curtains to see if there was any sign of him.

I picked up my cell phone. There were two more missed calls from him and a message that said, "I love you. Please answer the phone". I had half a mind to type "Fuck off. I hate you" but then I stopped myself. His penance was in him being ignored. I switched off the phone and carried on with the evening. I went into the kitchen. The maid who came to cook had made the watery *dal* that she was so notorious for. I had a small portion of it with rice and went back to my room.

My thoughts went back to our relationship. It was almost like destiny never intended us to be together and we had been trying to change its course. I wished that it didn't have to end. Even if it had to end, I wished that it could have been a better end. When it had been alive, it had been so beautiful that it deserved a better end.

I pretended that I was reading a book but the words would refuse to form a sentence. Sometimes, when they did, they flew past my brain. I read it and then reread it until I gave up and closed the book. I wanted to pee but didn't go to the washroom. I was besides the window again, looking for a sign of him. He wasn't there but there was the tree that the harsh summer had killed. It told me my story. The voice in my head returned and asked me why I couldn't hate him completely and forever.

I was still contemplating a definite answer when the doorbell rang. I didn't answer it. I rushed into my room and locked the door. Just as another precaution, I went into the washroom and locked that door too. Maybe, I was just afraid that if he came, I would succumb. When I had steeled my nerves and made my decision, I didn't want to be the wimp that I had always been.

I tried to hear if there were any sounds that resembled his voice or if the footsteps belonged to him. I pressed my ear closer to the door. There was stillness, no sound belied his presence. I stayed there, locked inside, sweating, unsure who I was hiding from. The bolder me said I shouldn't be hiding, but I stayed inside the bathroom for over half an hour. I finally came out, half expecting him to be sitting on the solitary chair in my room.

He wasn't there. I went back to the curtain and stole another look outside. There was nothing; absolutely no hint that he was here or intended to be. Maybe, he had just sent the message as a teaser. A sadists attempt to see if his victim was suffering enough. I came back to my room and turned off the lights. It was important that I get some sleep. I would have to join the Lucknow branch next week, which left less than five days to wrap up.

I thought if I should ask my parents, if I had made a good choice in moving to Lucknow. But, why even bother when I had nearly been estranged. Maybe, I didn't deserve happiness. Maybe, I was the creation of a lesser God whose creative abilities hadn't been developed enough to add happiness or colour into this life.

Aditya

I can't help feeling lucky with the offer letter in hand. It is a handsome salary that Axis bank is offering me. I know that being lucky and being happy are two different things. I remember when my boss gave me the promotion letter, right after my conversation with Radhika. I went to his room, still wondering if I could've been a little politer in that conversation. I had been harsh but if I hadn't been, it would've been detrimental. It would've made her feel that there was still room for reconciliation and I didn't want it. I had made my choice and my plan had been executed. Why else had I sat on the chair in the balcony when Radhika writhed in pain? Why else had I told Robin to tell her that I was at work?

For the first time, I looked down at the letter that my boss had given me. It was a handsome raise and I thought that now was a good time to buy a car. I imagined the car of my dreams and it's all shiny and bright, but it came with a vacant passenger seat. Suddenly, the letter was nothing but a piece of paper. It was meaningless and even in being able to break away from her, I hated my parents and myself.

I left the office early. My manager thought that I was going to celebrate my promotion. He couldn't quite understand why I still had a forlorn expression when I should have been rejoicing. I parked the car below the apartment and went upstairs. I knew she wouldn't be around, not after all that I had said. Robin answered the door. "Has she left?" I was half hoping that he would say no.

"Yes. She left in the afternoon." I nodded as if she had told me and it was all planned.

I changed into shorts and sneakers. There was so much negative energy that had to be drained. I had almost stopped running and I wanted to run today. Run until the last bit of energy was drained, until I would collapse, until I died. The emotions of anger, guilt, frustration and shame mixed up in a heady cocktail that kept me running. I ran away from a reality that I had been unable to face. It was past ten when I came back and crashed on the chair in the balcony and drank as I once had very long ago. In all the things that had changed since then, one thing remained. I was still without her.

The next day, I didn't go to office. I was expected to attend training. Through the morning, I had been unable to concentrate, preferring to doodle and think when the trainer had the others' rapt attention.

"It is your marriage next week, you want to look ravishing, and you walk into a store and look at about fifty suits. You find five in your size that you like enough to buy. You boil down the choice to two – the charcoal grey Armani and the navy blue Calvin Klein. Money's not a constraint, even though the Armani is a little more expensive." He continued, "You try on both, they're a perfect fit, but you are still indecisive. You settle for the Armani. You walk down to the teller, happy that you're about to buy what you wanted. The teller swipes the card, you sign for it and just as you are about to enter your car, creating images of yourself in the charcoal grey suit – a strange voice in your head tells you, 'you should've bought the blue one'. That is cognitive dissonance," the tall, cynical trainer said.

Now, with that last example, he had told me my situation. I wanted the Calvin Klein suit. I had broken up with her, and played the truant and the ideal son, but I wasn't sure where that left me. I thought that a breakup would help ease the stress, yet, it had only aggravated it. I longed for a date with her. I longed to meet her. Hell, I even longed to see her. I cursed myself for being stupid enough to take it to a point of no return. I was annoyed with myself that I had driven the relationship to this dead end.

I walked out of the conference hall at the Taj Hotel, the venue of the training. The trainer stared at me. Maybe he wasn't used to people walk out of his training. I didn't care to explain where I was going. On the way out, I grabbed my cell phone that had been kept aside this morning to deter deviant minds from reaching out to that distraction.

I reached the lobby that led to the many banquet halls. It was empty, even though the banquet halls seem to be occupied. I dialled her number; she didn't answer. I dialled her number again. No Answer. I dialled it a third time. A strange woman said in a sing-song voice, "The subscriber you're trying to reach is busy at this time". I dialled a fourth time, the same thing happened. The fifth time, the same woman said, "The number you are trying to reach is switched off".

I went back inside, momentarily, to retrieve the car keys from my table. The trainer didn't stare at me this time, he made a note and carried on. I drove like crazy from the Taj, almost running over the labourers who were busy trying to construct a fly-over at Dhaula Kuan. I had to see her. I would apologize; I would beg her to take me back. I would promise to never be a bastard again. If she agreed, I would marry her tonight. I knew that I had dug my own grave. In wishing that I spoil my relations with her, I had hurt her so grievously that she refused to speak to me.

*

It was over three days that I had not seen her, nor spoken to her. Even when we would pretend to be strangers in office, we would bump into each other – sometimes in the corridors, sometimes in the cafeteria. But it seemed that she had virtually become invisible. I went to the floor where she worked, but she wasn't there. I thought about waiting below her house when she entered, but what would that achieve. It was best for time to heal some wounds before I approached her again. I hated myself, not only because of my fickle mindedness, but also for my abjectly gross behaviour.

Radhika

There is something about Ranikhet that leaves me awestruck. I grew up in the hills, so it isn't unfamiliar to be in the hills, but Ranikhet is different. It has to be the snow-clad peaks in the distance, the forests around town and that wild leopard that crossed us one night. It leaves me enchanted.

A large part of me wants to stay here. I know that I can stay here and do everything that I am doing back in Delhi. I will be closer to Shipra, for sure. I chide myself that this is just a dream that will take a long time to accomplish. It isn't real. Very long ago, I stopped believing in dreams.

The last two weeks at Shipra's home were heavenly. Each morning would begin with a cup of tea on the lawns of her house and each day would end with drinks. I still don't drink, even though Divya was pushing me.

It has taken a lot to go back to reality. My reality is a makeshift school that I run out of the Gulmohar Park house. I bid my goodbyes and just as we leave the cantonment, Divya's phone rings. It has to be another one of her shady calls because she is talking about her commission.

I ignore her again as I had done on my way in, but this time she is adamant to tell me about it.

"I think it's important to have sex. It's human," she says.

I didn't know why she has vaguely and abruptly brought up this conversation with me.

"I couldn't live with my ex-husband, but that doesn't mean that I deprive myself. I even checked with the gynaecologist. She agrees," Divya continues.

I nod my head but don't say anything.

"You know, there are so many women who are faced with this same problem. I just help them," she says.

I wonder if the cause is so noble, why is she talking about her commission.

"You should try it too," she says.

This time, I don't nod. I'll be honest; it does cross my mind as an option.

Aditya

Finally, I saw her walking out of office on the fourth day. I walked up towards her, to accost her, to fall down on one knee and confess that I had been a fool for not understanding my emotions in time, beg her for forgiveness and to let me be a part of her life again. She saw me coming and instantly turned around, walking back into the crowd of people that would insulate her from me.

My ego should've died that instant and I should've followed her and done what I intended to do. I didn't. She walked with the crowd and I saw her leaving. I would have to wait for another chance. That chance never came.

I didn't know that when she walked away from there, she was leaving the city for good. I still didn't know that would be the end of my love story. I didn't even know that you could call this a love story. I didn't see her for a few more days. I thought that she was on vacation, to take time off work and to recuperate from my actions. It was much later that I discovered that she had taken up a posting in Lucknow. It was bizarre that she chose Lucknow when almost everyone in our generation wanted to move away from that city.

I thought about chasing her, going to Lucknow and telling

her everything that I wanted to in Gurgaon. It did cross my mind that she would be unwilling to talk to me in Lucknow, when she was hesitant to talk to me in Gurgaon. I just waited for the wounds to heal before I could approach her again.

It was a Saturday that I went back home and rang the bell. Robin answered the door, but didn't say anything. He wasn't used to seeing me come home alone on Saturdays. I didn't go out to drink. I switched the television on, surfing channels mindlessly. Nothing held my fancy. I switched off the TV as abruptly as I had started it. Nothing seemed good.

I had been here earlier, but I had someone to blame back then. It wasn't my folly that I had been left alone then. Now, there was no one else that I could blame. I picked up my cell phone and dialled her Delhi number, knowing that she wasn't here. But still, fervently praying that she had made a weekend trip to Delhi and switched on her cell phone. I wasn't lucky.

The days passed, abysmally slowly. It was nearly three months since she was gone. It wasn't only her going away that hurt so much; it was my guilt that burnt me inside out. I owed her an apology at the very least. I sat on my desk typing an e-mail. I had never been eloquent but when you write from the heart, it usually comes out well. I read it and re-read it. It was everything that I wanted to tell her. I explained my actions, my failures, my reasons. I apologized. I promised that I would never ever let her down again if she just forgave me. It was complete. In the global address list, I typed the surname Kapila; her name didn't come up. I typed Kapila, R; still no matches. I typed Kapila, Radhika; the name didn't exist in the Citigroup global address list. A little over three hundred thousand e-mail IDs were listed, but that elusive one that I needed to send the mail to was missing. There was only one conclusion that could be drawn – she no longer worked for Citibank. And if she didn't, where was she? In Lucknow? Chandigarh? Abroad?

Radhika

I go back to the porch of the Gulmohar Park house. The children don't come here very often. It's the middle of their Diwali vacation and they've gone back to their native. This setting is familiar. The weeds over grew in the monsoons and they still remain. They make me think about the weeds that grew in my brain when I decided to marry Vimal. The only reason that I got married a second time was to spite Aditya. There was no other reason that would justify my marrying a forty-three-year-old man. It had been a season of self-discovery. The ego that I never knew existed in me raised its ugly head. I had been scorned, demeaned and hurt. Aditya had left me for his career, for money and for everything materialistic. I was an impediment and a liability. I had played out every reason why he had left me and reached this conclusion. I wanted to show him that I could be richer than he ever would be and so, when I found Vimal Ahuja, an affluent businessman and a client of Citibank, I manipulated him to marry me.

It had been sudden and notwithstanding that he had a daughter Meera, who was just eight years younger than me, it was my chance to prove to Aditya that if money had ever been my motivation to love him, he was inferior. Stupidly, I had never been able to do that either. I had made a trip to Delhi three months after the wedding, about six months after I had moved to Lucknow to come face to face with him and enact the scene that I had played out in my mind, every day of those six months. He wasn't there. From my colleagues, I learnt that he had moved abroad on a foreign posting. I think he went to the Philippines. So, I was now caught in a loveless marriage that had ended with Vimal's death, leaving me an heiress of a large bungalow in Delhi – in love at various points in time with one man, twice married to men I didn't love, once divorced, once widowed.

It had happened so long ago, nearly eight years ago and yet, the memories are so fresh, as if it has happened only yesterday. Strangely, what I had thought of as improbable and impossible has happened. I have forgiven him. In the years that went by, time has done what it does best – heal.

In many ways, I have relived our relationship in my mind and even though the end was so bitter and disappointing, our moments of love always overshadow the bitterness. So many times, I am tempted to go back to him. I want to find him and tell him that he has been forgiven just like he forgave me. I looked for him on the Internet. There is only a LinkedIn profile that says that he used to work at Citibank. It's almost like he has disappeared. I wonder where he is and what he is doing.

Aditya

"Where are you from?" she asked me.
"India," I replied.

"India, big country?" rolling the R in the country like Filipinos do.

"Yes! Very big country" I replied.

"Bigger than Luzon?" she asked.

For God's sake, give me a break. Luzon was the largest island in the Philippines, a veritable speck on the world map, possibly smaller than India's smallest state and here I was lying in bed with this cheap whore who was asking me this question. I pushed her away in disgust, even more disgusted with myself that I was in bed with this filthy woman, who under the influence of alcohol and the dim light of the shady bar had looked worth picking up.

In some strange way, hardly patriotic, I was compelled to come back from the Philippines. The country had provided me with employment and the refuge from her memories. Alcohol was cheap, tobacco cheaper and there was an endless supply of women who would pretend to love you for your money. I couldn't even pretend. A dark, deep hole still existed within my soul, the corner where love used to exist.

I came back to India and I was coerced into marrying Jasleen, a Sikh girl that my parents had found for me. I had resisted and they had coerced. I had said that I didn't want to be married to anyone I didn't love, but they had insisted. I was indifferent and we were married. I eventually became the good son, at the cost of being a poor husband. As if to confirm my derangement, I had estranged my parents soon after I married.

The bank had a position open – as head of cards sales for north India and I gladly came back to India. I was doing very well professionally, being lauded as the best thing that happened to Citibank in India. My sales figures were the best: I was selling more cards than all the other regions combined. That was until the recession hit. The delinquencies that hit were in the same ratio as the sales. Overnight, I turned from a hero to being a villain. I was the cause why the bank was losing money.

The recession also brought with it an exodus of NRIs who had left India for greener pastures. The brain drain that had been plaguing India through the eighties and early nineties, was being corrected. A fresh slew of Non Resident Indians were claiming jobs in India that they hadn't thought were worth their while. Amongst them, was one man who resembled a mouse – Mr Abhinav Chandra. He joined as the head of the cards business in India and was my immediate boss.

It was an instant recognition for both of us, and the fallout was the same as it would've been if I had been in his shoes: Restructured.

Now, here I am, as cheap as the cheapest whore that I had slept with, once married, once divorced and still in love with only one woman, whose ex-husband, by a wicked quirk of fate, has rendered me into a gigolo.

I turn around to see Bhatoliya standing behind me, "Where are you lost stud?" he asks me.

"Nah, nothing. Tell me," I say.

"You've got to speak to this Divya woman. She wants a thirty-five percent cut on this client that she's sending you. Our overheads are high, we can't afford it," he says.

Overheads, wow! I haven't realized when my best friend turned into a businessman.

"I will," I promise.

Divya's greed is never-ending. While she is a damn good pimp, providing an endless supply of clients, her commission structure goes up every time there is a new client introduced. I will need to speak to her the next time we met. She is being greedy.

"And who is this new client? Is she coming over or is it a house call?" I ask Bhatoliya.

"She's coming over. Divya just said her name is… I don't even remember, some Ahuja. She is expected in at 3 this afternoon. First timer. Wants you to be gentle."

The business was doing well. Bhatoliya's dream of not selling toothpaste to make a living seemed on track. He was happy and I was sad. I was now in the trade for over a year and the ignominy of serving as a sex slave to the many women was beginning to take a toll. There are times in one's life that what you have is not enough and I was feeling like it too. Think about it, I was an out of job banker, who had become a male prostitute, making more money than I would have done at the job. I had craved for freedom from my wife, and I had gotten it. I wanted to be in a big city and I was, and yet, there was sadness. A deep melancholic sadness, that arose out of loneliness. Ironically, I would meet at least two women a day and yet, there was loneliness.

Radhika

"Just try it once. This guy is just great; you'll love him," Divya says.

"I am not sure," I say. I am shaking my head in disbelief that I'm having this conversation with her.

"If you're not comfortable there, I can send this guy over. You must try him. Trust me," she says. She's been trying her best to convince me.

At home, it will leave Laxman scandalized and I don't want the neighbours to see a strange man come in. I can't risk it and so, I decide to visit the place. She gives me an address in Greater Kailash. I look down at the address that she has scribbled down on a yellow post-it.

HappyEndingz Massage Parlor

M-201 Ground floor

Greater Kailash -1

New Delhi.

I am wondering why the name sounds so familiar. On the trip back from Ranikhet, Divya brought up the topic and I hadn't replied. I thought about it and for the same reason that I have chopped off my tresses, I agree. I think that a little promiscuity will do no harm to a bored widow. I am only thirty-three. How wrong can I go?

I don't ask Laxman to drive me that day. I just step out casually, as if I am going out for a stroll, but instead take an auto-rickshaw to reach the place. I recognize it immediately. I remember that it is the same place that we crossed when we came back from Chandigarh. I was so judgmental about the people who ran the place, not knowing that my new best friend had a stake in it.

I enter through the heavy wooden door into a neatly done up reception. A solitary thin man sits behind the desk. Somehow, he looks very familiar. I am not sure if I have met him before.

He ushers me in and politely asks me to wait while he checks on Aditya. I sigh. I am still wondering why this name is so popular when he comes back. He sends me in to one of the rooms. I am still unsure. One part of me wants to bolt out of the door and never come back. I have steeled my nerves in coming here and I don't want to act like a coward now. I enter the door, to see the naked back of a man. The gash on the back, over which I loved to run my finger, tells me that this is him.

Aditya

That we will meet was a certainty. Our destinies are too intertwined to be away from each other for long. We had never imagined that it will ever be in this setting. She my client, in want of lust; I, the gigolo, short on love but willing to accede. We just stand there, looking at each other, not saying a word, even while the clock ticks on. If she were just another client, it would've cost her a huge fortune, for doing nothing, for saying nothing. We don't make love, we don't even have sex – we just hug each other for the void that time and we have created.

She finally breaks the silence, "You don't have to do this".

The recession has ended and I have been offered a job, but I haven't taken it. This is my life – a life of penance that I will have to lead for all the sins that I have committed. Now, maybe this penance is over.

"Let's go somewhere else, just not here". I don't realize that she means a different city and not just the raunchy setting of the HappyEndingz Massage Parlour.

There is nothing the city hasn't given me – love, lust, a career, money, greed, corruption, hurt and pain. I nod my head in concurrence for I have nothing to give to the city anymore.

We finally do what we have been threatening to do for nearly a decade – marry. Our parents are estranged and nobody can blackmail us emotionally. There are no prejudices of religion or money to make us stop.

It takes us less than a month to move beyond the cantonment town of Ranikhet, where we run a school today, attempting to imbibe in the next generation, the virtues that we had so severely lacked in our lifetimes at those critical junctures – the strength of the soul and the courage to follow our convictions. It isn't commercially viable but it is our only hope of redeeming ourselves.

She says she can help get the funding from a Non-Government Organization to put a roof on the second wing. I want to come along, but she thinks it will be better if I stay.

She leaves on a Sunday, taking the driver along with her that she has brought along from Delhi, promising to return by Tuesday. She doesn't.

Her cell phone says that she is not reachable. I should be panicking, making phone calls to ascertain where she is; maybe, even make the drive to find out if she has abandoned me. I don't. I know she will come back - for what are we but homing pigeons that have that innate, uncanny ability to find their mate, no matter where you leave them on the face of this earth. She will come back.

Radhika

When I wake up on Wednesday morning, my first thoughts are of him. I check the phone to see, if miraculously, the network outage has been resolved. I haven't even been able to inform Aditya that I will need to wait another day before I can bring home a cheque from the NGO. The meeting has been a breeze and they have agreed to help us. Our cause is mired in nobility – imparting education to rural children. Little do they know that the education that we were imparting isn't bookish. It doesn't deal with debit and credit entries that no one will really use in real life. It is more meaningful than that – A strong backbone differentiates humans from jellyfish.

Srishti's all time bestsellers ₹ 100 each

- A Dilli-Mumbai Love Story
- A Feeling Beyond Words
- A half baked love story
- A Life that you knew..
- A Little Bit of Love...
- A Little Love Incident
- And then it rained....
- Anyone Else but you
- A Roller Coaster Ride!
- As Long as I Love you...
- A thing beyond forever
- A Walk Down the Lane...
- Because you Loved me..
- Beep you! you BeepHole
- Belong
- Boundless Saga of Love
- By the River Pampa I...
- Careful what u Wish for
- Coming up on the show..
- Can't Cook a Love Story
- Corporate Atyaachaar
- Crazy Bloody Thing LOV
- Dancing with Maharaja
- Everything you Desire

- Few things left unsaid
- Forever in these pages
- From Cubicles 2 Cabins
- Heartbreaks & Dreams!
- Here Sat A Key Maker
- I am Broke....! Love me
- I am Still Committed..
- If God Had A Desk Job..
- If God went to B-School
- If I Pretend I am Sorry!
- It Happened that Night
- In Course of True Love
- I too had a love story..
- It's all About Love...
- It Should Be u!! My Love
- It wasn't Love at First
- I will Love Once Again!
- Jab se you have loved me
- Journey of two Hearts
- Just Like in the Movies
- Life is What you Make it
- Love Happens Like that
- Love, Life & A Beer Can!
- Love, Life and Dream on

- Love, Life and Lust...
- Love Life & all the Dots
- Love, me and Bullshit!
- Love Power Politics!!
- Love a Rather Bad Idea
- Love & Urban Melodrama
- LUV is a Dirty Business
- My Love Never Faked...
- Nothing for you my Dear
- Nothing Lasts Forever
- Of Tattoos and Taboos!
- Oops! 'I' fell in Love!
- Ouch! that 'Hearts'..
- Patyala Down De Throat
- Plz.. Kiss me or Kill me
- Reality Bytes 'Bites'
- She is Single I'm Taken
- Simple Things Make LUV
- Something in your Eyes
- Sumthing of a Mocktale
- 34 Bubblegums and Candies

- That Kiss in the Rain..
- The Dev-D Syndrome...
- The Equation of my Love
- The Funda of Mix-ology
- The Idiot-Dudes.....
- The India I Dream of
- The Journey of Rock...
- The Journey to Nowhere
- The Lost Scraps of Love
- The Off-Site Tamasha
- The Other way Round
- The Quest for Nothing!
- The Thing Between U & Me
- Those Small Lil Things
- Three Times Loser....
- To Whom it May Concern:
- When Life Tricked me..
- What... if not I.I.T.?
- Will you Marry Me Cupid
- Your Place or Mine?

- Brain Building for achievement
  Herbert N. Casson

- Cheiro's : Language of the Hand

- Winning Personality:
  The Magic key to success
  F. Oss